A *Whisper* OF PEACE

A Mosaic Christmas Anthology IV

ELEANOR BERTIN ∗ LORNA SEILSTAD
SARA DAVISON ∗ ANGELA D. MEYER
STACY MONSON

WELCOME

TO THE MOSAIC COLLECTION

We are sisters, a beautiful mosaic united by the love of God through the blood of Christ.

Each month The Mosaic Collection releases one or more faith-based novels or anthologies exploring our theme, Family by His Design, and sharing stories that feature diverse, God-designed families. Stories range from mystery and women's fiction to comedic and literary fiction. We hope you'll join our Mosaic family as we explore together what truly defines a family.

If you're like us, loneliness and suffering have touched your life in ways you never imagined; but Dear One, while you may feel alone in your suffering—whatever it is—you are never alone!

Learn more about The Mosaic Collection at
www.mosaiccollectionbooks.com

Join our Reader Community, too!
www.facebook.com/groups/TheMosaicCollection

BOOKS

IN THE MOSAIC COLLECTION

The Third Grace by Deb Elkink
Crazy About Maisie by Janice L. Dick
Rebuilding Joy by Regina Rudd Merrick
Song of Grace: Stories to Amaze the Soul
Written in Ink by Sara Davison
Open Circle by Stacy Monson
The Heart of Christmas: A Mosaic Christmas Anthology III
Where Hope Starts by Angela D. Meyer
Flame of Mercy by Eleanor Bertin
Through the Lettered Veil by Candace West
Broken Together by Brenda S. Anderson
Every Star in the Sky by Sara Davison
Where Healing Starts by Angela D. Meyer
All Things New: Stories to Refresh the Soul
Into the Flood by Milla Holt
Through the Blaze by Milla Holt
A Whisper of Peace: A Mosaic Christmas Anthology IV

Learn more at
www.mosaiccollectionbooks.com/mosaic-books

PRAISE FOR AUTHORS

IN THE MOSAIC COLLECTION

Praise for Eleanor Bertin

Beautifully written! ... It was heartwarming, sad, happy, encouraging. I especially loved the ending! A mother's heart longs to hear her children call for her. The best so far from this author!

— jcrew

Praise for Lorna Seilstad

When I first saw the cover of the book it immediately intrigued me. ... So I knew I had to read it and I am so glad I did for I have found yet another author to add to my ever growing list.

— Sassy Bookish Mama

Praise for Sara Davison

What a suspenseful ride. I liked the international aspect of the story where the drama kept me on the edge of my seat. And I rooted for the couple to find out what happens, and hoped for the best. Excellent writing. Don't miss this one.

— Pirkko

Praise for Angela D. Meyer

A great story that encompasses a wide range of emotions. Characters so real that I felt I was there in each scene. I was so glad I got a chance to read this story. Definitely one of the best Christian fiction books I've read this year!

— L Palmer

Praise for Stacy Monson

This story is full of subtle reminders to heed that still, small voice of the Holy Spirit.... Heartwarming.

— Amazon Customer

CONTENTS

CHRISTMAS AT THE CROSSROADS

Eleanor Bertin

* * *

They say you become who you hang around with.

Myra and Sue are best friends. One is raised in a strict, religious home, the other permissively indulged. Which one will influence the other? When the teens are caught breaking the law near Christmas, the consequences force them to a crossroads with unexpected results.

> "I shall be telling this with a sigh
> Somewhere ages and ages hence:
> Two roads diverged in a wood, and I—
> I took the one less traveled by,
> And that has made all the difference."
> ~*The Road Not Taken,* by Robert Frost, 1915

To my first best friend,
Sandra
How grateful I am that Jesus got hold of us both.

"Today, if you will hear His voice,
do not harden your hearts as in the rebellion.
Today, if you will hear His voice,
do not harden your hearts as in the rebellion.
Today if you will hear His voice, do not harden your hearts."

Hebrews 3:7, 15 & 4:7 NKJV

Long before I ever became one of them, the first Hardy I met was Myra, sitting on the sideline bench in gym class the fall of Grade Five. I couldn't know, then, though I had hopes, that she would become my best friend, that our paths would intertwine for years until, well, until they didn't anymore. That fall, I was new to this small farming community and had already spent a few agonizing days trying to look like I had places to go and things to do in a school where everyone had grown up together and knew what they were doing.

Of all the tragedies that could befall me in the first week, I had sprained my ankle when I bungled getting out of the car. Yup. Stepped on my own foot. I mean, who does that? If there was any possible way to flub something, I, Klutzie-Sue, would manage it. Pain had shot through my ankle, but I'd still glanced around in every direction to make sure none of the cool kids were around to witness it before I collapsed back onto the front seat and bawled.

Myra, on the other hand, sitting on the gym bench in her brown floral peasant dress and tight braids, seemed fit enough. No crutches, no compression bandage.

I thumped down beside her on the low bench, propping my crutches against the concrete block wall, then leaned closer to her to be heard above the bouncy square dance music. "You got a doctor's note, too?"

She gave me a look I couldn't quite read. "No."

"How come you're sitting here, then?" I'd always been on the chubby side and was usually one of the kids picked last when teams were chosen for sports. But I tipped my head out toward the gym floor where our classmates were do-si-doing to the Teton Mountain Stomp. "It's the only part of Phys. Ed that's actually fun. Just my luck I have to miss out."

"My mom wrote a note to excuse me." Myra looked away, apparently fascinated by a big kid named Kevin who was goofing off at the far end of the gym, swinging his partner with a bit too much gusto.

"Really? Why?"

She shoved a braid over her shoulder, and I noticed her fingers were shaking. Then she turned to me and mumbled, "We're Christians and we don't believe in dancing."

My mouth dropped open. "Huh?"

But she turned away again, and I wasn't going to press for an explanation and risk messing up the first real conversation I'd had yet.

She pointed at the fiasco across the room where the clueless Kevin and three others had landed in a tangled heap on the floor. Evidently, I wasn't the only clumsy kid in class.

We both laughed, watching as they struggled to unpile themselves. And there we were: Fast friends, kindred spirits, bosom buddies bound together, as only two eleven-year-old girls could be, by our mutual misfortune and a superior disdain for our classmates' idiocy.

From then on, we were a unit. Myra-and-Sue, or Sue-and-Myra was how kids – and even teachers – referred to us. Never one without the other. Other than her always wearing skirts or dresses, we had a lot in common. We found out our birthdays were exactly one month apart. Practically twins. And although she didn't seem to know anything about my favourite TV shows, *The Brady Bunch* and *The Partridge Family*, we both loved reading. Some of her favourite books were a lot more complex than mine.

It was also great finding someone else who hated the inevitable recess dodgeball games. Like me, she couldn't wait to escape to a quiet corner of the playground to play with trolls. She didn't own any of the tiny, snub-nosed, bright-haired dolls herself, but I brought my collection in its treehouse-shaped case to school to share. I even got my mom to buy Myra a troll of her own so we could continue our ongoing troll saga. I liked how imaginative she was and the big words she used.

One day before leaving school, I noticed her stuffing her troll into the back of her desk.

"Aren't you going to take it home with you?"

Myra shook her head and went on pushing all the clothes and accessories she had made deep inside her desk.

I'd been so impressed with the little clothes she'd sewn for all the dolls – way better than my own paper and glue attempts. She knew things about seam allowance and snap fasteners that I had never heard of. But no surprise there, her mom sewed all her clothes.

"You're not going to leave your troll here overnight, are you? What if someone steals it?"

"I seriously doubt the janitor would purloin a two-inch doll with pink hair."

Yes. She really used the word purloin.

"Besides," she added, the corners of her lips tightening, "my mom would only confiscate it if I took it home."

"How come?"

"She despises the looks of them."

I puzzled over this for a minute. So far, what I knew about her mom didn't sound too nice. I was about to get her to explain when the final buzzer rang. Instead, I asked, "Wanna come over to my place for the weekend?"

"I doubt I'd be allowed." She took off outside to where the school buses lined up, leaving me to walk home alone.

When my mom came home after work that day, I waited until she'd had "a chance to get home" as she put it, before broaching the subject. She needed to shed her shoes and pantyhose, change out of her dress, and pull on a loose housecoat before settling into her recliner, and lighting a cigarette.

"Mom?" I nestled in the corner of the couch and stretched my legs along the length of it.

"Yes, Susie dear," she said with her eyes still closed.

"I asked Myra to stay the weekend."

"That sounds like fun."

"She didn't think she'd be allowed."

"Oh?" Mom finally looked my way. "How come?"

"She didn't say. All I know is, she said they're Christians and don't believe in dancing. And her mom doesn't like trolls."

Mom's eyes rounded, then she laughed. "The poor dear. All the more reason we should have her over. Ask her again. You know your friends are always welcome here. Now why don't you turn on the TV and in a minute, I'll see what I can rustle up for snackies."

I got up to begin our evening ritual. I turned on Mom's favourite show, grabbed a couple of Cokes, and settled back on the couch, trying to guess what would be on the plate she would bring us. Might be tuna salad with grapes, or maybe crackers and Cheez Whiz.

"Here you go, Lovey." She laid two small plates and a platter of peanut butter sandwiches, pickles, and potato chips on the coffee table, along with a couple of Kit Kat chocolate bars.

"Now then," she said, easing into her chair, "we're all set for a cozy evening just the two of us. Isn't this the bee's knees?" She always said that. And I always agreed that it was.

The very next day, before I had a chance to invite Myra to my place again, she beat me to it. "My mom said I could ask you over to our place this weekend. Wanna come?"

"Sure," I said, apprehensive but curious.

"Don't you have to ask permission from your parents first?"

Never having known my dad who took off when my mom

was pregnant with me, I automatically translated plural references to parents into the singular. "My mom won't mind."

Myra grinned. "Splendid! You can ride home on the bus with me."

Friday after four couldn't come soon enough. We whispered and giggled through recesses and lunch hours, scheming about the fun we would have, which turned out to be a handy diversion from the feud with two other girls we were involved in at the time.

Finally, we were hopping off the bus, mooing at some cows across the fence, and crunching our way down the leafy lane. Behind us, Myra's two older sisters and brother got off the bus, too. I hadn't yet met Dorcas and Esther, but Myra had told me about them. They both attended the high school. Dorcas, the eldest, was retarded, as it was then spoken of, on account of the cord wrapped around her neck at birth. I was familiar with Myra's seventh grade brother, Glen, known for his narrow-leg pants and crew-cut blond hair, so different from the shaggy hair of other boys his age. He sped ahead of us now, his metal lunch kit rattling against his knobby knees.

Myra's house was a starched and scrubbed white two-story with green trim. When she opened the door, I hung back a bit, suddenly aware of a feeling of inadequacy. What if her mom despised the looks of me? I glanced down at my striped, denim bell-bottoms and flower power top. Compared to Myra's plaid skirt and white blouse, I felt less than presentable. Thinking suddenly of our on-the-sly troll-playing, I worried that her mother might think I was a bad influence on Myra.

She tugged at my arm to bring me into the farmhouse kitchen. What struck me first was the sense of peace. Without clutter or the noise of broadcast voices, it was the kind of house that let you see the details. Something smelled like apples and cinnamon. A clock ticked, steady and reliable. Sudsy bubbles under the kitchen tap twinkled with rainbow colours in the fall sunlight that streamed through the window.

Myra's mom, tall and thin, turned from the sink and used her apron to dry her hands. Her brown hair, with gleaming wings of silver at her temples, was smoothed into a neat bun at the back of her head. She assigned each of the older kids some chores, even Dorcas, then turned her full attention on me.

"How do you do, Susan?" She took my hand in both of hers for a moment.

No adult had ever shaken hands with me before and I shrank a bit from her earnest gaze, feeling like she could see right inside me. At the same time, her placid smile put me at ease.

"Welcome here." She set a basket on the end of the kitchen counter, nodding at Myra. "When you've changed from your school clothes, would you girls please go out and pick the rest of those apples? After that, I thought you two might like to bake some oatmeal raisin cookies for tonight's dessert."

"Yes, Mom," Myra said, heading to the stairs. She beckoned me to follow her. I don't think her mother heard her deep, impatient sigh as we trudged up the steps, but I did.

In her room, everything was in peaceful order too, the double bed smooth with a pale green chenille spread, the few items on the small dresser aligned perfectly. It was a lot different from the loud chaos of my tiny room at home, where troll magazine photos covered the purple walls and paper snippings carpeted the floor. Myra changed rapidly, pulling on outdated green pants before taking her skirt off. I guess she was a little self-conscious about dressing in front of me, which I thought strange. Mom and I changed in front of each other all the time.

On the way out to the apple trees, I asked her what they would do with the fruit.

"Applesauce, apple jelly, apple juice, and canned apple pie filling for apple crisp and pies." She briskly gathered the ones on the ground and then turned to the tree.

I made an impressive start to the enterprise by pulling an apple off the tree along with half the leafy branch it was on.

"Here, like this," Myra said, showing me how to grasp the branch close to an apple with one hand and yank the fruit with the other.

I followed her lead, embarrassed at my inexperience, and tried to keep up with her speed. At least she didn't criticize. I had never done anything like this before and once I caught on to the technique, I found a deep satisfaction as the basket got fuller. "This is cool!"

Myra raised her eyebrows at me. "Glad you're enjoying yourself."

"I can't believe we'll get to make cookies. Do you get to bake a lot?"

She stopped picking to stare at me. "Get to? I have to. Don't you?"

"No. My mom just buys cookies and applesauce and all that."

"Must be nice."

We each took a handle of the basket and though I fumbled it once, spilling a few onto the grass, we managed to bring it safely into the house. By then, Myra's mom was ladling thick, golden applesauce into hot jars. I watched, fascinated, as she wiped the rims, put on lids, and screwed down the rings. To me, the growing line-up of shiny jars seemed a thing of beauty, made from nothing but her own two hands.

She finished scraping out the large pot, then looked at us. "Wash your hands, girls, and then you know where the ingredients are, Myra. Use the softened butter that's on the counter."

I followed Myra around the kitchen as she pulled out mixing bowl and measuring spoons, flour, sugar, and oatmeal. She asked me to get out the cinnamon and when I opened the cupboard she pointed to, the uniform row of gleaming spice bottles reminded me of a grocery store shelf. I thought of the nearly empty cupboards at home. My mother preferred to keep things handy on the counters, but we didn't own anywhere close to this variety and number of supplies.

"I'll measure and you mix, okay?" Myra cut off a large cube of the butter and dumped it into the ceramic bowl, then followed it with cups of brown and white sugar. "Cream that while I get the dry ingredients ready."

I stared uncertainly at the contents of the bowl. "Cream it?"

Her hands went still, and her eyes widened. "Just mush the sugar into the butter with the back of the spoon until there's no crystals left."

How was I supposed to know? More than that, how did Myra know so much? I did as she said and was pleased to watch the mixture became one soft mass. She handed me the eggs which I cracked into the mix – I did know how to crack open an egg – and I mixed them in. Then she poured in the dry ingredients. When she measured out the raisins, her mother said, "Don't muzzle the ox while it treads out the grain."

I searched Myra's face for a clue to the meaning of this. She rolled her eyes and poured out a couple of small piles of the raisins for each of us to snack on.

While we waited for the cookies to bake, we smacked our hands against each other's in a rhythmic game of Concentration, but quietly, since Myra's mom was at the table helping Dorcas with some homework.

22

Mrs. Hardy rose to check the cookies when we pulled out the last pan. "These look very nice, girls. I think Dad will enjoy them."

I glowed under her nod of approval, but the mention of Dad took me by surprise. It hadn't occurred to me before, but of course, Myra must have a dad. Where else would the money come from since her mom didn't have a job?

When we finally sat down to eat, I was surprised at how pretty the table looked. The tablecloth, edged with a sunflower design, held a centerpiece of a single branch of golden leaves. And there were matching sunflower cloth napkins. I hoped I wouldn't spill gravy all over everything. It all seemed so harmonious, the family sitting together, then joining hands while Myra's dad said a prayer. I liked the way a mom, dad and four kids filled in the spaces around the table, all balanced-like. Well, they would have if I hadn't been there. But they cheerfully made room for me, and I liked that, too.

The beef stew, corn on the cob, and home-baked buns with real butter were delicious. I had two of the buns and managed not to stain the tablecloth. After passing around the cookies, Myra's mom handed her husband a book. He looked down on it for a moment, then shook his head sort of sadly, I thought.

"That's alright dear. I'll read tonight," she said, patting his hand. She leafed through the thin pages and began to read. Her words spoke serenity to me. She read about Jesus who healed sick people but had no place to lay his head. It was sad, to me, to think of this man who did so much good having no home of his own.

I was following along with the story until I got distracted watching Glen folding his napkin. Before long, a fabric monkey appeared, its wide mouth flapping in perfect rhythm with their mom's reading. I had trouble keeping from laughing and, beside me, Myra's shoulders shook.

Mrs. Hardy finished reading and closed the book. "Congratulations on your stellar performance, Glen," she said. "It has earned you the honour of doing the supper dishes."

Glen's shoulders slumped and Myra and I stifled further giggles.

We all left him to his chore and went to the living room where Myra pulled out the Monopoly box. She dealt out the money to everyone except her dad who promptly fell asleep in his chair. Their mom said she would coach Dorcas. It was even more fun once Glen joined in. At one point, as we were all laughing about Glen's being sent to jail for a third time, I glanced around the room and noticed there was no TV. That must be why Myra only listened in silence when I talked about my favourite shows.

Getting into bed later, Myra asked me if I'd been bored that evening.

"Are you kidding? That was a blast!"

"Okay then," she said, pulling up the covers. "Good night."

Myra was never allowed to come to my place as often as I invited her. And when she did come, it was only for Friday night. I got used to the rule that she had to be in church on Sunday and never let it bother me. In fact, when her mom suggested they pick me up on Sunday mornings and take me to church with them each week I was quite happy to go along.

Myra sure loved spending time at my place, though. She laughed at all my mom's little sayings, even the ones I'd heard a million times. And she couldn't wait to watch whatever was on television, even boring shows about science or that dumb game show, *This is The Law*, where contestants had to guess which weird law was the real one. Did you know it's illegal to bathe a horse in a bathtub in Montana? Stuff like that. Myra especially liked eating meals in front of the TV. Which was strange, because the more time I spent at her house, the better I liked the way her family ate their meals together.

On weekends at her house, we had plenty of time to play and there were always interesting things to do. Climbing the bale stacks, playing with barn kittens, tobogganing, or helping Glen clear snow from the pond so we could skate on it. When it was too cold outside, we baked, or played board games. Some evenings, her mom would start a story and the whole family took turns, even Dorcas, telling the next part. Glen's twists on the tale usually had us splitting a gut laughing.

I always went to church with them on Sunday morning and evening, and after the first time, I knew to bring along a dress to wear. I liked Sunday school and the singing, and I tried to understand the sermon as long as Myra didn't get me giggling. Then her mom would clear her throat meaningfully, which was usually enough to shut me up. If it didn't, she might make us sit on either side of her. And if that didn't work, her mom's hand would clamp down hard around Myra's knee, which never failed to kill any fooling around. I had a growing awe of Myra's mother.

Things started changing when we turned thirteen. I wasn't outgoing or from a rich, well-known family. And not being an athlete or a brain, I had always thought I was one of the school low-lifes. But over the summer, my baby fat had begun shifting, making a whole new me, and I found boys starting to pay attention. Myra had always had status because she was one of the smart kids, but now her underdeveloped chest and broken-out skin left her less popular. Still, we experimented with my mom's makeup whenever Myra spent time at my place. We did each other's hair and put on fashion shows for Mom who would offer commentary into a rolled-up magazine as a microphone.

"Here comes Susie, ready for spring in a pink skinny-rib sweater and palazzo pants that show off her cute little figure."

Since talking about boys had replaced playing with dolls, Myra helped me take down all the troll pictures from my bedroom walls and exchange them for teen magazine photos of David Cassidy and Donny Osmond. We practiced kissing on the mirror, debating whether it was best to close our eyes before our lips touched the glass or after.

"You've got to know you hit the right spot, after all." Myra's confidence had nothing to do with experience since neither of us had ever been kissed.

"But what if you've got a cold and you can't breathe through your nose? How do you know when to come up for air?" This sent us into fits of giggles and provided us with plenty of knowing smirks during Mr. Whidden's next science class on the respiratory system.

Sleepovers had told me a lot about Myra, and vice versa. I knew, for instance, that she hated her name.

"I think my mother must have loathed me at birth giving me an old lady name like Myra."

"Oh, come on."

"I mean it. I'd even rather have had a Bible name like Esther or Ruth. Anything but Myra. It was her mother's name. She says it means beloved."

"Well then, she couldn't have hated you."

"I guess. But I looked it up," she added with a twinkle of mischief in her eyes, "and it also means rebellious."

Likewise, Myra had managed to pry out of me that I

thought her brother, Glen was cute. I made her swear never to tell him, and while we were friends, I don't think she ever did.

All our time spent together had led to devising our own language. Myra was the one who came up with it. She taught me how to exchange the first and last consonants of a word and we got fairly fluent in it. We could speak it in front of other kids, or even our teachers and they had no clue what we were talking about even if it was about them.

One Monday morning before classes, I stood outside the girls' bathroom cubicle as usual waiting for Myra to finish changing from her skirt into a pair of her brother's outgrown jeans. I asked her if she'd seen the poster announcing a Friday night Sock Hop at the high school.

She burst out the door, stuffing the hated skirt into a bag, her eyes imploring me. "Invite me to your place?"

"You really think your mom's gonna let you go to a dance?"

"What she doesn't know won't hurt me." Myra grinned.

It worked. Myra was allowed to spend Friday night at my place. All week, we schemed what we would wear and what boys we might dance with. She knew a lot more of them than I did, since she had older siblings and had grown up in the community. Walking home from school that Friday, we stopped at the variety store. As usual, we gravitated toward the make-up section. I fingered a package of peach frost Maybelline lip gloss, mentally calculating what was left of my allowance.

Myra nudged me. "Nurloip it," she whispered.

Purloin it? Shocked at the suggestion, I stared at her, a

churning beginning in my belly. I knew very well what she meant. I just didn't have the nerve.

The moment passed and she shouldered me towards the magazine section of the store, then out the door.

Outside, she turned on me. "What's the matter with you? You had a perfect opportunity. The clerk was looking the other way."

"I – I wasn't ready."

"She who hesitates is lost." She stalked down the sidewalk with such determined strides that I got winded keeping up. Not only was I puffing when we got to my house, I felt stupid for my lack of guts. But when we got to my room, Myra pulled the very lip gloss package out of her pocket with a triumphant smile. To say I was surprised is putting it mildly.

"You–how did you—?"

Myra flicked her index finger against the side of her nose and winked, just like I'd described to her from the movie, *The Sting*. "My treat." She laughed. "Open it."

I barely had time to think it over at the time. After a hurried supper of my mom's special cheese and walnut sandwiches, we dressed for the dance. When we came out to show ourselves to Mom, she smiled. But then her forehead wrinkled.

"Did your mom say it was okay for you to go to this dance?" she asked, tilting her head at Myra.

"Yes, she did." Myra's voice was strong and confident.

"You're sure?" I could tell my mom was still uneasy. She had met Myra's mother briefly at times when she had come out to the farm to pick me up and I knew she was intimidated by such a proper woman.

Myra looked my mother straight in the eye so that even I was almost convinced. "Quite sure, yes ma'am." You had to hand it to her. She had nerve.

But a war erupted inside me, as though I were struggling inside the web of lies we were weaving.

My mom hesitated for a tick, then slowly nodded. "Alrighty then. Hop in the car, girls, and I'll drive you over to the school."

And so the next few years went. In between all the usual friendship drama, teacher troubles, and junior high crushes, we had a lot of stories to keep straight with our sneaking around and lying to her mother so we could have the fun we wanted. I say we, but it was mostly Myra. I didn't have to lie to my mother since she pretty much let me do as I pleased. But watching Myra glibly fib to hers gave me the shakes. And though Myra never seemed bothered about it, I dreaded the day Mrs. Hardy saw through us. A whisper deep inside told me such a confrontation was inevitable.

In church on Sundays, that whisper grew louder, making me squirm. I'd recall what I'd taken part in through the week, and, conscious of Mrs. Hardy in the same pew, I'd resolve not to do that stuff again. But the next time Myra wanted me to invite her to my place so she could attend a movie or a dance I would stifle the whisper and go right along with her. Looking back, I know I was weak, but you had to know the strength of Myra's personality, the steely certainty behind her scrawny body. She was hard to say no to.

"Did you see who's going to be in concert next month?" Myra asked me, shoving a newspaper ad in my face just before Christmas of tenth grade.

By the excitement in her voice, you'd have thought it was

the Doobie Brothers or something. As if a big band like that would ever come to our small prairie city.

"Moodstone," I read from the ad. The Alberta-grown group had been making a name for themselves in Canada for the past few years.

"Only one problem. It's on a Saturday night." Myra tossed her dark hair out of her eyes and frowned.

"So, what do we do?"

She thought for a minute until the light of an idea slowly spread across her face. "We run away is what we do."

"What?"

"You invite me to your place Friday and then we'll sneak out of the house and hitchhike to the city to be there for Saturday night. While we're there we can do some Christmas shopping and even 'shop'" –she waggled her eyebrows—"for cute outfits to wear to the concert."

The audacity of the plan unnerved me, but I'll confess, it also excited me. The more she talked, the more brilliant it all seemed to me. Sneaking away and staying out all night was what you saw in the movies. And being free to roam the stores for as long as we wanted and do as we pleased sounded thrilling. Even I was getting tired of having to arrange exact times of meeting when my mom took us places. That and having to be home so early.

I shoved aside the nagging, inner voice of doubt, ignoring questions about how we would get concert tickets or where we would spend the night. The strategizing was part of the fun.

After another TV supper on the couch with my mom during which we girls tried to suppress our giddiness, Myra whispered to me, "It's all going off without a hitch."

"Until the part that comes next: the hiking." I elbowed her, snorting. "Get it?"

Naturally, Myra got the joke right away without my

having to spell out *hitchhiking*. Wit-wise, we were on the exact same page.

My mom shook her head at us with an indulgent smile. "You two should probably scoot off to bed now. And try to keep the chatter down to a dull roar."

"Sure thing, Mom," I said, and for a change we retreated to my room without protest.

Prying out the screen of my bedroom window was a simple matter, but when I looked down at the six-foot drop to the ground below, a warning clanged inside me. With my luck I'd break both legs. But Myra went first and then urged me on, so I bravely let go my hold on the window rim. I landed on my rear but without injuries and figured I was home-free. Only later did I wonder if the inner warning I'd sensed was about a different kind of fall.

For December, the weather was unusually mild, and the recent snow had mostly disappeared. The soggy earth muffled our footsteps as we left my tiny yard, but it did little to stop that voice of warning, almost louder than the pounding of my pulse. We kept to the shadows until we left my street, then hurried out to the main road leading to the outskirts of town. We turned to face the sporadic traffic and stuck out our thumbs. While I was conflicted inside, Myra seemed to have come alive, singing goofy songs in our private language. And though the temperature was above freezing, we were shivering from cold and nerves before a car slowed and pulled onto the shoulder about twenty minutes later.

The driver leaned across to wind down the passenger window. He was an old guy, at least forty, with nerdy glasses and a weirdly high-pitched voice. "Hello there, kittens. Need a lift?"

Myra stepped forward, reaching eagerly for the door handle. But I elbowed her back, taking a step back myself. For once, I paid attention to that voice inside. Something about the guy gave me the creeps. "No thanks. We're waiting for our friends."

"Whaddyou mean?" Myra hissed in my ear. "Let's get in the car. I'm freezing."

"Come along with me," Nerd-Guy wheedled. "I'll take you to the city and show you a good time."

"What is wrong with you?" Myra demanded, prodding my back.

"Look, you girls look cold," he said, his tone lower and impatient. "My car's nice and warm."

But the guy's insistence made me even more skittish. My teeth started chattering, on top of the shivers. I kept nudging Myra back from the car. In my hurry to put distance between us and the creep, I tramped on her foot.

"Ouch!" she yelped.

Out of the corner of my eye, I spotted headlights. I sighed in relief. "Here's our friends now."

Nerd-Guy checked his rearview mirror. Suddenly he was in a big rush. He straightened, put the car in gear, and took off without even rolling up the window, spinning his wheels and spurting gravel behind him.

Myra scowled at me. "How do we know this ride will be any better?"

"Anything's better than that weirdo." My insides relaxed. Maybe the alarm bell in my head had saved me from something awful with that guy.

Sure enough, the next car that stopped held some big-time operators from our high school—two guys and a girl. We hopped in the backseat of the car, grateful for the blast of warmth and the cranked-up stereo that kept us from having to explain anything. Or from hearing any more from the voice of conscience.

I noticed the others raise their eyebrows in recognition of Myra, likely surprised to find her hitchhiking, or heavily made-up, or both, but they said nothing. No matter what clique you were with, you could count on kids keeping the unwritten code of not snitching to parents.

"You girls up for a night on the town?" Doug, the driver, shouted over Credence Clearwater's "Bad Moon Rising."

"Sort of," I nodded, trying to thaw my chilled hands and legs.

"We're going shopping and staying over for the Moodstone concert tomorrow night," Myra yelled, unnecessarily.

I could tell she was compensating for her religious reputation.

Once we got to the city, we asked Doug to drop us off at the mall and thanked him for the lift, then headed inside. Christmas music and glitter and tinsel got us into the holiday mood.

"First we've got to buy something big, so we get a big bag." Myra marched ahead to a gift wrap display and tucked a couple of rolls under her arm before heading to the check-out.

"But what are we going to do with such a big thing all day tomorrow?"

"Never mind that. There's method in my madness." She grinned, shelling out a couple of bucks for the wrap and, predictably, receiving a large paper bag. "Now we fill it."

And we did. Ever so casually, a couple of pairs of earrings for me, a few nail polishes, eye shadows, a cute top, a Beatles album, and a lot of other odds and ends including gifts for my mom and Myra's siblings found their way into the bag. We sauntered out of the store into the mall without being stopped.

Lightheaded with success, we browsed the fashion and accessory stores with our backpacks and large department store bag in tow. In one shop, I felt a clerk's eyes on us as we held up a couple of cute tops against ourselves in their mirror.

I whispered *not here* in code, shooting a significant look at Myra to hold off in this place. But she slipped the red sweater into our bag and went on nonchalantly scanning the racks as we moved toward the entrance. We were about to take the last step out the door when a heavy hand on one shoulder of each of us stopped us. My heart pounded with the sudden weight of it.

"Girls, you're going to have to come with me." The middle-aged manager of the shop turned us around and steered us into her office in the back. She closed the door firmly. Her lips were a tight line, and she didn't offer us a chair. Instead, she held out a demanding hand. "I saw you put that sweater in your bag. Give it here."

I breathed a small sigh of relief, hoping that returning the item would be the end of it. Myra meekly dug into the bag and pulled out the sweater alone, closing the paper bag again in one motion.

The woman snatched the top, then sat at her desk and picked up the phone. We listened with sinking hearts, realizing she was calling police.

I picked at my hangnail, glancing at Myra's anguished eyes. "Oh no, oh no, oh no!" Myra groaned under her breath. I wasn't too happy about this either, but Myra squirmed like she was in mortal agony.

"I am in such deep trouble. Good-bye, cruel world!" Her voice wobbled with barely suppressed panic. She kept crunching the closed top of the paper bag. The rustling noise, added to my clamouring conscience, about drove me crazy.

"Quit that!" I finally snapped.

Just then, the store manager hung up the phone and sat back in her creaky chair, glaring at us.

I shifted from foot to foot, trying to focus on anything but her steely eyes, yet finding myself drawn to them anyway. Beside me, Myra gave low, intermittent moans while we waited.

I won't go into all the gory details except to say that the cop who showed up was a friendly old guy who gave us a talking to and then asked for one of our parents' phone numbers. Myra pleaded with me to give mine.

The officer made the call, then talked in undertones to the manager before leaving. That was the shopkeeper's cue to start her lecture. "Shoplifting is not a thrill. It's not a prank. It's a crime, and having a criminal record is a serious thing. Do you have any idea the effect it has on people like me who are trying to run a business and simply make a living? We have to pay more for security systems and staff, and we end up having to charge more for our products. Delinquents like you ruin things for everyone..." On and on like that it went. Finally, she shut up. But she still watched us with those hard, piercing eyes the whole time we waited.

Through the office window, I could see the shop lights starting to go out.

Finally, my mom breezed in and was I glad to see her.

She took a quick glance at the manager before shaking her head at us. "Tsk, tsk, you girls." She listened to the woman's accusations without comment and then to the cop who had returned with some papers for her to fill out.

"Come along girls," she said when she was finished. "Let's get you home."

Mom was unusually quiet, biting her nails as she drove. Closer to our hometown, she finally spoke in a serious tone. "Myra, I'll drop Susie off at our place and then drive you out to the farm. I have to explain things to your parents." That's when I realized she was likely as nervous having to give account to Myra's mom as Myra was.

Myra jabbed me in the ribs. "Please get your mom to let

you come with me," she whispered urgently. "Don't make me face my mother alone,"

I relayed the message to Mom, who nodded absently. In the rearview mirror I could see her chewing her lip. Perhaps she felt, like Myra did, that reinforcements would help in the showdown ahead of us.

As the miles flew by, my own apprehension started to grow. I hadn't liked the store manager's use of the word "delinquent" and had never thought of myself as a bad kid. I knew my mom would be a bit put out about all this and that I'd be grounded for a while, and I figured I deserved it. But now with the prospect of confessing to Myra's mother, a deep shame settled on me. If there was one word that described Evelyn Hardy, it was upright. By contrast, I began to stoop under the terrible weight of my sin.

It was no good telling myself it had been Myra's idea. I knew I was every bit as guilty as she was. Snatches of Bible verses I'd heard at the Hardy supper table and in church shouted condemnation in my head.

At last, we turned in the familiar driveway. Festive green Christmas lights outlining the porch only made me feel worse. A single dim light showed from the kitchen window. The three of us trundled up the steps in matching apprehension. I noticed that Myra had left the paper bag of purloined goods in the car. There was no time to question her because the door opened at Mom's first knock. We stepped inside.

On the table, a small lamp cast a yellow glow over the whole room. I repressed a groan when I caught sight of Mrs. Hardy's open Bible, her glasses sitting next to it. It reminded me that it wasn't just Myra's mom we had offended, but worse, we'd wronged God.

She glanced from one to the next of us with questioning eyes.

"Seems as though our little gals have gotten themselves into a spot of trouble," my mom began with a nervous smile.

"Oh?" Myra's mother asked, raising her eyebrows, and scrutinizing Myra and me.

While Mom stammered out the news, I shrank at Mrs. Hardy's look of growing consternation. At the same time, I was aware of a strange change in Myra's presence beside me. She stood taller and stuck her chin out. I could almost feel her hardening, the way soft syrup had hardened the time we made taffy. The merest glance out the corner of my eye showed defiance in her eyes and a stubborn set to her mouth.

And when I looked back at Mrs. Hardy, I was shocked at the change that had come over her, too, like something had sucked the air out of her. She backed up to the chair she had been sitting in and dropped into it, staring beyond us to a shadowed corner of the room. She looked shrunken, old, defeated. And strangest of all, she was completely silent.

My stomach churned. I had brought chaos into this haven of peace.

My mother shifted from foot to foot, finally stepping forward to lightly lay the police papers on the table next to the Bible.

"I'd best be getting on home now," Mom said. "I'm sure we'll be in touch."

There was no response. Mom tugged at my jacket sleeve and the two of us stumbled out to our car. My most powerful memory of that night is my backward glimpse through the kitchen window: Myra and her mother in a stand-off of wills that I now doubted Mrs. Hardy would win.

Never in my life had I had trouble sleeping. In fact, during sleepovers I'd usually found it hard to stay awake. But that night, my conscience worked overtime. I kept hearing the damning words *delinquent* and *crime*. At times, I broke into a sweat thinking over all that had gone on that evening. For that matter, what had been going on for the past few years. Every spiteful thought and dishonest word of my life piled together with this most recent sin shouting accusations at me. And they were all true.

Overheated, I flung my blankets off, only to feel cold moments later and cover up again. I found my thoughts screaming so loud I pulled my pillow over my head to shut them out. But it was no use. I was as guilty as Lady Macbeth whom we had studied in English class. I couldn't escape the inner charges.

Morning finally came, but no relief arrived with it. I padded out to the living room couch, wrapped in my comforter, to sit quietly in front of our silver Christmas tree. I switched on its lights to brighten the gloomy room. The twinkle and sparkle usually made me feel cozy and happy. Now they only added to the clamour in my head. All I could think was that someone like me didn't deserve something so beautiful and fun. Of all the times of year to have done such a thing, why did we have to pick Christmas? Because by now, I knew it was a celebration of Jesus's birth. Jesus, the perfect Man, who never did a thing wrong. I felt filthy by comparison and shut my eyes, squeezing out a trickle of tears.

When I heard my mom start stirring, I groaned. As I expected, when she came out of her room, she placed a hand on my shoulders and whispered, "Don't beat yourself up over it, honey. It was just kids being kids."

She was trying to help, but it didn't. That was the kind of thing she always said when I messed up and that day, all it showed me was that she couldn't possibly understand what I was going through.

And yet, underneath all my inner racket, the whisper of an idea that had occurred to me sometime in the dark hours of the night grew more insistent. There was only one person I knew who might understand my guilty feeling. Someone who wouldn't tell me it was nothing.

I turned around to look Mom in the eye. "Can you take me out to the Hardys' place this morning?"

Mom glanced at her watch. "It's only seven o'clock."

"They get up early. It'll be alright."

She stared at me. "Aren't you done with—"

"Please?" I pressed, more certain every second that Mrs. Hardy had the answers I needed. I jumped to my feet and grasped my mom's arm. "I need to …do something."

"Well now, I thought—"

"Mom! It's urgent. I need to go out there. Right now. Please!"

She looked doubtful, but slowly moved in the direction of her room.

I hurried to get dressed and had the car started and warming when she came out.

Again, Mom was quiet on the drive out, which was fine with me. My angst of the previous night had been replaced by a jittery anticipation. I felt like a string was pulling me there, or maybe like a fish being reeled in. A nervous giggle escaped me when I remembered a song I had learned in Sunday school. "I will make you fishers of men." Only, I'd never heard of a fish rushing headlong to the fisherman.

When we got there, I made Mom wait in the car for me, telling her I wouldn't be long.

Mrs. Hardy answered the door, and I was shocked by the deep shadows under her eyes. She was alone in the kitchen.

I blurted my question out straight away before Mrs. Hardy even got the door closed.

Tilting her head, she scrutinized me with her mouth open. "You want to know how you can get out from under the weight of your sin?"

She got it! I nodded, not trusting myself to speak. My throat swelled with the warning of impending tears.

She led me to the living room couch and spoke peace to me. And then *I* finally got it. Not only had Jesus come to live in this lousy world but He'd done so on purpose to be punished for the very things I had done last night. Now it all fit together. Now I saw how it affected me. I drank her words down in big gulps. They flowed into the parched crevices of my soul. They whispered peace to me, filling me with the assurance of forgiveness, the promise of love, the hope of freedom.

After praying together, I raised my face to her. "I'm so sorry, Mrs. Hardy," I sobbed. "I've been listening to the wrong voice. I'm sorry for not encouraging Myra to obey you. I'm sorry for being a bad influence on her. I'm sorry for disgracing you."

"Oh, Susan dear. I gladly forgive you." She took me in her bony arms and held me to herself for a moment, then released her hold to hand me a Kleenex.

I wiped my eyes and blew my nose, looking her right in the eye. "And one thing I promise you. I will never steal another thing as long as I live."

She patted my arm. "Remember that Bible I gave you when you first started coming to Sunday school? You keep reading and obeying it and you'll be able to keep that promise." She smiled. "But now, isn't your mom waiting for you in the car? Shouldn't we invite her in?"

"No, that's okay. We have to get home. But thank you so much for helping me understand how to be forgiven." I got up to go. Before heading back out to the car, I asked one last question. "What should I do with the other things we stole?"

Mrs. Hardy frowned before her face cleared. "Like I said, keep reading your Bible. You will find the answer there. Call me any time you have a question."

I had gone into that old farmhouse at war inside, a walking bundle of noise. I came out all smiles, walking on air. My mom's eyes popped wide when she saw me.

"Tell you all about it soon." For now, I wanted to bask in this amazing tranquility whispering comfort in my heart, not wanting it to end.

It never occurred to me to question why Myra didn't join her mom and me when we were talking that Sunday morning just days before Christmas. When I got home that day, I scarfed down my Lucky Charms in a rush so I could fling myself on my bed and start reading my Bible. Mrs. Hardy had been right. I read and read that first day and the more I did, the surer I was that I was going to have to go to the department store and return that bagful of items, confessing what I'd done. The prospect wasn't exactly thrilling, but more than anything, I wanted to preserve this peaceful, washed-clean feeling I had. So that's what I determined I'd do the next time Mom could take me to the city.

On Christmas morning, as usual, I opened my stocking and other gifts and promptly ran to the phone to see what Myra had gotten. Her mom answered and we chatted a bit, then she called Myra to the phone. Right away, I could tell something was different. She seemed stiff and not at all forthcoming. After a while I gave up, figuring she was uptight about talking while her parents were in earshot.

But in the new year, when school started again, it was obvious our friendship was kaput. I finally clicked into the fact that she had been avoiding me since the very morning after our debacle. This hurt me pretty badly. I cried on Mom's shoulder for quite a few nights after school. But after a while, I got busy making new friends. Myra, too, made other friends and from the people she started hanging out with, I knew she and I were headed in opposite directions. It was like we'd reached a crossroads that terrible night. But I couldn't figure out why she would walk the other way when she was so lucky to have the answer to her problems right in front of her, in her home, her family, and in church. To me it was thrilling to have Jesus with me everywhere I went, helping me with my problems, loving on me through what I read in the Bible. I still saw Myra at church, but her eyes had taken on a hard look. While she sat as far to the back as she could, I wanted to be near the front and involved.

We did commiserate with each other in February when we each had an appointment with a probation officer. Hers was first and she came out with a smirk, rolling her eyes at me. "Piece o' cake," she murmured.

Trembling, I stepped into the office. What was ahead of me couldn't possibly be worse than the humiliation I'd felt having to return all those items to the department store manager, could it? I was just grateful he hadn't pressed charges.

After a brief lecture telling me how lucky I was that the Young Offenders Act had just come into effect so I wouldn't have a criminal record, the probation officer closed the file on me and said I could go.

Passing by Mrs. Hardy, she clasped my hand briefly. I felt loved and reassured. At that moment, it occurred to me how strange it was that while she was slowly but surely losing her daughter, she was gaining me. I was a daughter to her long before I was ever part of the Hardy family by marriage. But that's another story.

Over time, as I watched Myra's life pathway diverge so far from mine, I clung tighter to her mom, hanging around the

Hardy home every chance I got. For the rest of my high school years and following, I often called Mrs. Hardy with questions about the Bible or about life. I guess if I think back hard enough, I can understand why others thought Evelyn Hardy sharp-tongued or crusty. But that usually said more about the conscience of the person who reacted to her arrow-straight integrity and thoughtfully worded wisdom.

Me? I had grown to love her. I revered her the way prisoners of war owe a debt of gratitude and love to the soldiers who rescue them. She had led me to peace.

A NOTE FROM THE AUTHOR

Dear Reader;

Christmas is always special to me because of the memories it holds, but not just the sparkle and glow of the season's trimmings. You see, it's not only the birthday of Jesus, it's my spiritual birthday as well. Like the girls in my story, I went through a rough patch of rebellion in my teens, deceiving and being deceived. Thank the Lord that, just like Sue and Myra, my friend and I were caught. God used that shame in my life to stop me in my tracks and change my direction toward following Jesus.

"Christmas at the Crossroads" is a bit of background on Lynnie's mom, Sue in *Flame of Mercy*, and explains why Lynnie's Grandma and her mom get along so well. And I hope it offers hope to parents of prodigals that God often uses the worst circumstances to bring about great good.

Your friend,

Eleanor Bertin

ACKNOWLEDGMENTS

A special thank you to Sara Davison for her work on the cover, to Brenda Anderson for her insightful suggestions, and to the Mosaic sisterhood for continual encouragement.

ABOUT ELEANOR BERTIN

Before raising and home-educating a family of seven children for thirty years, **ELEANOR BERTIN** worked in agriculture journalism. She returned to writing with her first novel, *Lifelines,* followed by *Unbound, Tethered,* and *Flame of Mercy.* The memoir, *Pall of Silence,* is about her late son, Paul.

Eleanor lives with her husband and youngest son in the Before of what will someday be a beautiful century home in central Alberta where she reads, writes, and sweeps up construction rubble.

Visit her website, www.eleanorbertinauthor.com, to learn more about her books and subscribe to her newsletter. Join her Facebook page, **Read with E's,** or find Eleanor on Amazon, BookBub, Goodreads, and Facebook.

TITLES BY ELEANOR BERTIN

THE MOSAIC COLLECTION
Ties That Bind series
Lifelines
Unbound
Tethered

A Flame of Mercy

THE MOSAIC COLLECTION: ANTHOLOGY STORIES
"Like Wool"
(*Hope is Born: A Mosaic Christmas Anthology*)
"Grounded"
(*Before Summer's End: Stories to Touch the Soul*)
"Love and Unexpected Stress Responses"
(*A Star Will Rise: A Mosaic Christmas Anthology II*)
"A Portion of Grace"
(*Song of Grace: Stories to Amaze the Soul*)
"No Night There"
(*The Heart of Christmas: A Mosaic Christmas Anthology III*)
"How Life Begins"
(*All Things New: Stories to Refresh the Soul*)
"Christmas at the Crossroads"
(*A Whisper of Peace: A Mosaic Christmas Anthology IV*)

NONFICTION
Pall of Silence
(a memoir)

THE MAGIC OF CHRISTMAS

Lorna Seilstad

* * *

Occupational therapist Shayna Winters will do anything to create some magic for her pediatric patients this Christmas. But when an accident on the gridiron lands Dante Gallo's nephew in her care, she has to find a way to make her former boyfriend see that peace is more than an illusion.

CHAPTER ONE

Water splashed, drenching the hospital's overbed table.

Shayna covered the fourteen-year-old's trembling hand and helped him lower the pitcher to the table. "Good work, Luca." She used a hand towel and mopped up the spill. "Now, drink from the cup."

Luca's brow scrunched as he reached for the plastic tumbler, wrapped his fingers around it, and slowly lifted it to his lips. He took several swallows.

Shayna applauded. "Look at that! You didn't spill a drop! You'll be home in no time."

Water sloshed when he sat the tumbler down far too hard. "Home . . . by . . . Christmas." His language processing was slow but according to the speech therapist, no longer slurred and improving every day.

With the towel in hand, she swiped at the water. "That's a good goal, but we'll have to see. The kind of injury you suffered takes time to heal. Remember? Be patient."

"No!" Luca drew back his arm and knocked the tumbler off the table. It bounced across the wood laminate floor and came to a stop in the doorway.

Shayna looked from the cup to her patient. A flare of anger was not uncommon with those who suffer a brain injury, but having to relearn so many simple tasks was even more difficult for the once cocky freshman football player.

After pulling her chair close, she met Luca's eyes. "I know you're frustrated, and you have a right to be angry. I know this feels like it's taking forever, but you have to believe me. You're making great progress. You will be home soon."

"By...Christmas." He hit his fist on his leg.

"We'll do our best."

"What's this, sport?" A deep voice said from the doorway.

Shayna heard the plastic tumbler scrape across the floor as it was scooped up. She turned and stared.

The man marched up to her. "What are you doing here?"

No, no, no. Her patient could not be related to Dante Gallo. Or could he? They had the same last name. Why hadn't she noticed that before? But there's no way Dante had a son Luca's age.

He glared at her. "Shayna, what are you doing in my nephew's room?"

She stood and took a steadying breath. "I am Dante's new occupational therapist. I started here at Oakcrest before Thanksgiving."

"I come every day. How did I not know this?"

She shrugged. "I imagine there's a lot of things you don't know."

Ugh. That was a bit over-the-top. Still, the wound she'd had since high school opened afresh at the sight of him.

Not a boy now. A man.

She collected Luca's tennis shoes from the end of his bed, removed the laces, and replaced them with special-colored laces. "We were just about to work on shoe tying."

"I'm sure there are other OTs here, Shayna. I'll just request a change. It will make things easier for both of us."

51

Shayna bit her lip. It would be easier. "Maybe, that's not a bad idea."

"No!" Luca shouted. "No. She's mine. Not yours."

It was the most fluid sentence she'd heard from Luca, and her heart swelled. What was she thinking? She'd already connected with this young man. She got him, and she had no intention of leaving his care to anyone else. "You're right, Luca. I am here for you."

She turned and pointed to her shirt which read, "Yes, I have a ball pit, a swing, and shaving cream in my office. Yes, I play all day. Yes, I have the coolest job ever. I'm an occupational therapist." With her finger, she underlined the words. "Luca, do you see what this says?"

He nodded. "Do . . . you . . . really . . . have a ball pit?"

He could read and the words were making sense to him. "I do, and a lot of other cool gadgets." She lifted her eyebrows and flashed Luca a big smile. "Just give me a chance to work my magic."

Magic? Dante dropped into one of the chairs in Luca's room and crossed his arms over his chest. What was Shayna trying to pull? Cheerleader turned miracle worker? He refused to believe that was possible. He knew Shayna Winters too well. Everything in her world was lollipops and moonbeams. Sure, she'd been smart, but how could he leave Luca's rehabilitation in the hands of someone who once covered his entire car with sticky notes before a big game?

The big game that had ruined his life.

Shayna awkwardly bent and slipped the sneaker onto

Luca's right foot, placed a small wooden block beneath it, and sat back in her chair.

He studied her. She hadn't changed much in the last eight years. Her golden blonde hair was pulled back with a scrunchy into a messy bun. Was scrunchy the right word? He wasn't exactly an expert on girl—or rather women—stuff. Instead of the contact lenses she wore in high school, she had on a pair of retro looking, navy blue cat-eye glasses which matched her occupational therapist t-shirt. The combination made her steel blue eyes pop.

He shook his head. Stop watching her like some sort of stalker.

Switching his focus to Luca, he found himself flexing his own fingers. The accident had impaired the use of his right, dominant hand, and it now curled inwardly. The therapists said he had muscle weakness, but assured him the brain was very adaptive and rehabilitation would give Luca the best chance of a full recovery.

At first, the right arm hung loose like a noodle. Now, however, Luca had regained some use of it, but he was a long way from being able to hold a pencil or throw a football.

His chest grabbed at the thought of a potentially sports-less life. It was all so unfair, so wrong. Tying his shoes one handed was yet another thing Luca would have to relearn. Shoes today. Passes tomorrow.

"Let's do it again. Cross the green lace over the red and tie a knot." She waited for Luca to comply. "Now, what do you do?"

"Step on the red lace." Luca lifted his foot and placed it on top of the lace, then pulled the green lace until the knot tightened. "Here . . . comes . . . the hard part."

"Yes, but you got this." She pointed to the free end. "Take the green lace and slide it under the red one and form a small

53

loop. Then, make a second small loop and slip that into the other one and pull."

Luca chuckled. "One bunny ear."

"Now, lift up your foot and thread that lace through the knot to form the second loop."

Luca's eyebrows knit together as he struggled to get the second lace into the knot. "I can't do it."

"Take a deep breath. Close your eyes. Picture it in your head and try again when you're ready."

Luca complied. After three more attempts, he managed to get the lace in place and form two overly large loops.

"Outstanding." She put his other shoe on, moved the wooden block beneath that foot, and coached him through tying the second sneaker. "That's great for today. I'll leave you to visit with your uncle."

She stood and gathered her bag.

Dante pushed to his feet and went to Luca. Before she could stop him, he untied the boy's shoes.

"Excuse me?"

"Luca needs the practice."

She bent and tied Luca's shoes, then stood. "He needs to rest."

"Shayna—"

"This isn't a football field, Mr. Gallo. He's recovering from a brain injury. Finding the right balance of work and rest is imperative. You're going to have to trust me. I know what I'm doing, and I know how hard to push my patient."

With that, she whirled, her bag brushing his shoulder as she stalked out.

He stared after her. What was that Mr. Gallo bit? And didn't she understand that the only way to get back in the game was to push through when things got difficult?

Luca chuckled. "She . . . told. . . you."

"As long as you remember who your real coach is."

Luca pointed at him with a shaky right hand. "You."

"That's right." He moved the overbed tray away. "Now, let's get you back in bed. The lady said you needed your beauty rest."

"Did not."

He helped Luca stand, and because his balance was still iffy, he held the cumbersome gait belt as his nephew made his way to the bed.

"Shoes on or off?"

"Off."

Dante removed each sneaker and set them at the end of the bed.

Luca's eyes began to close. "She's pretty."

"Yeah, she is."

"And nice." He opened his eyes and looked at Dante. "Don't . . . make her . . . go away."

"We'll do what's best for you, buddy." Dante ruffled his hair.

If that proved to be Shayna, then he'd support her. But if it wasn't her, he would let her go. After all, he'd done it before. He wouldn't make promises he couldn't keep to Luca. Maybe Shayna had changed, but he doubted it. The girl he knew always went where the fun was or where the breeze blew her. In late November in Nebraska, that wind might blow her right out of his life by tomorrow morning.

He could only hope.

CHAPTER TWO

Papers lie strewn across the dining room table. Shayna rubbed the knot in her neck and made a notation on a legal pad, before closing her laptop. There had to be more she could do for her pediatric clients at Oakcrest Pediatric Rehabilitation Center.

Pediatric patients always required a special touch, but with Christmas fast approaching, so many of her patients seemed listless or despondent. Like Luca Gallo, they wanted to be home opening presents on Christmas morning, not learning how to tie their shoes.

Luca was making remarkable progress, but what would happen if Dante kept pushing him? Should she speak to the boy's mother? Apparently, she lived a couple of hours away, so she was only able to come once a week or so, but Dante lived close enough to visit daily. Often one of the hardest things for teenagers to handle was the feeling they were letting family members down. She knew firsthand how Dante's high expectations could weigh on a person. "If you can't outplay them," he'd told her time and again, "outwork them."

Ironically, she learned later that the motto she'd given

Dante credit for originating came from an old golfer named Ben Hogan. She doubted Dante even realized that.

She rubbed her eyes and squeezed them shut, but Dante's image remained fixated in her mind. The boy she'd known in high school had become a man with broad shoulders that looked great in the crisp white shirt he'd worn today. His Italian lineage provided him with an attractive olive complexion, velvety brown eyes, and a charming smile. According to him, his heritage also made him passionate about anything that mattered to him. His intensity had scared her in high school. He knew what he wanted, and nothing was going to stop him from getting it.

But it had, and he couldn't pivot.

She glanced at the television where a newscaster was predicting a possible snow-mageddon for the first week December. She'd believe it when she saw it. She pushed back her chair and went in the kitchen to make herself a cup of hot chocolate. Now for a much-needed soak in the tub before Nicki got home.

As if the mere thought of her sister signaled her arrival, Shayna heard the beeps of the keypad and the click of the door unlocking. Nicki entered and deposited her oversized gym bag on top of Shayna's papers in the dining room.

Nicki took a bottle of water from the fridge and downed half of it. "Hey, guess who I just ran into at the gym?"

"Serena or Venus Williams?"

Nicki rolled her eyes. "No."

"Michael Jordan?"

"Shayna, no."

"Simone Biles, Apolo Ohno, Patrick Mahomes, Tom Brady, Aaron Rodgers?" She took a sip from her mug. "Want me to keep going?"

"Don't waist your breath. I ran into your ex, Dante the

Hottay from high school." She snagged a yearbook from the bookshelf and plopped down on the couch.

"So?"

"And aren't you curious about what he's doing now? Or how he looks? You two were quite the couple. Prom king and queen." She pointed to a photo in the yearbook. "You remember that, right?"

"Of course I do." She plucked the yearbook from Nicki's hand and returned the volume to the shelf. "I also remember how much I hated my hair that night and how much I loved my dress."

"And how much fun you had?"

"Sure." Shayna took another swallow from her mug. "I'm going to go take a nice long bath."

"But you aren't going to ask me about him?"

"No. Did he ask about me?"

Nicki shook her head and withdrew the purple towel from around her neck.

"Let it go, Nicki. The past is the past. You know as well as I do that I'm not the same person I was in high school, and I doubt if he is either."

The art therapist had been busy helping the patients make decorations for the tree in the reception area over the last few days. Shayna stopped to admire an angel made from a lacey paper doily. Since she had started at Oakcrest only a week before Thanksgiving, she hadn't even had time to set up a nativity scene at home, let alone buy gifts. Maybe she and Nicki would have to plan an evening of decorating, and she needed to get a start on gift selection. If she wasn't careful, it would be silly socks for everyone.

She laughed to herself as she zigzagged through the lounge's stylish gray chairs. Everyone? Her small family could hardly be considered a gift-buying burden. There was a high probability that Mom and Dad would be off on one of their many cruises over Christmas, and Nicki had a boyfriend who had hinted at whisking her away for a ski trip with his family.

Now that she thought about it, maybe the deserters deserved the silly socks for abandoning her. Just once, she wished she could experience a big family Christmas filled with traditions, lots of gifts, and an annoying relative or two.

She pushed her Christmas thoughts aside and joined the rest of the therapy team to discuss the patients. After the meeting concluded, Shayna made her way to the occupational therapy room. She'd rearranged her schedule the day after she'd first run into Dante. Since most visitors came at the same times each day, she hoped that if she avoided seeing Luca at that particular time, she would miss Dante. Five days. So far. So good.

She snagged the virtual reality system case and a short pole before heading to Luca's room. It was time for him to have some fun. In the last few days, he'd appeared more despondent than ever. When she could get him to talk about his feelings, his frustration seemed to come from missing out on all of the things his friends were doing like hanging out, going to school, and especially playing sports. Some of them were supposed to be visiting this Saturday. If things went well today, he'd have something to tell them about.

The team had discussed Luca's progress, and it was decided that after today, all of his therapies would occur outside of his room just as if he were going to work or school. Of course, they'd make sure he had adequate rest as well.

"Good morning, Luca." She was pleased to find him sitting in a chair, fully dressed. "Did you dress yourself?"

He nodded. "And tied shoes."

She glanced down at his sneakers. "Bravo, Luca." She flipped the television off and plopped the carrying case on his bedside table.

"What's . . . that?"

"Have you heard about virtual reality goggles?" She waited for his response. "That's what is inside this case, and today, my friend, you're going to go kayaking. You told me you loved doing that, right?"

Luca nodded, his eyes wide. "Me?"

"Yes, sir. This will make you feel like you're on a vacation. It's so real, there are even fish to see. All you have to do is paddle." She opened the case, removed the two controllers and attached one to each end of the pole. "This will be your paddle."

Once he accepted his "paddle," she began to tuck the Bluetooth earpieces in place and told him to tell her immediately if he felt any discomfort whatsoever. "You're all set."

"Don't I . . . need directions."

"Sure." She slipped the goggles over his eyes. "Don't drown." She pulled the app up on her phone and started the program. "I've cued the Christmas version, so watch for Santa flying over you. I've set it for the relaxing free-roam mode so enjoy the journey."

It took Luca a couple of minutes to catch on, but soon he was exclaiming over the stingrays beneath his kayak and rock formations he was paddling through. He'd completely forgotten he was working both his left and his right arms to maneuver the kayak.

Shayna sat down in the chair and watched her young patient. His right arm still cooperated less than it should, but his left could make up the difference with the makeshift paddle.

Luca would not be the same person he once was, but there was nothing stopping him from embracing who he was now. God had a plan for him, and Shayna took this break to ask God to grant Luca strength and courage as he faced his future. Before she said "amen," she added another request. "Father God, please whisper peace into Dante's heart."

Dante wheeled his Ford F-150 Lightning into a parking space and climbed down. The visitor's parking spaces were nearly empty. Too early in the morning, he guessed. His own schedule varied a great deal because real estate agents did not have nine to five jobs. While that might be difficult for some families, Dante currently considered it a blessing. He could drop in to see Luca any time he found himself with an hour or two of unscheduled free time.

He strode down the hall, but halted abruptly at the door to Luca's room. His nephew sat with some white contraption on his face and held a broom handle in his hands. Luca swung the right end of the broom handle in an arch, then ducked his head. "There's . . . a cave."

Shayna sat in a chair beside him with her back to the door. "Are you going inside it?"

Luca grinned and nodded.

Dante eased into the room and laid a hand on Shayna's shoulder. She jumped and pressed a hand to her chest.

He pointed to the contraption on Luca's head and whispered. "What is that?"

She motioned him into the hallway. "Luca is using a virtual reality system to kayak." She kept her voice low.

"I thought I made it clear that I expect him to be working at this rehab thing." He sounded genuinely surprised Shayna wasn't doing exactly what he'd asked for. "You remember what work is, don't you? Not that you were working that hard sitting next to Luca in there."

Shayna drew in a deep breath and released it slowly. "He is working. Look at him." When he didn't move, she turned him and nudged him toward the door. "Go on. Look."

He peeked around the doorjamb into the room.

She patted his shoulder. "What do you see?"

"My nephew swinging a broom handle."

"No, he's using his upper extremities to paddle, both his left and his right arms. He's interacting mentally and making his mind and body work together, and most importantly, he's enjoying himself." She placed a hand on Dante's arm. "He's a kid. His rehab needs to be fun."

"I know he's a kid." He kept his eyes fixed on his nephew. "But I just want him to get back in the game."

"Which game do you expect him to get back into, Dante?" she asked softly. "He's had a traumatic brain-injury. Playing football on the field is no longer an option for him, or he'd risk re-injury. But if you mean the game of life, that's my goal, too."

"Does this—" Dante waved his finger in circle, "—really make a difference?"

She stepped beside him so she could watch Luca, too. "Yes, it makes a difference. In a normal OT session, we might get twenty repetitions of an activity. Using a VR system, we can get over two hundred repetitions. Even better, the patient doesn't feel like they're working. The gamification makes it fun and makes them feel successful. It's good for his body and his spirit."

Luca let out a whoop. "I found Santa!"

Dante turned to face her, his eyebrows raised.

She grinned and shrugged. "I couldn't resist selecting the Christmas version."

"I haven't seen him smile like this since before the accident." Dante flashed her his trademark, award-winning, dimpled grin. "Are there other VR programs? Can he go skiing? Throw a football?"

"Make spaghetti?" She giggled. "We have several other options, but Dante, enough with the football. I know how much football means to you, but I've read Luca's file. I know he was injured on the gridiron. It might be too traumatic for Luca to engage with football even in the metaverse right now." She glanced at her patient. "I'm trying to introduce him to things which can be a meaningful part of his future. If he loves sports, we'll make sure it's part of his life, but we don't know if he'll be able to compete again the same way he could before. It's too early to tell."

A lump formed in Dante's throat. She didn't understand. It wasn't that he expected Luca to play football again, but he needed him to be okay. A weight pressed down on his chest. He was the reason Luca was here. What if she was right and Luca lost his ability to participate in sports? What if he could never drive? Date? Or go to prom? What if college would now be too difficult?

It would all be his fault.

CHAPTER THREE

It was her fault.

Shayna struggled to keep the mood light with the mercurial Dante, the black hole, sucking the life force from the room. One minute he seemed to be fine, and the next his mood had darkened. She shouldn't have pushed the football issue. Why had she mentioned it just when Dante seemed to be softening toward her treatment plan?

"Okay, sport, one more minute," she said. When the time was up, she eased the VR googles off Luca's head.

Luca blinked as his eyes adjusted to the light. He spotted Dante. "That was awesome!"

Warmth spread through her chest. Not a bit of hesitation in his speech when he spoke that sentence. His excitement was palpable.

Dante placed a hand on his shoulder. "I'm glad you enjoyed it, but you know it's back to work tomorrow."

Shayna's mouth gaped. Did he not hear anything she'd said earlier? Well, she would put a stop to this now. Dante had always been a hands-on learner in school, so that's what she'd do. "Actually, Luca, tomorrow you are going to have a snowball fight."

Luca grinned.

Dante crossed his arms over his chest. "I realize snow is coming, but—"

"It's a VR snowball fight. The program is called 'Merry Snowballs.'" She helped Luca into his bed and drew the blanket up. "PT has a good workout planned for you today, so while you're taking a quick nap, I think I'll give your skeptical uncle a taste of defeat."

Luca pumped his fist. "Beat him."

"That's my plan. A generous dose of humility. Unless he's afraid to take on my challenge." She quirked a brow in Dante's direction. "You game?"

Dante moved to stand in front of her and leaned forward. "On one condition."

"Which is?"

"The loser buys lunch."

Inwardly, she moaned. Lunch? Together? Could she handle that? Her gaze darted from eager Luca to self-assured Dante. His unfair advantage as a football player would mean he'd most likely trounce her even in the metaverse, but if he began to see how the exercises she was doing would help Luca, it might be worth it. Besides, she wanted to ask him to help her with something and lunch was the perfect place to broach the subject.

She struck out her hand. "It's a deal."

Dante knew he looked ridiculous.

He stood in the occupational therapy room wearing a set

of white VR googles, holding a controller in each hand. Only one person could play at a time, so Shayna would watch this time—and probably spend the whole ten minutes laughing at him.

"You block with one controller and throw with the other." She tapped each of his hands and he was surprised by the current her touch triggered. "The goal is to become Master of the Snow. There are different levels like Gingerbread Destruction which you may or may not reach."

"Have you?"

"Destroyed gingerbread men? Of course." Shayna smirked. "Most of them were in cookie form, but I made sure there was nothing but crumbs remaining. Click the arrow when you're ready to start."

As Dante hurled snowballs at stocking cap-clad cartoon children in the metaverse, he soon forgot how he must look to Shayna. He spun and swooped. He took out a snowman. The more he scored, the faster the pace became.

"Ah!" He lifted the goggles. "I ran out of time." He rattled off his score and dared her to beat it.

She stepped to the center of the room and took the proffered goggles. "Did you cap any gingerbread men?"

"No. In fact, I don't think there are any."

"Hmmm." She held a controller in each hand. "Well, my friend, let me show you how the cookie crumbles."

He wished he could, in fact, see what she was seeing, but he loved watching the expressions on her face when she clearly made a successful shot. Her head reared back and he guessed she'd had a snowball thrown in her face.

She chuckled and drew her arm behind. She appeared to throw the imaginary snowball. "Take that gingerbread man!"

Was she serious about the gingerbread man? How would he ever know?

She ripped off the googles and held them aloft. "Beat you

by 500 points!" She set the controllers in the case. "And I'm hungry for—" She tapped her chin. "—a Runza."

Half an hour later, he found himself following her into the fast-food restaurant native to Nebraska. She'd always liked Runzas, a yeast dough bread pocket filled with seasoned ground beef, cabbage, and onions. Today, she ordered one with cheese and a side of onion rings. He chose one with a Swiss Mushroom Runza and a side salad.

"Are you limping?" he asked as they made their way to an empty table.

"Maybe. My foot fell asleep on the way over." She sat down and sipped at her Diet Coke. "Give me your honest opinion of Merry Snowballs."

"I enjoyed it."

"But?"

"No buts, I can even see its merits as a form of therapy. You can't help but get into it and want more when you're done." He leaned forward. "Honestly, is there really a level with gingerbread men?"

"I guess you'll have to ask Luca after he plays." Her lips curled and her eyes twinkled.

An all-too-familiar twinkle.

Alarm bells sounded in his mind. While Shayna had never been far from his thoughts, he'd carefully packed her away with the rest of his high school memories. Sure, they'd been good together. Great actually. And they'd been as in love as two eighteen-year-old kids could be, but he needed to be careful now. Shayna's creativity, confidence, and wholesome nature made her nearly irresistible. Fun-loving, she'd made him less serious. In return, she used to say he was her anchor.

But the one thing he hadn't been able to deal with was her flightiness. She bounced around from one fun adventure to another like a ping pong ball. Even after he blew out his knee during the state finals, ending his college football career,

Shayna wanted him to "look on the bright side." Where was the bright side when all of his dreams had been destroyed in one bad tackle?

Shayna jerked her head up. "Isn't that the number of our order they're calling?"

He shook his head. "Oh yeah, I'll get it." He returned with the tray and set it on the table.

After she passed out the paper wrapped food, she paused and looked at him, a question in her eyes. "I know we used to—"

"Yeah." He clasped his hands together to keep from reaching for hers. "Let's pray."

CHAPTER FOUR

It had been hard to concentrate on the words of prayer when fireworks were going off in her head.

Shayna offered Dante a quick goodbye when they returned to Oakcrest. She made an excuse of needing to get back to work and hurried inside. In truth, she was struggling with the long-buried feelings that surfaced at being near Dante. Her world had been turbulent in the last few years, and she'd found herself yearning for his solid strength. She'd pushed those feelings aside. After all, feelings didn't dictate her choices.

Still, she knew one thing: having lunch with him had been a mistake.

Dante had been open to talking about Luca's care, but he'd stopped short of saying he trusted her. He'd asked about her training and seemed surprised at all the places she'd volunteered even before entering the occupational therapy program. She'd asked about what he was doing now and learned he had his own real estate agency with four agents in his employ.

He asked where she lived and frowned when she gave her

address. "You should really let me hook you up with a place in a better neighborhood."

She'd explained that she rented and wasn't ready to purchase a home since she had no idea how long she'd be in Oakcrest. His disapproval had been obvious, but she'd managed to change the subject by asking about his family.

Now, as she climbed out of the car, she remembered she wanted to ask for his help with her Christmas plans for the children. The timing, however, didn't feel right.

Timing had never been their forte.

She hurried inside and arrived back in the OT room in time for the aide to roll ten-year-old Ansleigh in. A fall from a slide had left Ansleigh with a fractured vertebrae. Physical therapy was working with the girl to walk again, but Shayna was focused on the girl's fine motor skills. Bright and bubbly, Ansleigh usually embraced any activity with gusto, but when Shayna spread shaving cream across the tray for Ansleigh to write her name in, she made a half-hearted attempt.

"What's the matter, sweetheart? You seem sad."

"Tonight is our school Christmas concert, and I'm missing it. I want to go to school with my friends."

Shayna placed her hand on Ansleigh's arm. "Of course you do. And you will get there."

Fat tears filled the girl's eyes. "But I won't be there tonight."

"No, you won't." Shayna leaned back in her chair and sighed. "No, but I do have an idea of how you can perform."

Shayna hurried to a cabinet and withdrew a small, black case. She brought it over to Ansleigh and set it on the table. "This, my friend, is a magic kit." Shayna nodded and opened it wide. "Let's learn a trick so that you can show your parents later."

A broad smile erupted on Ansleigh's face. Shayna showed her how to make three balls penetrate the solid cups. The girl practiced her "trick" over and over again—sometimes successfully and mostly not. Still, she kept on trying to master it, even begging to take the cups and balls back to her room.

An idea began to take shape in Shayna's mind. The children were missing out on so much this Christmas, but what if all pediatric patients worked on something special— something magic?

Bright and early Friday morning, Shayna arrived at Oakcrest prepared to present her ideas to her fellow occupational therapists. While the concept of using magic tricks in OT had been around for quite some time, the idea of making a magic event for the families would be unusual. They'd done proms, played hide and seek, and even had their patients model in a fashion show. Would this be all that different?

She needed everyone to be on board. If anyone had their doubts, it wouldn't work. The last thing she wanted was for one child to feel left out at Christmas.

The other OTs filed into the meeting room and took their places. They looked quizzically at the magic kits she had stacked on the table, but didn't ask her any questions. They covered a number of topics, and finally, it was her turn to speak. She explained the need for the children to have something to look forward to. She talked about how magic tricks allow a child to do something others cannot, and that performing magic allows the child to know the "secret."

She pulled out metal rings from the kit. "We all know David Copperfield's Project Magic is endorsed by the American Occupational Therapy Association, but what I'm suggesting is on a much smaller scale. After all, we only have three weeks to get the kids ready."

To her delight, everyone loved the idea, and an animated discussion began about each of the OT's experiences using magic tricks with patients.

"I've always been impressed at how much a child's self-esteem improves when they master a trick," thin-faced Jeremy said. "In addition to their dexterity, of course."

Rita, a frizzy-haired woman who'd been at Oakcrest the longest, pulled one of the kits closer. "We can catalogue all of the magic tricks available and decide which one would best meet our patient's needs right now. Shall we set a date for the families to come?"

Amanda, the softest-spoken OT, pulled up the calendar on her phone. "December twentieth would give us over three weeks to practice."

Rita tapped her pen on the table. "What should we call it? It's your baby, Shayna. Any ideas?"

Shayna took in all of the eager faces and her spirit soared. "What do you think about 'The Magic of Christmas Extravaganza'?"

CHAPTER FIVE

With snow forecasted for the end of the day, Dante decided to visit Luca early.

He wasn't surprised when he found Luca's room empty. He asked at the desk to find out where his nephew was. A few minutes later, he located him in the gym, working with the physical therapist. Ned, the balding, middle-aged physical therapist, had Luca standing on a balance board and reaching across his body to retrieve puzzle pieces from Ned's hand. After Luca collected a puzzle piece, he would place it in the correct spot on the board in front of him.

"Hi there!" Ned waved Dante over. "We haven't seen you for a couple of days. We're working on Luca's core strength, his balance, coordination, and muscle memory, and he's doing great."

Dante eyed the gait belt still strapped around Luca's midsection and winced. When could he get rid of that thing? Every time Dante saw that belt, the guilt nearly crushed him. It was such a stark reminder that Luca was not safe on his own, a thought that tore at Dante day and night.

"Why don't you step up here and give me a hand?" Ned

stepped aside. "Just hold out one of the puzzle pieces like this." He demonstrated by holding it aloft. "Now, Luca, use your right hand and reach across your body to get it."

Luca followed the directions and retrieved the puzzle piece.

"Good job, buddy." Dante picked up another piece and held it a little farther away.

"Easy." Ned pulled Dante's hand in closer. "We're working on balance, not trying to make him fall."

Once the puzzle was complete, Ned had Dante move to a different area. He then directed Luca to step sideways, keeping his knees slightly bent and a shoulder length apart. "Dante, you hold the belt just in case he needs to be steadied."

Dante swallowed hard and grasped the belt. Luca assumed the squatted position, and with determination etched on his face, took five sidesteps to the right, then repeated it with five sidesteps to the left. The sidesteps were a far cry from what Luca could do a month ago at practice, but at least this resembled the workout he was used to.

"Slow." Luca glanced back at Dante.

"You're doing great." Dante clapped him on the shoulder. "Focus."

When Ned said he believed Luca had worked hard enough for the day, Dante fought the urge to encourage his nephew to do a few more reps. The therapists knew what they were doing. He was working hard to remember that. They had the training, and Luca needed their expertise to get his life back.

As part of his new plan, Luca was wheeled from PT straight to OT. Dante followed, wondering when Luca would be able to walk from one location to another. Maybe once he was more steady on his feet.

"Luca, how's it going?" Shayna walked in and stopped short. "Oh, hi, Dante. I didn't realize you were here."

"Hello, Shayna." He casually leaned against the wall. "I'll just watch from over here."

Shayna got a button-down shirt from a hook and laid it on the table in front of Luca. "Today, we're going to work on buttoning and unbuttoning a shirt."

"If . . . you . . . say so." Luca's head lolled forward when he laughed. "I don't wear these."

Shayna pushed up her glasses. "I do say so, and you might when you go to the next dance."

"Who . . . would go . . . with me?"

"By the time we're done here, the girls will be fighting over you." Shayna pointed to the shirt, then cued him to take hold of the fabric in one hand and try to push the button back through the hole with the other. When he struggled, she glanced at Dante. "It's takes bilateral coordination."

"But his right hand isn't working that well." Dante moved closer.

"That's why we're doing this." She continued to encourage Luca's efforts until the shirt lay open. "Awesome! Now, let's see if you can button it."

Five minutes later, Luca still hadn't managed to get one button through the buttonhole. His face reddened. He wadded the shirt into a ball.

Shayna put her hand over his. "Close your eyes. Take a deep breath." She waited while he self-regulated. "Now, let's take a break. We'll work on buttoning the shirt tomorrow. Do you want to show Dante your surprise?"

He nodded.

Shayna scooped up the shirt, put it on the shelf and brought back four metal rings. She turned to Dante. "Luca is learning a magic trick. Watch."

Luca fingered two of the rings until he had them where he wanted them. He held up a ring to show it was solid, then he struck the two rings together. On the third strike, the rings linked. Excitement bubbled in Luca's face when he looked at Dante.

"Wow!" Dante was truly impressed, and Luca was clearly proud of his accomplishment.

"We're going to . . . have a show."

Dante looked at Shayna for confirmation. "May I be the first to invite you to Oakcrest's very own *Magic of Christmas Extravaganza*. All of our pediatric patients will be participating."

"Was this your idea?"

She gave a little bow.

It figured. Magic tricks were right up there with fairies and unicorns making this another one of Shayna's fanciful ideas. Still, did it have merit? What could it do for Luca's recovery?

He glanced at the balled-up shirt on the shelf and then at Luca with that ugly gait belt secured around his waist. Anger simmered inside him. How could Shayna justify taking the time to teach his nephew magic tricks when Luca couldn't even button a shirt?

"Absolutely not." The anger simmering in Dante's chest threatened to explode, but at least he kept it under control until Luca had gone.

Shayna stared at Dante in disbelief.

"Who do I need to talk to in order to get this show stopped?" he demanded. "Luca can't tie his shoes or button his shirt, but you have him doing magic tricks?" Dante ran his hand through his hair. "Shayna, this isn't a game! Don't you understand you're playing with lives here?"

Her face reddened. "I am not playing with anyone's life, and I know better than anyone that this isn't a game."

"Luca needs to be coached, not coddled. No one is going to wave a magic wand and make his problems go away." He pointed his finger toward the rings on the table. "*That* is not what he needs."

"How do you know what Luca needs? Have you ever faced a life-changing trauma?" She stiffened and met his gaze with steely eyes. "And I'm not talking about a career-ending knee injury. I'm talking about something that changes how you do every . . . little . . . thing in your life. How you dress. How you feed yourself. How you go to the bathroom." She sucked in a breath. "No, Dante Gallo, you haven't. You cannot possibly understand what Luca needs."

This was ridiculous. He waved his hands in the air. "And you do?"

With her jaw clenched, she walked to a chair and sat. Slowly, she lifted her pant leg to reveal a prosthetic leg. She knocked on it and the resounding thunk seemed to fill the room. "Yes. I do."

The color drained from Dante's face. "When did— How did—"

"Sit down, Dante." Her tone softened, and she waited until he'd sunk into the chair across from her. Then, she pulled her pant leg down. "I was in a motorcycle accident my sophomore year of college. The bike belonged to my boyfriend at the time. He was driving, and thankfully, was not badly injured. That wasn't the case for me. They couldn't save my leg, and I had a below-the-knee amputation."

"I'm so sorry. I had no idea." Tears shone in his eyes, and he rubbed the back of his neck. "Why didn't you get ahold of me?"

"You know why. We didn't exactly end on a good note." She leaned forward and rested her arms on the table. "It was my journey. I had to relearn everything from walking to driving to swimming. It's what made me want to become an occupational therapist. God was with me every step of the way."

"I would have been there for you."

"Like you're there for Luca?"

He drew in a sharp breath.

"Dante, I'm sorry. I know you have his best interest at heart, but I need you to understand I'm not the same person. In high school I might have bounced around from one thing to another, but that was eight years ago—a lifetime ago. I am not that girl anymore. You have to trust me. Not just because I'm a professional, but because I know what it's like to have your world spin out of control. He needs to believe in himself. He needs to find his own strength. You can't force him to find the motivation. Sure, he also needs to work on his fine motor skills and his bilateral coordination, but right now, he needs something to look forward to. This magic show can do that."

Dante's brows pulled slightly together, and he tilted his head to the side. "Shayna, I am so sorry."

She stood abruptly. "Don't you dare. I don't want your pity."

"But if we hadn't broken up."

"Losing my leg was not your fault. Luca's brain-injury is not your fault." She jammed her hands on her hips. "Newsflash. The world does not revolve around Dante Gallo and it never did."

His Adam's apple bobbed. "I feel responsible."

"And it's tearing you up." She sighed. "Let God be God, Dante. None of this—not your knee injury, not Luca's accident, and not my amputation—surprised God. At some point you have to 'be still and know that He is God.' When are you going to be still, Dante? When are you going to let God give you the peace you need?"

Dante's chest heaved, and his words refused to align and form sentences. He had always believed in God. He had believed God had plans for Him, but did he trust Him? And when was the last time he sat in the stillness of God's presence.

CHAPTER SIX

Shayna climbed out of her car and drank in the fresh scent of snow on the ground. Thankfully, the weather forecasters had been wrong—again--and the latest snow-mageddon had turned out to be only three inches of fluff. The blanket of snow cast an instant Christmas aura on everything.

She scanned the vehicles in the visitor's parking area for Dante's truck. It had been two weeks since she spoke to him, and she didn't see his Ford today. The last thing she thought he'd do was abandon Luca. Over the weekend she'd even called Luca's unit to see if Dante had visited and the clerk said Luca had a parade of family visitors including his mother, but there'd been no sign of Dante. The clerk added that Luca's mother said she was staying through Tuesday so she could be at the magic show. While Shayna was excited for her to see Luca's progress, she worried about what Dante had shared with her. Would she be the one to have her pulled from Luca's care even at this point?

And where was Dante? Had she pushed him too hard?

A familiar ache formed deep inside her, and she could no longer deny it. She missed him. Even as stubborn and unyielding as he was, she wanted him in her life. She covered her lips with her gloved hand. She didn't miss high school Dante, she was missing the man she knew today. "Oh, Lord, please help me protect my heart."

She crossed the reception area and walked to her office. A snarl of worries, doubts, and questions tangled inside her like a string of Christmas lights. This was not an emotionally safe path for her to go down. Dante had demons to deal with, and if she got involved right now, she'd be collateral damage. For whatever reason, Dante seemed tormented by Luca's accident on the field.

She pulled her gloves off, hung up her coat, and sighed. Hot tears spilled from her eyes. "Lord," she prayed, "I want Dante to be happy, but he'll never change, will he? He needs control too much to rest in Your perfect peace. Please, Lord, whisper peace into his heart."

She sank down into her office chair and spotted the poster she had hanging on her office wall. She'd put it up when she first arrived. It been an office warming gift from Rita. The words on the poster, now so familiar, hit her hard. "Never say never because limits, like fears, are often just an illusion."

Goose flesh prickled her skin. Had God just used Michael Jordan to speak to her heart or was it just wishful thinking?

Shayna stood back and watched Luca complete the task of dressing himself. With his mother looking on, Luca did up every button on his shirt without assistance. He then slid his feet into his tennis shoes and had them secured with loopy bows.

Shayna's heart swelled. That morning in their therapy

meeting, Luca's remarkable progress had been discussed. His physical therapist believed he'd "turned the corner." His gait and balance had improved significantly as had his speech. She, too, had to admit the young man had mastered the necessary self-reliance skills in record speed in the last week.

"It's the magic," Rita told them during the meeting. "Shayna saw he needed to see what he *could* do. Not what he couldn't."

Currently, the main thing stopping him from being released from in-patient care was the concern over outpatient services in the small town where his mother lived. The social worker on the case said she was going to examine the options and how his small school was set up to handle his return.

"I can't believe how much progress you've made." Sofia, Luca's mother, kissed her son's cheek. "You have the heart of a champion."

The aide walked in and asked Shayna if Luca was ready to go to physical therapy.

"Yes, we're done for now. We'll work on your handwriting this afternoon." Shayna glanced at Sofia. "I'm sure you'll want to go along so you can watch his PT work, too."

"Actually, I'd like some time to speak with you." Sofia indicated the empty chairs. She waved at Luca. "I'll be down shortly."

Shayna lowered herself into the chair and drew in a deep, steadying breath. Was this it? Perhaps Sofia simply wanted more insight into Luca's prognosis or information on how to assist him once he was home. "What can I do for you?"

Sofia leaned forward in her chair, resting her elbows on her knees. "You can start by telling me where my brother is."

Shayna sucked in a breath. "I honestly don't know."

"No one has seen him all week, and Luca said the two of you had words."

"We did." Shayna removed her glasses and fiddled with

them. "Dante seems to be struggling with a lot of guilt concerning Luca's situation. I was encouraging him to—"

"Stop playing God?" She leaned back in her chair and pulled a mass of dark curls to one side of her neck.

"Not in so many words, but that was the gist of it."

"Did you know that Luca worshipped Dante?"

"I can tell they're very close."

"They are and I'm grateful." She met Shayna's gaze. "As a single mother, I knew my son needed a male role model and Uncle Dante was there for him. Dante's first gift to Luca was a football shaped rattle. Naturally, Luca grew up loving football because Dante shared his passion with him." She paused and reached for a Starbuck's cup. After she swallowed, she returned to her story. "And it was all great. Dante is a good role model. He's a man of integrity. He's hard working, and he's fiercely protective, but you know all that."

Shayna nodded.

"And Luca showed a great deal of athletic promise, just like Dante had. My Luca began playing football in middle school. By the time he reached high school, he was already on the coach's radar. The whole season, he'd done well as a tight end. He started in every varsity game even as a freshman." She stood up and walked to the window. "During the championship game, he got hit hard, but he wasn't knocked unconscious. The coach took him out, but it made Dante mad. He wanted him to walk it off and stay in the game. Then, on the sidelines, Luca collapsed and had a seizure." She turned. "It was a brain bleed. We learned later that he'd taken a hard hit two weeks earlier in a practice that he didn't tell anyone about."

"So Dante feels responsible for what happened to Luca?"

Sofia nodded. "I believe he does. It's not his fault. It's not anyone's fault, but this is tearing Dante up."

83

"He kept saying he needed Luca to get back in the game. Do you want him to play again, too?"

Sofia's eyes widened. "No, absolutely not, and I don't think that's what he meant. At least that's not what I understand from when we talked. I think Dante just wants the boy he loves to come back. When he first came here, it seemed as if we'd lost that boy, but now we can see he's in there, thanks to all of you."

"And thanks to Dante." Shayna met Sofia in the middle of the room. "As much as Dante's 'work harder' mentality drove me crazy, I know Luca wants to make his uncle proud. It's the real reason he's made leaps and bounds this week. He wants to show Dante what he can do." She took Sofia's hands in hers. "I can't imagine how difficult this has been for you."

Sofia's eyes brimmed with tears. "My heart was here with my son, even if I couldn't be. I couldn't have let Luca stay if I didn't know Dante was with him."

"Come on." Shayna linked her arm with Sofia's. "Let's go find your son so you can see for yourself how good he's getting around. As for Dante, we have to trust that God's working on his hard head and on his heart."

CHAPTER SEVEN

Shayna stood beside eight-year-old Timothy as he showed an empty black top hat to the audience at the Magic of Christmas Extravaganza.

He set the hat back down and waved a wand over the hat with his weaker hand. "Abracadabra!"

Then, he reached into the felt hat and withdrew a stuffed rabbit. He held it aloft, and those in attendance applauded. She reminded him to take a bow and steadied him as he did so.

As Rita brought a freckled faced Ethan up, Shayna returned to her seat and looked around at the extravaganza. The front table had been draped with a plastic black tablecloth. Behind it, the art therapist had had her patients design a banner with the words "The Magic of Christmas" displayed in glittery, swirling letters. Sofia had helped by adding strings of white lights around the staging area.

To Shayna's delight, the gym was filled with patients and parents. Only one person was missing.

Dante Gallo.

Little Ethan held the ends of two brightly colored scarf

chains in his postured hands and Rita pulled down on each of them. The colors "magically" changed, and the crowd cheered.

Child after child took their place in the spotlight to display the mastery of their magic trick, aided by their occupational therapist "assistant." Decks of cards magically revealed the correct card, pens slid through dollar bills, and wands danced in the hands of the young illusionists. Oos and ahs from the audience only added to the joy in the room.

Shayna had saved Luca until last in hopes of Dante making an appearance. He walked to the stage table with his rings in hand. She stood back and let him clink them together and make them magically link, then add more links to the chain. He played to the audience like a pro and delivered a dazzling smile that reminded her so much of Dante's.

She turned to Sofia and Shayna's heart leapt. Two men stood beside Sofia's chair. One was Dante, who clapped exuberantly, but who was the other man in the flashy orange satin shirt?

When the applause died away, she started to thank everyone for coming, but Dante stepped forward and held up his hands. "If you'll forgive me, I have a surprise, too."

"If you tell me you've learned how to saw a woman in half in the last week, I'm not volunteering," Shayna muttered.

He ignored her. "Ladies and gentlemen, boys and girls, may I present to you, Mr. Johnny Impossible!"

Two of the aids carried in a new table laden with magic equipment, and the man beside Sofia stepped forward and bowed with a flourish. Dante took hold of Shayna's hand and tugged her off the stage.

"How did you plan all this?" Shayna breathed in Dante's ear once they were seated. "And where have you been?"

"We'll talk after the show."

The illusionist lauded the young "magic apprentices" he'd

just watched and then awed them with a show filled with fun, laughter, and hoards of magic tricks.

Dante draped his arm around Shayna's shoulders and drew her close.

Maybe it was the excitement of the kids or maybe it was the magic in the air, but she let herself relax into his embrace.

Tomorrow, she'd be facing her sparce Christmas plans, but tonight, she was in a room filled with the happy, victorious children she loved.

CHAPTER EIGHT

Shayna rolled the last of the plastic tablecloths into a ball. The other OTs had gathered the magic tricks and put them away. Johnny Impossible had remained after his show to talk more with the children. He also made them elaborate Christmas balloons shaped like trees, elves, reindeer, snowmen, and Santa to carry back to their rooms.

Dante walked over to her. "Sofia told me to tell you goodbye. She has to head home tonight."

"I wish she didn't live so far away."

"I'm working on that." Dante took the tablecloth ball from Shayna's hands and tossed it in the trashcan, lay-up style.

"Impressive." Shayna grinned. "Basketball is not exactly your sport."

"Hey, I can pivot."

She hiked her brows. "Since when?"

"I'm evolving. You'll see."

Rita thanked Shayna for all of her hard work and thanked Dante for sponsoring Johnny Impossible's appearance. "It was the icing on the cake or should I say on the icing on the Christmas cookie. Now, you two go on and get out of here."

Ten minutes later, Shayna walked out of Oakcrest with Dante beside her. He seemed so different. Maybe he'd suffered a head injury—a good one. Questions filled her mind, but she wasn't sure if this was the time or place to ask them.

He walked her to her car. "I've got something to show you." He took a dollar bill from his pocket and folded it in half. Then, he made another fold and covered his creation with his other hand. When he pulled his free hand away, he revealed an origami heart. "This is for you."

"A dollar tip?"

"No, not a tip. You were right. I was trying to control it all and not letting God be God. It's just when Luca got hurt, I felt so responsible."

"I know."

"I didn't realize how angry I was with God. I said I trusted Him, but I didn't really. So this week, I've been in the scriptures, letting God heal my heart." He paused and held up the origami heart. "So that I can give it to you."

"Cheesy but adorable." She took the heart and blinked away the tears in her eyes. But what if he changed his mind tomorrow?

"This isn't as Johnny would say a 'presto chango' thing for me. I've done some real soul searching. I've spent days in prayer and God has opened my eyes to what I've done." He cupped her cheek. "I'm sorry I hurt you—then and now."

She pressed her hand over his. "Never say never." The words of the poster came back to her. God had heard her prayers and answered them. Dante had changed, and the best part was that she could see the peace and love in his eyes.

Her heart raced. Her head told her to get in the car, but her heart told her to take a chance. Her heart won.

"Dante Gallo, you already know you've got me under your spell, so stop apologizing and kiss me."

"I don't have any mistletoe."

"You don't need it." She stood on tiptoe, one leg lifted behind her, and pressed her lips to his.

He pulled her close, one strong arm encircling her waist and the other reaching behind her neck. He kissed her again, softly at first, then tilted his head, and deepened the kiss—a kiss that magically silenced all the noises in her head.

CHAPTER NINE

Shayna had the best Christmas gift ever to deliver. She carried the cardboard box into Luca's room and plopped it down on top of the checkerboard.

"Pack it up, boys." She motioned to Luca and Dante. "Luca Gallo, the doctors and therapists have all agreed it's time for you to go ho-ho-ho-home."

Dante chuckled, but Luca seemed too excited to appreciate her Santa impression.

"I'm going home?" The pitch of Luca's voice was high.

"Sort of." She smiled. "You're headed to your grandparents' home for a while until we can get outpatient services arranged, but you'll be with your family for Christmas."

"But where's my mom?"

"Your mom said Dante could do the honors of delivering you to their doorstep. She's making fish with your grandmother." She couldn't keep the incredulity at making fish on Christmas eve from her voice. Sofia had made the fish-making sound important. "So, let's get you packed up."

She untacked photos and posters from the walls, while

Dante cleared the closet and dresser. When they were nearly done, Shayna handed Luca his jacket. "Last test. Put this on."

He stood and spread the jacket flat on the bed.

"Does he still need that?" Dante scowled.

Shayna looked where Dante was pointing. "The gait belt?"

Dante nodded. "I mean if he does, it's okay, but—"

"I think he'll be fine." She smiled and unclipped the belt. She handed it Dante. "A souvenir so you can remember we all need help sometimes?"

"Funny." He rolled the belt and set it in the box with Luca's other things.

Unlike a hospital, Luca did not have to ride in a wheelchair to leave. In fact, therapists, aids, and nurses lined the halls and applauded as he walked with a slight limp out of Oakcrest . Dante walked beside him, carrying the cardboard box. Shayna wheeled Luca's suitcase behind them.

Getting up into the Ford F-150 proved to be quite a feat, and she made a mental note to mention that to PT. He had practiced putting on a seat belt, and her chest warmed when he managed doing so without any prompting. Dante shut his door and walked over to her.

"Thank you for everything, Shayna." He kissed her cheek.

"You're welcome." She pulled her coat more tightly about her. "Now, go be with your family."

Dante knocked on Shayna's door.

Almost two minutes later, she opened the door wearing leggings and an oversized hoodie with a gingerbread man in a Santa's hat on it. The gingerbread's left foot had been eaten and a speech bubble proclaimed, "Seriously?"

"Cute shirt." He nudged her aside and came indoors. "But unless you want to meet my family in that, I suggest you change."

"What? Why aren't you home with them?"

"Let me use what I learned from you." He opened the fridge and took out a can of whipped cream. He squirted some of it on the table and wrote. "Christmas eve with me and my family?"

"You're incorrigible."

"And bossy and stubborn and a whole host of other offenses, but you still love me." He flashed her a grin and turned her towards the bedroom. "You've got ten minutes."

It took her fifteen, but when she emerged from the bedroom, he decided every minute had been worth it. She had on a red and green plaid jumper over a white turtleneck. Around her neck, she wore the heart necklace he'd given her in high school.

"Sorry," she said, snagging her coat. "I had to switch legs."

He'd forgotten about her prosthetic entirely. They had yet to talk about the experience. In fact, they still had so much to talk about.

He glanced down and noticed she was wearing chunky, black healed boots. Very attractive. "You look great. Shall we?"

She looked at the kitchen table where the whipped cream had puddled. "After you clean up your mess."

Not that Shayna had ever heard of the Feast of Seven Fishes, but she noticed Dante seemed unusually proud to proclaim this was her first.

Shayna sat at the large dining room table surrounded by

Dante's parents, his paternal grandparents, his sisters, several aunts and uncles, and of course, Luca. Dante squeezed her hand under the table. On the way over he'd explained that the Feast of Seven Fishes was an Italian Christmas tradition where only fish was eaten. However, while fish might be the only protein, his mother, his nonna, his sisters and his aunts did not believe *only* fish should be served.

They started with appetizers which included fried calamari, a seafood salad, and shrimp cocktail. The scents wafting from the next round of dishes set before her made her mouth water. The pasta and risotto dishes waited for no one, according to his aunt. Dante told her the names of each item presented, but the only one she remembered was her favorite —the lobster fra diavolo. Shayna thought she was in heaven when she tasted the spicy, tomatoey lobster-packed spaghetti dish.

The main dish was fish piccatta or fish fillets with a bright, caper studded lemon-butter sauce. When Shayna reached the point where she felt like she'd burst, she leaned back in her chair and listened to the family surrounding her, sharing stories of Christmases past and laughing together in a way that only a large family can do.

She glanced at Luca, and he grinned back at her. This was why he wanted to be home.

After another half an hour had passed, Dante's mother announced it was time for dessert. She hefted a tray filled with delicate cookies, tiny cups of panna cotta, and thick slices of pannettone, his nonna's specialty. "This is amazing," she told his grandmother after taking a butter slathered bite.

"Pannettone is a labor of love." She winked at Shayna. "Crafted by tradition and a passion to please the senses. Italians are passionate people, you know."

"So I've been told." She took another bite.

Dante's grandfather leaned forward. "We love fiercely. You'll see."

Her cheeks heated, and Dante pressed a kiss to her temple and whispered. "Are you ready for a break from the family madness?"

She nodded, and he excused them from the table, insisting for privacy in the living room. That only brought out more whoops and comments, but all in good fun.

They went into the living room, and he sat down on the floor with his back pressed against the sofa and facing the Christmas tree. "Come sit with me."

She eyed him. "I can get down, but getting back up might not be pretty."

"Everything you do is beautiful."

"We both know that's not true." She sat down on the couch, then eased to the floor, and scooted until she was in front of him, propped against his chest. He draped his arms around her, and they sat in silence, listening to the raucous chatter in the other room. She exhaled slowly. "I love your family."

"You always wanted a big family."

"I wouldn't change my family for the world, but yes, I've always wanted to be surrounded by family like this on Christmas. Thank you for bringing me."

He pulled her closer and he pointed out different ornaments on the tree that were heirlooms from Italy. "And that one," he pointed to a baby shoe, "is from Luca's first Christmas. Did I tell you that I found the perfect house for Luca and Sofia? It's one-level and nearby. A great price, too. She's been looking for a job in the metro area and has an interview after the first of year." His breath tickled Shayna's ear. "It sounds great to me, but I know Luca misses his friends, too. I'd love to have them closer, but I'm trying to leave it in God's hands."

"What else are you trying to leave in God's hands?"

"Us." He kissed the top of her head. "I love you, Shayna Winters. I never stopped. I just let my own frustration and anger drive you away. Everything in me wants to get down on one knee and ask you to share the rest of my life with me, but that's me taking charge again. We need time to grow closer to Him and to each other."

She laid her hand on his forearms and felt the solid muscles beneath her fingertips. She could feel the beat of his heart, steady and true, against her back. She wanted that security. It would be so easy to tell him she was ready to be with him forever, but he was right. They needed more time. "I'm at peace with that. Are you?"

He brushed her hair aside and kissed the back of her neck, then laughed when she shivered in his arms. He hugged her so tightly it felt as if he'd hold onto her forever.

And if God answered her prayers, Dante would do exactly that.

ABOUT LORNA SEILSTAD

LORNA SEILSTAD brings history back to life using a generous dash of humor. She is a Carol Award finalist and the author of the **Lake Manawa Summers** series and the **Gregory Sisters** series. Her stories are also part of several novella collections. When she isn't eating chocolate, she teaches women's Bible classes, volunteers with 4-H, and is a wedding planner. She and her husband have three adult children and live in Iowa.

Learn more about Lorna at www.lornaseilstad.com.

TITLES BY LORNA SEILSTAD

THE MOSAIC COLLECTION
Watercolors
More Than Enough

THE MOSAIC COLLECTION: ANTHOLOGY STORIES
"Claus-trophobic"
(*The Heart of Christmas: A Mosaic Christmas Anthology III*)
"The Magic of Christmas"
(*A Whisper of Peace: A Mosaic Christmas Anthology IV*)

THE GREGORY SISTERS SERIES
When Love Calls
While Love Stirs
As Love Blooms

THE LAKE MANAWA SUMMERS SERIES
Making Waves
A Great Catch
The Ride of Her Life

NOVELLA COLLECTIONS
Seven Brides for Seven Texans
Seven Brides for Seven Texas Rangers
First Love Forever Romance Collection

Victorian Christmas Brides Collection
The Soldier's Lady: 4 Historical Stories

A SINGLE SPARK OF LIGHT

Sara Davison

* * *

a two sparrows for a penny prequel

God had abandoned him a long time ago. And Ty didn't blame him one bit.

Tyrone Jones will never forgive himself for the people he hurt in the past. And he has no reason to believe that God will ever forgive him either. Until he meets a stranger on a bridge one night a couple of weeks before Christmas.

A stranger who sends Ty on a quest that just might change his life—and his heart—forever.

The light shines in the darkness,
and the darkness has not overcome it.

~ John 1:5

CHAPTER ONE

It was possible that prison hadn't done as good a job of knocking the darkness out of him as Ty had hoped. The colorful Christmas lights twinkling in store windows and decorating utility poles and pretty much every other available surface in the downtown Toronto core only highlighted that fact. Reminded him that any glow *he* might once have carried inside him had been snuffed out the night he'd pulled the trigger on that unsuspecting kid.

Zach McConnell. Not an innocent, a rival gang member. Still, the drive-by attack had caught the eighteen-year-old unaware, and he'd had no chance to defend himself. His life had been snuffed out as easily as any remaining embers of light inside Ty.

Was it possible to re-ignite that flame once it had gone out and the coals had grown cold? His brother, Laken, would doubtless insist that it was. So would their mother. Even given their love and support, Ty struggled to believe it. The God he'd grown up hearing about in Sunday school had turned his back on Ty a long time ago.

And Ty didn't blame him one bit.

He'd been out a few months now. For the most part, he'd managed to avoid trouble, to stay away from his old friends and everything that hanging out with them involved—drugs, alcohol, women, violence. Not to mention more jail time, which was the last thing Ty wanted. Partly because he couldn't stand the thought of being back in that dark hole again and partly because of the embarrassment it would cause Laken, who'd graduated from the Academy and joined the Toronto police force while Ty was behind bars.

He'd believed—hoped—that he was done with that life. But Christmas was a couple of weeks away. And the fake Santas ringing bells next to the Salvation Army kettles on every corner, the people tromping through slush while loaded down with bags and packages, the cheerful season's greetings every time he stepped into a store, were not exactly filling him with holiday joy. Pretty much the opposite, in fact. They were making him feel more alone than ever.

Which was causing the pull of his old life to rise like a desert horned viper. A serpent that had camouflaged itself beneath the sand for a while but was now slithering sideways in his direction, preparing to sink its fangs into him once again.

At least, with his gang, he'd felt as though he belonged somewhere. With someone.

Ty trudged through the ankle-deep snow that had fallen over the city the last few hours, his bare hands stuffed in the pockets of his jacket. *I will not go back there. I will not go back there.*

Succumbing to the magnetic draw of his old life might provide him with that false sense of belonging again, for a little while anyway, but it would cause a lot of people a lot of heartache. His mother and his brother most of all. But not only them, all the victims of the stupid stuff he would be required to do before being let back in—the collateral damage of his weaknesses and terrible choices and inability to stand up to peer pressure.

He'd left a trail of victims the last time. Done damage he could never undo. Ty swallowed. Maybe, if God had left him and all he could offer the only people who truly cared about him was more pain, it would be better if he just ended it all. Tonight. Took his chances that what he'd heard in church about his eternal prospects was actually a myth and all he would face at the end of his life was utter darkness. Oblivion. Nothingness.

Anything was better than this endless pain and guilt. He chewed on his lower lip, contemplating the various options. How should he—

A soft light to his right caught his eye and he stopped abruptly. A manger scene had been set up in the front yard of one of the countless old stone churches in the city. The soft white spotlight shining on it lit up the scene so that the faces of Mary and Joseph, the little baby in the manger, gave off an ethereal glow that felt almost otherworldly.

Ty studied them a moment before his gaze shifted to the shepherds, the cow and sheep lying in the hay behind the trough, the wise men approaching on camels. Memories of his childhood Christmases drifted through his mind. He'd played one of those wise men once, in a pageant at a church not far from this one. The robe the director had draped over his shoulders had been the nicest article of clothing Ty had ever worn.

Until he'd learned how to get his hands on enough easy money to buy all the designer clothes and shoes he wanted. He had stopped going to church by then, so it had been a long time since he'd seen the Christmas story acted out.

A sign nailed to the crosspiece of the wooden stable caught his eye. *Peace on Earth.* Ty snorted. That earth had to be an entirely different planet than the one he lived on. There was no peace here. Not for him, that was for sure. Had he ever known a moment of peace?

His gaze fell on one of the wise men, the one in the turban who was the only person in the scene who looked anything like him. Maybe, when he was a kid. He'd had fun being in that play. Of course, Christmas had meant something then. Although their dad had left them when Laken was four and Ty was only two and they never had much, their mother had done everything she could to make the holiday special for them. There were always a few gifts waiting under the tree on Christmas morning. And she'd read them the story of the manger and the shepherds out of her worn Bible over a breakfast of pancakes and syrup.

So yeah, back then, he might have known what peace was.

But that was a long time ago. A lot had happened since then. He knew too much now about the world, what people were like, what one had to do to survive.

What he was capable of.

And he had come to understand that shattered peace was like extinguished light—no power on earth could ever bring them back.

CHAPTER TWO

The river flowed beneath the bridge on the edge of the city, a snake slithering from view as it wound its way beyond the soft glow of the lampposts spanning the metal structure. It was after midnight, so traffic crossing the metal structure was sparse, which suited Ty fine. A delivery truck rumbled past behind him, and for a few seconds the cement beneath his feet vibrated.

Ty rested his arms on the four-foot wall at the edge of the bridge and peered over the side. Was it high enough to do damage if he jumped? Or should he keep it simple? He stuck a hand into his jacket pocket and fingered the cold handle of the pistol he'd picked up a few days ago.

Groaning, he propped his elbow on the railing of the overpass. "Oh, God." He rested his forehead on his hand. He didn't want to die. Not really. The last thing he wanted was to hurt Laken and their mother more than he already had. And he definitely wasn't ready to face his maker, if that was what happened at the end of a person's life.

He wanted to live. He just didn't want to live like this. Not anymore. He groaned again as he closed his fingers around the handle of the pistol and tugged it free.

"You okay, kid?"

Ty shoved the weapon into his pocket and whirled around. A middle-aged man, sandy-brown hair tussled in the wind, worn coat hanging on his too-thin body, was hunkered down on the cement a dozen feet away, his back pressed to the wall.

Ty's eyes narrowed. What was the man doing here, sitting in the slush at the side of the road? Pretty far from the downtown core where he might be able to find shelter for the night and a hot meal. The wind was bitter tonight, sending whorls of snow spinning across the road like tiny tornadoes. So why was this guy sitting up here? "I'm good."

"You don't look good. And you didn't sound good a minute ago."

Heat surged through Ty's chest. What right did this stranger have to listen in on his conversation with God—if it could be called that when it was strictly a one-way deal? He shook his head slightly. It wasn't this man's fault Ty hadn't noticed him sitting there when he'd stopped at this spot. He leaned a hip against the cement wall. "Well, *good* might not be the right word. But I don't need any help, if that's what you're asking."

"And yet you're up on a bridge late at night in the freezing cold, calling out to God. If that's not a cry for help, I'm not sure what is."

Ty repressed a sigh. He couldn't argue with the man's logic.

The stranger inclined his head toward a spot on the ground next to him. "I've been told I'm a pretty good listener."

Did Ty want to talk? Maybe he did need to unload a bit of the garbage pressing down on his chest like the proverbial elephant people always described when they were having a heart attack. Pouring out his heart to a perfect stranger would be crazy though. He contemplated the man. Or it might be the sanest thing he'd done in a long time. Besides, what did he have to lose? Anything sounded better at the moment than taking that gun out of his pocket, pressing it to his temple, and ...

Another blast of wind roared past Ty, sending a frigid cyclone of snowflakes pelting against his cheeks and slithering down his neck. "All right, look. Maybe it would help to talk. But could we go somewhere warmer? I'd be happy to get you a cup of coffee, maybe something to eat."

In the glow of the streetlamps illuminating the bridge, something flitted across the man's face. Surprise? Apprehension? Whatever it was, he shook it off as he rose and brushed wet snow from the back of his jeans. "Coffee does sound good."

Nothing sounded particularly good to Ty at the moment, but if he wasn't going to follow through on his plans tonight, then getting in out of the cold was as appealing an idea as any.

They made their way across the bridge to where Ty had parked his car on the side of the road. When they reached his old black Corolla, he opened the driver's door and gestured for the stranger to get in the other side. The man didn't hesitate, only slid onto the passenger seat and did up the seatbelt. He was quiet as Ty pulled onto the road and headed into the city, as though leaving the door open for Ty to accept his invitation to talk about whatever it was that had driven him to the bridge in the middle of the night. Ty hadn't slept well in days, though. He needed that cup of coffee if he hoped to get his thoughts in order enough to share them. If he did decide to share them. He was still more than a little on the fence about that. Prison had taught him many things, not the least of which was to be careful who he opened his mouth around and what came out of it when he did.

He ran his fingers over his left ribcage, feeling the phantom ache there still from the last time he'd mouthed off a little too freely, a couple of weeks before he'd been released.

He brushed off the thoughts like the man sitting next to him had brushed the snow off his jeans. It might be after midnight, but, in the heart of the city, that didn't mean much. A number of coffee shops were still open. Ty parked near the first one he saw, and he and the stranger climbed out into the cold. Bells jangling announced their arrival when he pulled open the door, although no one glanced over. He held the door until the man had gone through and then followed him inside, the rich, nutty aroma inside the shop swirling around him in a mist of comforting warmth.

They ordered coffee and sandwiches, Ty waving the man away when he started to reach into his pocket. "I've got it."

The man nodded. "Thanks."

After Ty paid, they grabbed the food and drinks and he followed the stranger to a table in the back corner, partially shielded from the rest of the shop by a large potted plant on the floor, draped with strings of twinkling white lights. Although only a couple of other tables had people at them—a young guy engrossed in a book on the other side of the room and a couple, fingers entwined on the table, gazing so deeply into each other's eyes they likely had no clue anyone else was in the place anyway—Ty was grateful for the small bit of privacy.

The man took the seat facing the back wall, leaving Ty to settle on the wooden chair angled toward the exit. Ty slid a glance in the man's direction. Did he know, somehow, that Ty would be more comfortable facing the door? If he did, he didn't say so, only set his cup on the table, tugged off his gloves and shoved them in his pocket, and then reached for the ham and cheese sandwich. He'd worked the plastic wrap free and taken a big bite before Ty had unzipped his jacket. When was the last time the guy had eaten? He had to have been pretty hungry to accept Ty's invitation, since Ty was a few inches taller and a lot more bulked up, thanks to the prison gym. Throw in the short dreads he'd pulled into a ponytail and the tattoos creeping up his neck above the collar of his long-sleeved black T-shirt—metallic gold and crimson designs gleaming against his dark skin—and even if the man hadn't caught a glimpse of the handle of the gun, Ty would have thought he'd be quite a bit leerier of him than he appeared to be. Instead, he was scarfing down the sandwich as though his empty stomach was his only care in the world.

Ty studied him over the rim of his paper coffee cup. The man's slightly sunken cheeks were reddened from the cold but not terribly weathered for someone who spent a lot of time on the streets. Had he recently lost his job or his home or both? "What's your story?"

The man shoved a small piece of lettuce into his mouth with the tip of his finger before reaching for a napkin. "I believe you're supposed to be telling me your story." He swiped the napkin over his face. When he set it on the table, his lips had quirked up at the corners. "I'm sure it's considerably more interesting than mine."

Interesting was likely not the right word for what Ty was going through any more than *good* was, although he wasn't sure he could pinpoint the exact one to sum up his situation. Dire, maybe? Although he'd felt the need to unburden himself on the bridge, now that the moment was here, he had no idea how to begin.

As though he understood, the man set his sandwich on the piece of plastic on the table, brushed crumbs off his fingers,

111

and held out a hand. "Let's start with introductions. My name's Con."

Well, that's ironic. Ty grasped the man's fingers, cool and slightly wet, as though his gloves had been soaked from the snow. "Ex-con."

The man let go and pointed a finger in his direction, his pale blue eyes twinkling. "I see what you did there."

Ty managed a grin. "It's Tyrone, actually. Although everyone but my mother calls me Ty."

"What does your dad call you?"

He sobered. "I don't really know what he'd call me if he was around, since he hasn't been since I was two years old."

The twinkle faded from Con's eyes. "I'm sorry to hear that."

Ty shrugged. "What are you gonna do?" He played with the plastic tab on the lid of his cup. "So, you want to know what had me up on that bridge tonight, calling out to God?"

"If you want to tell me."

He contemplated the words imprinted in the plastic lid. *Caution. Hot.* Such a clear warning to be careful to avoid getting hurt. Why couldn't the really big dangers in life be plastered with signs like that? He sighed. "I used to be in a gang."

"Okay." Con picked up his sandwich and took another bite. Obviously, the revelation hadn't shocked him.

Don't get too comfortable, buddy. I'm just getting started. Ty ran his thumb over the textured side of the brown cup, the feel and warmth of it soothing him. A little. "I had to do a bunch of terrible stuff to get in, stuff I'm definitely not proud of."

"Like what?"

"Little things at first. Shoplift. Spray paint graffiti on a church. Ambush the leader of another gang and beat him up."

"Did you hurt him?"

"Yeah. I mean, I was on a meth high at the time, so, while

he did get in a few punches, I managed to send him to the hospital."

"Huh." Con still held the remnant of his sandwich in one hand, but he hadn't taken a bite in a while. "Was he okay?"

"I don't really know. I think so. He didn't die; I know that much."

Con studied him for a few seconds before sticking the last of the sandwich into his mouth and wiping his fingers on his napkin. "Anything else?"

Ty took a deep breath. "I had to start a fire in a dumpster, and it ended up doing quite a bit of damage to the back of a restaurant."

"You ever get caught?"

"I did a few months in juvie for the dumpster fire, but no. Not for those other things, anyway."

"For something else?"

"Yes. For the last test."

"Which was?"

Ty offered him a rueful smile. "You sure you want to hear this?" Maybe, now that he had a little food and a hot cup of coffee in his belly, the man would no longer feel the need to sit here in this makeshift confessional like some kind of ragged, unshaven priest. Ty wouldn't blame him for taking off, any more than he blamed God for leaving him.

Con folded his hands together on the table as though there was nowhere else in the world he wanted to be. "If you're willing to tell me, I'm willing to listen."

"All right." Ty couldn't bring himself to look at the man across from him when he confessed the next part. The worst part. The part he would never forgive himself for. "A bunch of us were in a car one night. I was high again, and someone handed me a gun, told me I had one more test to pass, and then I would be a full-fledged member of the gang. I had a pretty good idea what it was, and the thought of it started to make me feel really sick. I tried to give the gun back, but the guy pushed it away, told me I was in too deep now, and there was no way out. All I had to do was take out one kid, a guy from another gang they were pretty sure had been talking to the cops, giving up a bunch of our names."

There was a tiny splotch of dried icing on the table. Ty dug his thumb nail through it, scraping it off the wood and leaving tiny curls of sugar lying on the surface. "The closer we got, the sicker I felt. My heart was pounding so wildly I could hardly breathe. Then I saw him, standing on a street corner with a couple of other guys. There were four other members of my gang in the car, all older, and all screaming at me to take the shot." He closed his eyes. Even now, their shouts reverberated through his head, like they did most nights in his dreams. He could smell the interior of the car—thick, hot air permeated with cigarette smoke and weed and alcohol—feel the cool glass beneath the fingers he'd pressed to the half open window.

He opened his eyes, trying in vain to erase the images flashing before them. "I couldn't do it. I told them that and suddenly one of them shoved the barrel of a gun against the back of my head. And I knew if I didn't take the kid out, they'd shoot me and dump me out of the car right in front of him. One way or another, they were going to teach him a lesson that night. I still didn't want to, and I hesitated until it was almost too late, until the guy holding the gun on me clicked off the safety, and then I forced myself to stop thinking about it and just aim and fire." His voice cracked and he stopped and took a swig of coffee. It didn't help. "It was the wrong choice."

"You had a gun to your head."

"Even so, I chose to pull the trigger. I played God. I decided my life was worth more than that kid's. And I was wrong. I had no right to exchange my life for his. I regretted

114

it the second I did it, and I've regretted it every moment since."

Con's knuckles had whitened, the only sign that Ty's words were having any kind of impact on him. "What happened next?"

Ty drew in a breath that shuddered a little. He set the cup on the table and rested his hand on top of it, the steam curling through the hole in the lid dampening his palm. "We took off. The cops showed up at my mother's door the next morning. One of the guys with the kid had seen my face and knew who I was. They arrested me in front of her and my big brother. I pled guilty and spent six years in Toronto South. Just got out a few months ago."

Con didn't speak. Ty contemplated the pattern in the wooden tabletop for a moment or two before forcing himself to look up and meet the man's gaze. Something swirled through Con's eyes that hadn't been there before, although Ty couldn't decipher what it was. Not fear, which kind of surprised him. After all, he'd just found out the big guy across from him was a cold-blooded murderer.

If that didn't freak him out, what would?

The man's voice, when he spoke, rasped a little. Maybe he was slightly more affected by Ty's revelation than he was letting on. "So, you've paid your debt. You're a free man."

"Am I?" The last thing Ty felt was free. Although metal bars no longer hemmed him in, he felt every bit as much a prisoner as he had the last six years.

"You don't feel that way?"

"No."

"Why not?"

"I guess because everything I do—going for a walk, cooking my own food, being with my mother and brother—reminds me that I'm out and that I have no right to be. No right to be alive, even, when that kid who'd been standing on the street corner isn't. Six years behind bars doesn't feel as though it begins to make up for what I did. Not only the shooting, but the other stuff too."

"What would?"

Ty slumped against the back of his seat. "That's just it. I don't think anything would. How could it? All I've been able to think lately is that the only thing that might come close would be if I took my own life like I took his."

"Which is why you were up on that bridge tonight."

"Yeah."

Con unclasped his fingers and pressed the tips of them to the table. "Have you thought about making a list?"

Ty rubbed trembling fingers across his forehead. "A list?"

"Yeah. I mean, you just told me about all the things you did. What about writing them down, trying to do something about them? That might be a way to help deal with the guilt."

Guilt. Ty couldn't deny that it did hold him captive and that he had doubted he could ever be free of it. Was it possible he could be? Something warm sparked deep inside him. That tiny ember of light he'd thought had been extinguished for good? "I wouldn't know where to start."

"Sounds to me like you already have."

Ty furrowed his brow. "I have?"

"Look, I don't know where you and God stand, but you did call out to him tonight, which suggests that, on some level, you recognize he might exist and can hear you."

"Yeah, I guess I do. My Iya brought my brother and me up to go to church and believe all that. Although I've gotten pretty far away from it the last few years." *But I miss it.* He blinked, the thought catching him by surprise.

"Iya?"

"That's what we call my mother. It's a Nigerian term of endearment."

"Ah. Well, as long as you're breathing, it's not too late to get back. If you truly want to be free of your past, you need to work out your relationship with God. He sent his son to atone for those sins of yours. It's already done. Believing that, accepting it, is the only way to truly be free of them. But, as long as it's safe to do so, you *can* try to make amends for what you've done, go to the people you hurt, ask them to forgive you. There's a lot of healing in that."

Amends. The word resonated with Ty. That was what he needed to do. If he could figure out how, he might be able to find a way to go on living. The tiny flicker of warmth deep inside his chest spread a little, and he pressed his hand flat against the spot.

Ty pondered the list of wrongs he'd committed in a desperately misguided attempt to make it into that gang. The thought of trying to make up for all of them was dizzying, and he pressed harder against his chest, trying to dull the painful thumping.

"Don't think about the whole list at once or it will be too overwhelming. Start with the first thing and take it one step, one item at a time."

Ty scrutinized the man across the table from him. Could he actually read Ty's mind? This wasn't the first time it had felt as though he could. Maybe he wasn't a homeless guy, like Ty had thought. Maybe he was some kind of messenger from God. The thumping beneath his palm intensified. Could God have sent an angel to him like that old guy in his mother's favorite Christmas movie? What was his name, Harold?

Arthur? Ty lowered his hand to the table. Clarence. That was it. Was Con his own personal Clarence?

Bells jangled and his head jerked. Bells ringing? Seriously? Maybe God had more of a sense of humor than Ty had realized. He shot a look at the entrance. A middle-aged couple stepped into the shop, flakes of snow dotting their wool caps and winter coats. He said something to her as they strolled toward the counter, and she laughed. A lovely but very human laugh. Ty turned back to Con. A smile played at the corners of the man's lips, as though he knew what Ty had been thinking.

He didn't comment on Ty's theory, though, only clasped his hands together again. "What was the first thing on your list?"

Ty retreated back along the crazy trail he'd started down, dragging his thoughts with him to the start of their conversation. "Shoplifting."

"Right. Do you remember what store you stole from? What you took?"

He might have been doing drugs occasionally at the time, but every detail of his past transgressions still stood out starkly in Ty's mind. Too starkly. "Yes. It had to be something substantial, not a candy bar or anything. I took an iPod Touch from that small electronics shop on Danforth. IT World."

"Is it still in business, do you know?"

"It is, actually. I walked past it a few days ago."

Con unclasped his fingers and held up both hands, palms up. "I suggest you start there, then."

Ty nodded. He could do that. Go back, confess what he'd done, and pay for the item he'd stolen. A knot formed in his stomach. They could easily refuse to accept his amends and call the cops on him. What if Laken showed up and had to arrest him? The thought dragged stinging bile up the back of Ty's throat. His heart rate picked up again. Could he do this? He was out on parole. One call to the cops, one accusation of wrongdoing, and he would be behind bars again.

I can't keep going like this. The thought of the desperation he'd felt on that bridge, the hopelessness, the certain knowledge that something had to change, something had to give, gripped him again. This was it. It was his past he needed to go back and change.

"Of course, you can't change the past."

Con's quiet words drew Ty into the present, and he gaped at the man. "How do you do that?"

Con's smile went deep into his blue eyes. "Do what?"

"Read my mind like that."

He chuckled. "I'm not reading your mind. I'm reading your face."

"My face?"

"Yes. It's a particular talent of mine, I've been told. Comes from some of the things I've been through, according to my therapist. Trauma and loss will send you in one of two directions. Into a state of numbness or bitterness that causes you to block out the people around you, erect walls to keep them distant so they can't hurt you like others have. Or it will give you an increased empathy and understanding, a deep desire to reach out to people, especially hurting people, because you know how they feel and you want to help in some small way."

"Sounds scary."

Con smiled again. "It is. But usually well worth the effort." He reached across the table to grasp Ty's forearm. "*You* are worth the effort, Ty. To me and to God. And, it sounds like, to your family."

Ty's throat tightened. He hadn't cried in years. Crying was the fastest way to get beat up on the streets. Or in prison. The ultimate sign of weakness. Although … His gaze locked on Con's. The man's eyes glistened a little, as though his own words and the compassion behind them had moved him to tears. Except nothing about this man felt weak. Maybe he didn't look that strong, physically, but he'd clearly been through a lot in life, been beaten down. And he'd not only survived, he'd emerged from his trials with a strong faith in God and a solid belief in the value of other human beings. What could shake a man who had that kind of steel core running through him?

Nothing that Ty could think of.

That was the kind of man he wanted to be. The kind of man that his older brother was. Laken had gone through the same childhood Ty had. Harder even, since, when their dad abandoned them, four-year-old Laken had taken on the role of the man of the family. He'd always tried to protect their mother and Ty, always taken care of them. When he and his brother had found themselves at the same crossroads in life, what had compelled Laken to take one pathway and Ty another?

God.

The answer came to him in a blinding revelation. Laken had a strong faith in God too, like the man across from him. A faith that informed every decision he made, every action he took.

Had Ty ever had that kind of faith? Maybe, as a kid, but somewhere along the way he'd lost it, or shoved it into some dark shadowy place inside him and then held his hands over his ears every time he thought he might hear God trying to speak to him, to call him back.

No wonder he'd ended up in one heap of trouble after another. But he was still breathing. Was Con right and, as long as that was true, it wasn't too late for him to answer that call? To change his life? Find his way to that crossroads and, this time, choose another path?

The coffee shop was spinning around him a little. Con

tightened his grip on Ty's arm. "One item at a time, Ty. One day, one moment at a time. You can't change the past, but you *can* find your way out of the darkness."

Exactly what he needed to do. "How?"

"Focus on the light, no matter how dim or far away it may seem. While you are seeking amends, trying to atone for the things you've done, fight the darkness that *will* come for you and keep your eyes on that light. You can do it. It's not too late."

Focus on the light. He pressed a palm to that spot of warmth in his chest again.

"Here." Con let go of him and undid the top button of his coat. He slid his hand beneath the flap and withdrew a worn black notebook from an inside pocket. After flipping it open, he tore out the first few pages, covered in looping handwriting, and stuffed them into his pocket before sliding the book across the table. "Use this. There's something cathartic about writing down that list, seeing it in black and white, crossing off one thing at a time. Feels as though you are taking steps forward on your journey."

"Thanks." Ty picked up the small notebook, warm from being next to Con's chest, and stuck it into the back pocket of his jeans. He probably should buy his own, not take this man's from him, but he was suddenly anxious to start, to take the first step on that journey Con had mentioned. As soon as he got home, Ty would write out his list.

A teenage girl started stacking chairs on top of the empty tables, so he and Con dumped their garbage into the receptacle and made their way out of the coffee shop. The temperature had dropped even further, and Ty pulled up the hood of his jacket as a frigid breeze swept along the sidewalk, sending a crumpled paper takeout bag rolling past them end over end like an urban tumbleweed. It ended up in the street and, seconds later, was crushed beneath the wheels of a city bus shooting up sprays of brown slush in its wake as it rumbled by.

Con worked a glove out of his pocket and pulled it on before reaching for the other one. Ty frowned. "Do you have somewhere to go?"

Con slid on the second glove and tugged his wool cap down a little farther over his ears. "I'll be fine."

"No, really. Do you need a place to stay? I don't have a big apartment, but you're welcome to crash on my couch if you want. It's too cold to be outdoors."

"I'm all right, honest." Con slapped him on the back. "You're a good man, Ty. Don't let anyone, including yourself, tell you otherwise." He touched his fingers to the side of his head. "Take care now. And thanks for the coffee and sandwich."

"Thank you for listening. And for all your advice. I think it actually helped."

"I hope so. Next time, coffee's on me."

Next time? "So, I'll see you again?"

Con smiled that smile that went deep into his eyes. "Oh, I'm sure we'll run into each other. Merry Christmas, Ty. And remember, all it takes to beat back the darkness is a single spark of light."

Before Ty could respond, the man had turned in the opposite direction Ty needed to go and started off. Before he'd walked half a block, the thick, driving snow had nearly blocked him from Ty's sight.

With a heavy sigh, Ty zipped his coat to the top and shoved his hands into the pockets. Could he do this? Could he atone for his past actions?

All he had to do, as Con had suggested, was fight the darkness and keep his eyes on that faraway, distant light showing him the way that he should go.

How hard could that be?

CHAPTER THREE

The *l* had burned out on the neon sign above the door of the small electronics shop, so it now read *IT Wor d.* Ty wasn't surprised, since the place had been around a lot longer than most small stores in this area of town lasted. His theft hadn't driven them out of business, at least. Which was something. When he'd first been told he had to steal something, he'd consoled himself the way most thieves did—with the lie that it didn't cost the store anything because it was built into their insurance plan.

When a quiet voice deep inside—the one Ty had gotten pretty good at muzzling over the years—tried to whisper that petty thieves like him drove up those insurance rates until a lot of small businesses couldn't afford the monthly payments or compete against the big box chains, Ty ignored it.

He held a hand to his abdomen. Could he do this? *You're a good man, Ty.*

The memory of Con's quiet words, his firm grasp on Ty's arm, bolstered him. A little more bolstering couldn't hurt, though. He shot a look at the clear sky, soft white clouds drifting against a backdrop of icy blue. *Okay, look. I know you and I haven't been on speaking terms for a while, but if you can hear me, I could really use your help right about now. Any chance you could give me the strength to do this?* Despite the intense cold, his palms had grown damp, and Ty rubbed them across the front of his jeans as he waited for an answer.

Only the bitter north wind brushing across the back of his neck responded to his silent pleas. He did feel that small spot of warmth in his chest again, which was something. *All right, then.* He squared his shoulders and marched to the door.

No bells this time, thankfully. Although, no one stood behind the counter and, after thirty seconds of standing around waiting, Ty was starting to wish there had been. He wandered over to the counter, pressed his palms to the glass surface, and leaned over it, trying to see to the right into a hallway that led into the shadowy recesses of the staff area. The side of his hand brushed against a silver call bell, and he contemplated it. Really? Now he had to actually summon someone to come so he could apologize, offer payment, and then wait to see if whoever it was planned to press charges that would immediately send him back to prison?

His hands closed into fists against the glass. No way he was going to simply stand here and wait for that to happen. Ty scowled as he shoved away from the counter. He'd tried. No one could expect him to—

Fight the darkness that *will* come for you.

Great. Was Con's voice planning to provide the soundtrack for this entire journey?

Ty shook off the black cloud threatening to surround him and choke out his desire to somehow try and make things right. *Find the single spark of light.* He'd already taken a few steps backwards, away from the counter, but he stopped when the thought struck him. Before he could move, a woman around his age emerged from the back hallway and took up residence behind the counter. She pushed her long, dark hair back over one shoulder. "Sorry about the wait. I didn't realize anyone was here." She spoke with a slight Spanish accent. Was she Mexican? South American?

Completely irrelevant. Ty issued himself a stern rebuke. *Amends. Focus.*

"It's fine." His voice came out a little hoarse, and he cleared his throat as he walked back to the counter. The woman's eyes, the color of rich, dark chocolate, locked on his, and suddenly the air in the place felt a little thick, difficult to draw in. "Uh, would it be possible to speak to a manager?"

Amusement flitted across her face. "That would be me. Owner. Manager. Entire staff, to be honest." She spread slender arms out to her sides. "We're a small operation."

We? She and her husband? Ty glanced at her left hand as she lowered her arms. No ring. Which didn't mean she was available. Not that her relationship status was relevant to this moment either. A framed picture of a boat floating on a calm lake hung on the wall over her shoulder with the words *Be still and know that I am God* scrolling across the water. Interesting. A flag with a blue stripe at the top and bottom and a white strip in between, a bright yellow sun in the center, was draped on the wall next to the frame. What country was that from? Ty met the woman's gaze. "The last time I was in here was about seven years ago. Were you the manager then?"

"No, that would have been my dad. I was here though, working for him or with him, depending on which of us you asked." Her voice held a hint of laughter.

"Oh. Then I think it might be your dad I want to talk to."

The amusement in her eyes faded. "You and me both. He passed away last year."

Ty winced. "Oh man, I'm sorry."

"Thank you." She inclined her head slightly, her long, silver earrings brushing against her shoulders. "He did teach me everything he knew about electronics, so I should be able to help you find what you're looking for. Or did you need something fixed?" She glanced at his empty hands before meeting his gaze again.

"I am trying to fix something, but it's not electronic." Ty was usually pretty good with his words, but for some reason, the right ones weren't coming to him now.

Confusion flitted across her face. "Then maybe you're not in the right store?"

He took a deep breath. "I am, but I'm not here to buy something. At least, not something new. I'm here because, when I came in last time, I stole something, an iPod Touch. A brand-new 6th Generation. I came in today to apologize for that and to pay you for it."

"Ah." The woman crossed her arms and pursed her lips, studying him. "I have to admit that's a first."

"First time someone stole from you?"

She laughed, although the sound held less humor than either her eyes or her voice had a moment earlier. "I wish. No, that happens quite often. No one has ever come back to say they're sorry, though."

"Well, I am. Really sorry. Not only for taking the iPod but for not coming here in time to be able to apologize to your dad. I'm trying to make amends for all the stupid stuff I did back then, and I'm starting with you." Ty reached into his back pocket and pulled out his wallet. He'd gotten a job in a factory after getting out and, while he didn't have a ton of money, he was more than happy to compensate this woman for whatever she felt he owed her for the iPod, plus six years of interest, of course.

She didn't uncross her arms but continued to scrutinize him, so intensely that Ty had to work not to squirm. "You know I could call the police."

"Yes." Although the statute of limitations had likely run out on the petty crime, Ty had no desire to take that risk.

The woman jerked her head toward the corner of the ceiling. "I have you on record, confessing to stealing from us."

His heart sank a little at the sight of the video camera mounted there. "Okay."

She uncrossed her arms and reached under the counter. When she straightened, she held up a cell phone. "Would you leave if I called them?"

He met her gaze steadily. "No." Good. He'd meant that. Which suggested he'd been able to fight off the darkness. This time.

Her eyes narrowed. "Amends. So, this is a twelve-step, check-the-boxes-so-you-can-clear-your-conscience kind of thing?"

Ty blinked. He wasn't following any kind of recovery program, and this was definitely not about checking off a few boxes. How could he convince her of that? Honesty might be a good way to go. "It's more than that for me. I'm genuinely remorseful for what I did. I know I can't undo any of it, but I'm trying everything I know to do and hoping and praying it will help, somehow."

"Help whom?"

"The people I hurt. Me. The ones who care about me."

She studied him in silence for several long seconds. Could she read his face as easily as Con had last night? Maybe, because after what felt like an eternity, she tossed the phone back under the counter. "How much are you planning to pay me?"

"What would you charge for it now?"

"We don't sell those anymore. Not new ones, anyway. Apple has discontinued them. A classic one still in packaging can go for three hundred or more on eBay though."

Ouch. Back when he'd stolen the thing, he could have gotten it for less than two hundred. That was a steep rate of interest for six years. "So, you think three hundred would be fair?"

"What would have been fair would be you paying for it seven years ago, before you walked out the door with it."

He ducked his head a little, acknowledging that.

"Why did you steal it?"

Ty hesitated. The honesty thing had felt pretty good. Was that God, offering him tacit approval? If so, Ty wouldn't mind a little more of that. "It was part of an initiation."

"For a gang," she said, her voice flat.

"Yes."

"I take it you did a lot worse things, then."

He swallowed. Would she push him on what those things were? Whatever she asked, he would answer. "Yes, I did. Much worse."

"Did you do time?"

He nodded. "Six years."

She blew out a breath, lifting the bangs away from her forehead. "I'm sure that wasn't easy."

"It wasn't. But I deserved it."

Her gaze flicked past him, toward the door. Was someone coming? Ty didn't turn to look. Her eyes fixed on his again. "All right, look. Give me two hundred for the iPod and we'll call it even."

The muscles that had knotted across his shoulders as he'd waited for the verdict unwound slightly. Ty flipped open his wallet. "That's great. Thank you." He pulled out the twenties he'd withdrawn from the machine before coming here. After counting out ten of them onto the counter, he shoved the remaining two into the wallet and stuck it into his back pocket.

Behind him, a scraping sound and a whoosh of cold air let him know a customer had entered the place. The woman behind the counter scooped up the money, hit the button to open the cash register drawer, and stuck the bills into one of the slots. When she spoke, she had lowered her voice, so only he could hear her. "What's your name?"

"Tyrone Jones. My friends call me Ty."

"Well, Tyrone …" a little of the humor had crept back into her dark eyes, "I'm Gabriella. My friends call me Gabby."

"Good to meet you," Ty hesitated before adding, "Gabriella." The customer who had come in was rustling around in the back corner, but no doubt he or she would soon come to the counter.

A smile played around her lips. "Well, I appreciate you coming in. I'm sure it was hard for you."

"It was. But I deserved that too."

She grabbed a business card from a plastic holder on the counter and held it out to him. "Given what you've told me, I suspect it's only going to get harder from here. And I happen to know a bit about difficult journeys. My number is on there. If you need someone to talk to, you know where I work. Or we could go for coffee or dinner or something."

Really? She was asking him out after everything he had told her? Ty narrowly resisted the urge to glance up at the ceiling. That could only be God. "Thank you." When he took the card, his fingers brushed hers and electricity tingled across his skin. *Wrong kind of spark. Focus.* He lifted the card in the air. "I'll call you."

"I hope so."

Footsteps approached. Time for him to be on his way. Ty smiled at Gabriella before sticking the card into his pocket, nodding at the middle-aged woman in a ski jacket and long, red scarf who had come up to stand behind him, and then skirting around her as he headed for the door.

A blast of arctic air struck him when he stepped outside, but Ty barely noticed. That had been way more difficult than he'd anticipated. And, somehow, way better. He stuck his hand into his pocket and fingered the card the woman had given him.

His smile faded as her words stemmed the slight rush of euphoria. No doubt this journey was only going to get harder from here. The next guy might not be as willing to put his phone away and simply allow him to pay his debt. Not in cash, anyway.

One item at a time, one moment at a time.

Apparently, Con's voice *was* going to be his constant soundtrack. Fine. Maybe that was for the best. The man's quiet wisdom had started him on this quest; it might be helpful to have the constant reminders of what he'd said as Ty maneuvered his way through this uncharted and potentially treacherous territory. And maybe God would decide to come along for the ride, too.

Between the two of them, and possibly that cup of coffee Gabriella had suggested, Ty felt cautiously optimistic that he might make it through to the end. To whatever it was that waited for him in the future when he'd done everything he could to make up for his past.

CHAPTER FOUR

Ty stood on the sidewalk at the corner of the property where the old stone church loomed, gusts of cold wind sending shards of ice blowing across his cheeks and throat. From this angle, he could see the side of the building, and he winced. While the ugly words he'd scrawled across the stone years ago were long gone, what looked like fairly fresh ones had been painted over the spot. Had he started something with his stupid stunt back then?

At least he knew what he could offer to do to make his amends here. Although spending hours in the freezing cold cleaning spray paint off a wall hadn't been on his agenda for the day, it was now. Someone else had needed to do the same thing with his handiwork back then, which made him feel sick. Hopefully the church would allow him to atone for his past sins this way, which might help to ease the stinging guilt burning a hole in his gut at the sight of the scrawling on the wall. Whoever had said words couldn't hurt was way off base. These ones weren't even directed at him, and he felt the punch of them anyway. Like others had felt when they'd read what he'd written.

Ty ran a hand over his head. He couldn't stand here thinking about that. He needed to do something to make up for what he'd done. He made his way to the walkway and then to the large, double, curved doors, painted burgundy, at the front of the building. They were locked, so he pressed the buzzer set into the frame and waited. What was he going to say to the faceless voice that answered his call?

Before he could think about it too much, a staticky "Hello?" came through the speaker.

Ty leaned closer. "Uh, hi. I wondered if I could speak with the pastor?"

Silence followed. He glanced up at the small camera fixed to the upper right corner of the doorway. No doubt whoever belonged to that voice—and maybe everyone else working at the church—was studying him now, trying to determine if he posed any kind of threat. Like he'd told Con, he hadn't been caught for spray-painting the church, so they wouldn't know him from that. Although, he had made the news more than once for his other crimes, so maybe someone would recognize him that way. Which would mean the chances of them letting him through the door would be pretty slim.

"One moment, please." The staticky voice came through the speaker again. Ty sighed and propped a shoulder against the stone side of the church. If he had to apologize over the speaker, he would, but if they cut him off and refused to let him come inside, there wasn't much more he could do. Maybe he could look up the church's website, email the pastor. He pushed away from the wall. Probably should have done that in the first place.

He took a step toward the stone stairs but stopped at the sound of a couple of deadbolts sliding open followed by a lock clicking before one of the heavy doors swung open. A woman who was maybe in her sixties stood there in a thick, cream-colored sweater and brown pants. Remarkably, she had a warm smile on her face beneath glasses with large, tiger-striped rims. "Can I help you?"

Ty clenched and unclenched his fists, trying to relieve a little of the nervous energy coursing through him. "I'm sorry to show up like this. I probably should have made an appointment."

"No, it's fine. You shouldn't have to make an appointment to come to church." She tapped the lock on the door. "I'm not a fan of locking up the place either, but the board worries about security. In any case, I'm Reverend Milson." She held out her hand.

Ty stepped closer to the doorway and shook it. "Tyrone Jones."

Something flashed through her eyes at that, although her smile didn't waver. Did she recognize his name?

"Did you want to come into my office, Tyrone?"

"Sure." Probably shouldn't lie to a reverend, but walking through the church, past everyone watching him surreptitiously, to sit and face this woman in her office while he confessed his crimes was pretty low on the list of things he *wanted* to do at the moment. Top of the list of things he needed to do, though, so hopefully God wouldn't consider it a complete deception.

He trailed after the woman through one side of the sanctuary and out the other into a maze of hallways. They did pass three or four people who, as Ty had guessed they would, looked away quickly when he glanced in their direction, but the reverend didn't slow her pace until they reached a door at the end of a long corridor and she pushed it open. He'd assumed she would leave it that way in case she needed to call for help, but she held it as he passed by and then closed it firmly before gesturing to a plastic chair in front of a large wooden desk covered in books and piles of papers. "Please, sit."

She rounded the desk to take the worn leather seat behind it. When they were both settled, she folded her hands on a small, cleared area on the wooden surface. "What brings you here today?"

"I came to apologize for something I did a few years ago."

"Which was?"

"I spray painted graffiti on the side of the church. It was extremely stupid, and I'm really sorry that I did it. If you'll let me, I'd like to clean off the graffiti I noticed out there earlier to make up for it in some small way."

Reverend Milson didn't look as surprised as Gabriella had at his announcement. She only tilted her head a little, as if intensely interested in what he had said. Or maybe in him. "What did you paint?"

Heat crept up his neck when he recalled what he had written. "A bunch of things I wouldn't want to repeat. Plus, I painted a picture." That part hadn't been obscene, like the words. And he hadn't planned to include it, but, standing there, paint cans filled with several different colors propped against the wall at his feet, the idea had come to him, and he hadn't been able to resist.

"A picture of what?"

"A lion in a cage, roaring at a little boy standing on the other side of the bars looking at him, hands behind his back."

Her face lit up. "I remember that painting. It was very powerful. The board wanted it taken off with the rest of what you painted, but I talked them into keeping it there. It was only removed a couple of years ago, when it had faded and all the stonework in the building was re-done."

"Really?"

"Yes. I was sad to see it go. Still have a picture of it somewhere." She rifled through a couple of the piles of papers on the desk before spinning the chair around and pulling open a low drawer in a metal shelving unit behind her. After

134

digging around in it for a minute or two, she called out, "Aha," and spun the chair back around, her arm thrust in the air in triumph, her fingers clutching something that looked like a Polaroid picture. "Might be a new record. It usually takes me a lot longer to find what I'm looking for."

Ty contemplated the photo, or what he could see of it as she waved it around before finally lowering it to the desk. She pressed a fingertip to the white border and slid it between two piles to him.

"Huh." Ty picked it up carefully by the edges. He hadn't had a lot of time to study the scene after he'd finished painting it. As he'd applied the last bit of spray, the distant wail of sirens had risen above the hum of traffic that never seemed to ease off entirely downtown, even in the middle of the night. He had tossed the can he'd been using onto the ground, shot one last glance at the wall, and then sprinted around the back of the church, through a dark alley, and up and over a metal fence before taking off for home.

Reverend Milson sat back and rested her clasped hands on her stomach. "The boy looks like you."

"Yes."

"What does the lion represent?"

"I'm not sure. Life, maybe?" Ty hadn't given it that much conscious thought, only recreated on the stone the images that came to him from somewhere deep inside.

"And the bars?"

He reflected on them a moment, glistening silver in the picture. "Whatever it is that protects me from the lion, I suppose."

"Or whoever."

Ty didn't respond.

The reverend leaned forward. "Have you painted any other pictures?"

"You mean legally?" Ty offered her a small grin as he set the photo on the desk.

Her smile reappeared, something that—given the lines of laughter radiating from the corners of her eyes—apparently happened often. "Yes."

"Not with spray paint, but I have a few sketchbooks I've filled with drawings. I did a lot of them in ..." Telling her where he'd been the last few years might have her opening her office door fast.

"Prison?"

He blew out a breath. "How did you know?"

"I recognized your name when you told me. Drive-by shooting a few years ago, right?"

His chest tightened. "Yeah. That was me. Almost seven years ago. How could you remember my name?"

"Something about that story stuck with me. I've prayed for you over the years."

He blinked. "You have?"

"Yes, although I didn't expect you to turn up at the church, I have to admit. That's a lack of faith on my part, isn't it?"

Her warm smile hadn't faded, which Ty was struggling to comprehend. "I can't blame you for that. I'm pretty shocked myself that I'm here."

The reverend laughed outright at that. "Well, since you are, I will take you up on your offer to clean the side of the church. That bit of handiwork appeared a couple of days ago, and the janitorial staff hasn't had a chance to get to it." She pressed her palms to the desk and pushed to her feet.

"I'll be happy to do it." Ty stood too. Maybe *happy* wasn't entirely accurate, but it did feel right.

"Here." She leaned across the desk to retrieve the picture and then carried it over to a photocopier in the corner of the office. After making a copy, she lifted the lid and removed the original. She crossed the room and held it out to Ty. "To remind you."

He took the photo from her and stuck it into the back pocket of his jeans. "Of what?"

"The beauty you are capable of creating." Warm, surprisingly strong fingers grasped his wrist. "You can only do that when there is beauty inside you, you know."

His throat tightened. For most of his life, he'd believed that the only thing he was capable of creating was a mess. Havoc. Pain. Anything but beauty. Had he been wrong? "Thank you." Those were the only words he could force out, so he hoped she understood that he meant for more than just the photo.

They started down the long hallway, the reverend waving as they passed by windows set in the closed doors, likely other offices. "You know, I would very much like to see some of your sketches."

"You would?"

"Yes." They reached a set of stairs and she started down. "You have a lot of talent, Tyrone. And we're in need of someone like that to do work for us around here—murals on the Sunday school room walls and illustrations for our newsletters, a new logo for our church, that sort of thing. Would you be interested in a little work on the side? We'd pay you, of course, although I can't promise it would be much."

Ty couldn't believe what he was hearing. After his confession to her, and given what she already knew about him, she wanted him to do work for the church? And she was offering to pay for his art? As much as he loved drawing— something that had kept him sane and out of a lot of trouble in prison—he'd never considered trying to make any money at it. Could he do that? Maybe even make a career out of it? He'd taken art and graphic design courses while incarcerated and loved them, so maybe.

"I've never considered anything like that."

"Well, think about it. My email address is on the church website. Send me a message and we'll set up a time for you to come in and show me your work. We can discuss various options then."

"I will. Thanks." He definitely would. The moment she'd mentioned the possibility, his heart rate had accelerated.

They reached another door that she stopped and pushed open. The small room on the other side was clearly a janitor's closet. The reverend grabbed a bucket, filled it with hot water at the laundry sink attached to the wall, dropped a hard-bristled brush into the water, and handed it to Ty before grabbing a bottle from a shelf. She held it out and Ty took it and glanced at the label. Graffiti removal chemical. He grimaced. Obviously, this happened a lot, since the church was prepared for it.

The minister led Ty to a nearby exit and held the door open for him again. "Thanks for doing this, Tyrone."

"You're welcome. It's the least I can do. And it's Ty."

She smiled again. "All right. You can set the bucket outside the door when you're done. And I'll be watching for your email, Ty." With a wave, she disappeared into the building. For a moment, Ty could only stare at the door, trying to wrap his mind around what had just happened.

Then, gripping the bucket tighter, he started for the side of the church and what he knew would be at least a couple of hours of back-breaking work.

Exactly what he deserved.

CHAPTER FIVE

Ty dropped onto his couch and tugged the phone from his shirt pocket. He hesitated, his finger poised over the keypad, then, glancing from the phone to the business card he clutched in his other hand, he punched in the digits. Was there a chance he'd misunderstood the offer Gabriella had made a few days ago? Maybe she had a boyfriend and had only meant that she would be willing to listen if he was in crisis and needed to talk. She might even be a therapist or somehow trained to deal with people having a mental health breakdown, and she meant that he could contact her in a professional capacity. Although going for coffee or dinner wasn't all that professional.

He sighed as the call went through and started to ring. Too late now. He couldn't really humiliate himself any more than he had when he went to her store to apologize and pay for the iPod Touch, so he had nothing to lose at this point.

"Hello?"

His heart rate picked up at the sound of her voice, the light Spanish accent. "Gabriella? It's Tyrone Jones."

"Tyrone, hi. I was hoping you'd call."

Meaning that, if he was only meant to call her when he was in crisis, she'd been hoping he'd have one, which wouldn't really make sense. The tightness in his shoulders eased a little.

"I, uh, was just thinking about you, and I wondered if you might want to go for that coffee you mentioned."

Was that a slight hesitation? If it was, she pushed past it quickly. "Yes. I'd like that."

"Great. How's tomorrow evening?"

"That would work." Something creaked, as though she had sat down. Was she at home? At the store? "How is it going with the amends?"

"Pretty well, actually. I went to a church a couple of days ago that I had spray painted graffiti on. The pastor remembered my artwork and said they might have some work for me to do, painting murals in the kids' rooms and stuff like that."

Gabriella's laugh was light and musical, and Ty's fingers tightened around the phone. Tomorrow suddenly seemed a long way away.

"What's next on your list?"

Ty grimaced. Each item got harder, and he really wasn't looking forward to the next one. "I started a dumpster fire in an alley one night and it did a lot of damage to the back of a restaurant. Going there to apologize is next on my agenda."

"Hmm. Would you like some company? We could go for dinner tomorrow night instead of getting coffee."

Ty was completely torn. As much as he'd love to have a whole meal with her instead of only coffee, was he ready to make an apology for his past actions in front of her? What if the owner of the restaurant didn't take it well? The audience there would likely be quite a bit larger than it had been in her store. He cleared his throat. "I usually like to save my public humiliation dates for a little later in the relationship." He winced. Likely shouldn't have used the *r* word already.

To his relief, Gabriella laughed. "If you are publicly humiliated, then we'll just go somewhere else to eat."

"All right then. If you're sure." It might be nice to have a little back-up. And Gabriella's company would be a serious consolation if he did have to slink out of the place. Besides, his first two amends had gone far better than he could have possibly imagined. He'd met an incredible woman and might be given the opportunity to use his art to make a little money on the side, which could lead to bigger and better things. Maybe something great would happen at the restaurant as well, and it would turn into a celebration dinner. "Pick you up at the store at seven?" He may or may not have checked the hours on his way out last time, so he'd know when she finished work.

"Make it seven-thirty. That'll give me time to make myself a little attractive before you get here."

"I promise that won't take anywhere near thirty minutes. Thirty seconds, tops."

When she replied, her voice held the amusement it had the day they'd met. "Thank you for that, but I'm going to take the half hour anyway."

"Okay. I'll see you at seven-thirty."

"Looking forward to it."

"Me too." Ty disconnected the call and tossed the phone onto his coffee table. That was a massive understatement. As slowly as time had moved in prison, he suspected the next twenty-four hours were going to be the longest he had ever experienced.

Ty rubbed his palms across the front of his navy dress pants as they approached the double wooden doors of what appeared to be a much fancier restaurant than he'd remembered. He didn't begrudge what it would cost to bring Gabriella here, but it wasn't the type of place he'd grown up going to, and he wasn't that comfortable starting now. Should he have worn a tie?

Of course, that would have required him going out and buying a tie, and that thought hadn't even occurred to him. They reached the door, and he grasped the large, scrolling metal handle and pulled it open. Too late now.

They left their coats at the check-in counter near the entryway before heading for the hostess station. He'd made reservations, and although the woman in the black pencil skirt, white blouse, and bright red lipstick did gaze at him head to toe, a slight look of disdain on her face, she didn't comment, only led them to a quiet table in the back corner. Gabriella looked stunning in a royal-blue dress, but she did tug at the sides of it a couple of times while she walked, as though she was as uncomfortable all dressed up as he was. Which for some reason he loved. The hostess set a laminated menu at each of their places before nodding slightly and leaving them.

Ty held Gabriella's chair out for her, and she flashed him a smile before sitting down. So far, so good. He wiped his palms on the front of his pants again before taking the padded chair across from her. Soft music played in the background, and a vase of flowers and a flickering candle sat in the center of the table. Definitely not the type of place he usually ate at.

Gabriella scanned the room before her gaze settled on him. Holding the menu to her chest, she leaned forward and lowered her voice. "Did you have to choose the ritziest restaurant in town to burn down?"

Ty would have laughed if his stomach hadn't been so tied

up in knots. A first date, especially when he knew this had the potential to become something great, was nerve wracking enough. Add to that the confession he'd come here to make, and he couldn't remember feeling this sick with anticipation since he'd stood before the judge waiting to hear his sentence.

"For the record, I didn't burn it down. It only got damaged in the back from the fire I set in the dumpster."

"Did you get caught?"

"Yes. There were video cameras on the back wall of the restaurant that I wasn't smart enough to check for at the time."

"Is that what you went to jail for?"

He shook his head. "No, although I did a few months in juvenile detention for it. I was only sixteen when I started the fire in the alley."

"Ah. So what—?"

The arrival of the server granted Ty a reprieve. Was he ready to tell Gabriella what he had done his hard time for? Maybe she wouldn't ask again, although, if she did, he would tell her. Absolute honesty. And maybe it would be better if she knew now, before things went any further.

The same hint of disdain he'd seen on the hostess's face flickered across their server's—a tall, clean-shaven man with blond hair, also dressed in black and white. Ty narrowly resisted the urge to glance at himself. His light blue button-down shirt didn't hide the tattoos on his neck or part of the scar running across his chest. He glanced around the room. All right, he didn't look like the restaurant's usual clientele. Still, his money was good here, and they weren't causing any trouble. Yet. His eyes met Gabriella's. She was glancing from the server to him, a slight frown creasing her forehead. If she was uncomfortable, maybe they should go somewhere else.

"Can I offer you anything to drink this evening?" The man's tone was icy as he tapped two fingers on the wine list in the holder on the table, something neither of them had looked at yet.

"I think we'll need a minute to decide." Ty kept his voice low and even. Might be a good idea to get his mission accomplished now, in case things went sideways here. Which it definitely felt like it might. "Can you tell me if the owner is here tonight?"

"She is, but she's extremely busy." The server's voice had grown even colder, if possible.

"I don't want to bother her, but I wondered if I might be able to speak with her for a moment."

The man pursed his lips and scrutinized him a moment as though trying to figure out what, exactly, Ty could have to say to the woman who owned this establishment. "I'll ask her, but I doubt she will be able to get away. She's very busy."

So you said. Ty nodded. "I'd appreciate it. Thank you."

The server nodded curtly and spun around, striding away without another word.

Ty started to reach for the wine menu but stopped when he caught the look on his date's face. A storm cloud had settled over her features. He left the menu where it was and pulled back his hand. "It's okay, Gabriella."

She shook her head slightly, her long, dark hair swishing over her shoulders. "It is not okay. He has no right to treat you that way when you have been nothing but calm and polite."

Ty shrugged. "It's not worth reacting to. With people like that, nothing you do or say helps; it only tends to make things worse." He reached across the table and touched the side of his hand to hers. "I'd rather ignore it and enjoy a nice dinner with you."

The storm cloud lifted. Slightly. "If you're sure. I'm happy to go somewhere else, though, if you'd prefer."

"Let's see how this conversation goes and then we can decide." Ty inclined his head toward a woman in a gray jacket and blazer, short, red hair perfectly coiffed, crossing the room toward them, their server at her heels.

Ty drew in a deep, steadying breath and pulled his hand away from Gabriella's. He half-rose as the woman approached the table. When she nodded at him, he sat back down.

"I am Jacqueline Lemieux. Henry said you wished to speak with me?" She had a strong French accent, which fit the décor perfectly.

"Yes." Ty cleared his throat. "Thank you for coming out."

She nodded again and rested a hand on the back of a chair at the empty table next to them. "Is there a problem?"

"No. I actually came here tonight to apologize to you."

"Apologize? For what?"

"A few years ago, I set fire to the dumpster in the alley behind this place, and I know it did some damage to this building. I'm not sure if you were the owner at that time, but—"

The woman drew herself up to her full height, her eyes blazing as hot as the server's voice had been cold. "As a matter of fact, I was. Although I nearly lost the place back then when we had to shut down for a couple of months." Her accent had abated considerably, which was interesting.

Ty swallowed. Clearly this amends was not going to go as smoothly as the first two, which he could have guessed the moment he walked in the door. "I'm really sorry about that. I was just a kid back then and I did a lot of foolish things I truly regret. If there's anything I can do to make it up to you, I'd be glad to do it."

She fingers tightened on the chair. "What exactly did you have in mind? Can you repay the thousands of dollars that fire cost us in insurance or compensate the people who didn't receive any wages while the restaurant was closed down or bring back all the customers we lost during that time period?"

Her voice had risen. Ty didn't have to look around the

room to know that everyone in the place would be staring at them, wondering what was going on. "I would if I could, but no, I can't do that."

"I didn't expect so." The woman let go of the chair. "I think it would be best if you left."

Ty had been thinking the exact same thing. Gabriella shoved back her chair and stood. "You know, he didn't have to come here tonight. He was trying to do the right thing."

The woman whirled on her. "Well, it's too bad he didn't do the *right thing* a few years ago and not set my place on fire." The accent—and any façade of civility—had vanished.

Ty rose quickly. Things were escalating fast. They needed to get out of here now, before the situation spiraled as out of control as that dumpster fire had. "Gabriella ..."

He took a step toward her, but she lifted a hand to stop him. "Maybe so, but it took a lot of integrity and decency to apologize to you, something your staff could use a little training in. They have treated him like a second-class citizen since he walked through the door."

"Likely because they could tell that was exactly what he was, even before he attempted to ease his guilty conscience with some lame—" She broke off when Gabriella took a step toward her, her fists clenched.

Ty stepped between the women and wrapped an arm around Gabriella's waist. "Okay, easy, Ronda Rousey. Let's just go."

"Yes, go." The owner hissed the words in Gabriella's direction. "And I would appreciate it if neither of you set foot in my place again."

Gabriella bent over Ty's arm a little to stick her finger in the woman's face. "This is definitely going into my Yelp review."

Before the woman could respond, Ty guided his date gently toward the door. Behind him, he could hear the owner assuring the other patrons, her strong Parisienne accent miraculously restored, that *the problem* had been dealt with. He gritted his teeth a little as he grabbed the coats the smirking host held out to him and pushed open the door.

Gabriella stormed outside ahead of him. "Here." Ty followed her and held up her coat. "You'll freeze."

"I doubt it. I'm burning up." She shoved an arm into the sleeve.

"I can see that." Ty held onto her coat until she had wrangled her other arm in, and then he let go and slipped his own coat on.

Her fingers shook and she fumbled with the top button. "How is it possible for someone to be that cold and unforgiving?"

"I don't know. But those are her issues to deal with, not mine."

When she couldn't work the button through the hole, he stepped closer. "Here." He did up the buttons for her and then grasped the lapels and tugged them a little closer to protect her throat from the icy wind. Her eyes met his and something passed between them that definitely helped banish the coldness of the night air. For a few seconds, Ty didn't move. Then he forced himself to let go and brush a long strand of hair from her face. "Better?"

"Yes. I'm sorry. I can get a little … passionate when I see someone being treated unjustly."

"Don't apologize. Other than my family, I can't remember anyone ever standing up for me like that." He touched a finger to her flushed cheek. "Although, it wasn't completely unjust treatment, you know. I did set her place on fire and cost her and her employees a lot of money."

"Which you were sincerely apologizing for."

"Even so, she was right about that much; there's no way I can make up for the damage I did or the people I hurt." The truth of that stung and burned like the blade had when the gang leader he'd beaten up had slashed him across the chest before Ty could wrest the knife from his grasp and toss it into a nearby bush. He took a steadying breath. No use dwelling on that now. He was doing what he could, which was all anyone could ask of him. All he could ask of himself. "Want to go somewhere for a burger and fries?"

"Yes. Please."

He grinned at the obvious relief in her voice. His kind of girl.

"Do you like Mario's?"

"I've never been."

"It's about time, then. They serve the best burgers in the city." They started walking in the direction of his favorite burger place. When they passed Ty's apartment building, he pointed it out to her, although he didn't suggest they go inside. "I'm sorry I got you banned from that other restaurant."

She snorted. "I wouldn't go back there if you paid me."

Ty appreciated the loyalty. Although, as they made their way through the snow, past the Santas ringing bells on every corner next to a Salvation Army kettle and the shoppers trudging in and out of shops laden down with packages, his brief spurt of elation dissipated.

His past was a disaster. Gabriella hardly knew about any of it, had only spent a few hours with him, and she was already paying the price.

Did he have any right to ask her to wade any deeper into the muck with him than she already had?

CHAPTER SIX

Ty spent an entire night tossing and turning before deciding he had to break the commitment he'd made to himself—and Laken—not to make contact with any former members of his gang. If he wanted to make amends for the next item on his list—sending the leader of that other gang to the hospital—he had to know where the guy was. He sent a text to Antonio, probably the only real friend he'd had back then, asking him if he knew where he might be able to find Hanh Lo Kongh.

Antonio hadn't responded by the time Ty left for work, and when he checked his messages at lunch there was still no response. It had been years. It was quite possible Antonio didn't have the same number anymore. He could even be dead, for all Ty knew, a thought that twisted his stomach.

After an interminably long shift and subway ride home, he dropped onto the couch and pulled out his phone. The text icon had a red tag. Was that Antonio, getting back to him? Ty wasn't sure whether to hope he had or not. If he couldn't reach Antonio, he had no real way to track Hanh down, not without putting himself in extreme danger, which Con had told him he wasn't supposed to do. Meeting up one on one with the guy he'd beaten was dangerous enough—heading somewhere a bunch of his old gang members were likely hanging out when he didn't plan to join them was borderline suicide.

Ty hovered his thumb over the icon for a few seconds before tapping on it. Antonio. His heart rate picked up a little. *H hangs out at The Red Planet on Granby.*

Nothing personal, just the facts, which suited Ty fine. Before he could reply, Antonio sent another text. *Careful.*

Ty typed *thanks* and hit send. His friend didn't reply. Maybe he was as determined as Ty to get out of that life. Ty hoped so, for his old friend's sake. He tossed the phone onto the coffee table and grabbed the TV remote. Slumping against the couch cushions, he pointed the remote at the television but didn't turn it on. What was he waiting for? It was Friday night. Chances were good Hanh would be at the bar now. It was December 21st. If Ty didn't go soon, he'd have to wait until after the holidays. As tempting as the thought of putting off the coming confrontation was, it would probably be better to get it over with, not give himself too much time to think about it.

Ty dropped the remote onto the couch, grabbed his phone, and pushed to his feet with a groan. What he'd really love to be doing tonight was crashing on the couch with Gabriella, eating a pizza and watching a movie. Not tracking down some guy in a seedy bar who was, more than likely, drunk and nursing a years-long grudge against him.

The thoughts pulsing through his head slowed his steps as he grabbed the coat he'd tossed on a chair and headed for the door. Really, was it worth putting himself at risk just to tell Hanh he was sorry for beating him up so badly years ago? So what if Ty had someone out there he had wronged and hadn't apologized to? He'd never make everybody happy, right? And the guy wasn't exactly a model citizen. All Ty had really done was take him off the streets for a few weeks, likely preventing a bunch of car-jackings or assaults on innocent people.

He shook off the doubts threatening to sabotage his mission, along with the inner voice warning him that this was not a good idea. He'd come this far in his journey—something deep inside compelled him to finish, whatever the cost. And the truth was, whoever the guy was, whatever he'd done, the pain, fear, and drug-induced fury Ty had unleashed on him had not been justified. And he hadn't only ambushed and injured Hanh, he'd humiliated him. He was an older, veteran leader of his gang. He would have lost a lot of the respect he'd earned over the years, which was a far bigger blow than any physical damage Ty might have inflicted. He paused, his hand on the doorknob.

As much as it is in your power, be at peace with everyone.

Con's wise words scrolled through his mind as they had so often done since that night in the coffee shop. He pulled open the door. Wait. That wasn't Con. That was from the Bible. A verse he'd learned when he was ten or eleven and gotten a candy bar for repeating in Sunday school.

Was he replacing his old soundtrack with a new one? Of course, those words weren't new, they were old. Ancient words of wisdom, in fact.

Even so, they infused Ty with a rush of fresh energy, and he stepped into the hallway and pulled the door closed before striding to the stairwell. A fifteen-minute drive later, he stood on the sidewalk in front of The Red Planet, a place he'd heard about but never entered. The bar looked pretty rundown, but someone had still strung multi-colored lights around the posts at the top of the stairs and along the porch railing. A bedraggled wreath hung on the large wooden door, the red bow at a forty-five-degree angle from the top.

Ty tromped up the two cement steps and reached for the handle. He took a deep breath before pulling open the door and stepping inside. A wall of hot air and Bob Seger's raspy voice belting out "Old Time Rock and Roll" greeted him. Most of the tables in the small, dimly lit bar were full. Ty walked past several guys standing at the arcade game machines that lined one wall, flashing and beeping. A place like this would have definitely been his scene a few years ago. Now the only thought in his head was how fast he could get in, conduct his business, and get out.

He meandered to the bar against the back wall, scanning every table as he passed by. No sign of Hanh. When the bartender headed toward him, Ty slid onto an empty stool. "Ginger ale." Probably better to keep a clear head in case Hanh did show up. Plus, Ty was driving. No need to add DUI to the list of possible reasons for the police to arrest him tonight.

The bartender nodded and grabbed a glass from a shelf over the bar. When he set the drink and the machine in front of Ty, Ty tapped his debit card to it. The bartender left to serve someone else, and Ty searched the room again. No one he recognized. How long should he wait? It was already after ten. If Hanh was coming, wouldn't he be here already? Ty sipped his drink slowly, sitting sideways on his stool so he could watch the door. A few people came and went as he sat there, but no Hanh. By the time he'd finished the soda, it was almost ten-thirty.

Ty slid off the stool. He'd tried. Other than this lead, he had no idea how to find the guy. Maybe he'd come back tomorrow or next week, try again. He made his way to the exit and stepped onto the porch. The wreath banged lightly against the wood when he closed the door behind him. At the bottom of the stairs, he stepped aside to let a group of guys brush by. Ty's stomach tightened when he caught a glimpse of the man in the middle of the pack. Hanh. Hanh's dark gaze lasered in on him, and he shoved past a couple of his friends to reach Ty. "What are you doing here, Jones?"

"I was looking for you, actually."

"Why? You planning to kill me too?"

Ty flinched. "No. I just want to talk."

Hanh edged closer, until his chest nearly touched Ty's. His buddies had all stopped when he did. A couple of them had reached the top of the porch but three or four stood behind Hanh. Looked like an Asian gang, which wasn't the one Ty remembered him being in. Had he left that one? Or been kicked out? If so, and it had anything to do with what Ty had done to him, Hanh was likely holding more against Ty than he'd realized.

"Talk about what?" Hanh stood so close to Ty that he felt the man's hot breath against his cheek.

"I wanted to apologize."

Hanh's nearly black eyes narrowed. He didn't speak for a moment, as though Ty's words had caught him so off guard he didn't know how to respond. Then he spat out, "For what?"

"For hurting you that night."

Another long pause, before Hanh let loose with a racist, curse-word-laden tirade letting Ty know what he could do with his apology.

Ty's jaw tightened, but he heard Hanh out and then stepped back. "All right then. I wanted you to know I was sorry, and now you do." He'd done what he had to do. Hopefully Hanh would be willing to leave it at that and head inside.

He wasn't. Instead of retreating, he stepped closer. Planting his palms on Ty's chest, Hahn shoved him back a few steps.

Ty held up his hands. "I don't want any trouble."

"Then you shouldn't have come here, Jones."

Probably true. The door to the bar opened and a couple of people came out, talking away. Their voices died off as they stopped on the porch. Ty shot them a look. The man and woman were both taking in the scene, clearly attempting to figure out what was happening. Would they intervene? They didn't, only retreated inside. Ty was on his own.

He faced his old adversary. No walking away now. "Look, Hanh, I—"

The man shot out his fist, connecting with Ty's jaw. His head jerked to the side, but he recovered quickly. He'd been a decent fighter before he'd gone to prison, and he'd only honed his skills there. And he had a couple of inches and maybe twenty or thirty pounds on Hanh. If the guy's friends stayed out of it, he could likely give him a decent run for his money. Drop him again, although he'd stop short of the complete thrashing he'd given him the last time.

Which would nullify his apology and do far more harm than good.

God, could you maybe help me out here? I need—

The rest of his prayer was cut off when Hanh's fist drove deep into his gut. Ty bent forward slightly as pain shot through his abdomen. His fists clenched. Everything in him longed to pummel the guy, but something held him back.

Really? He narrowly resisted the urge to look up at the sky, which would only open him up to another piston punch to the face. *I'm just supposed to stand here and—*

Hanh landed a jab squarely to his ribs. Ty gritted his teeth but didn't hit back, only tried to stay on his feet as Hanh hit him again in the jaw and then landed a flurry of blows to his abdomen and one to his kidneys that had Ty groaning in pain.

The keening wail of a police siren broke through the thick haze swirling around him. Hanh shot out his fist one more time, slamming into Ty's ribs with enough force that Ty was pretty sure he heard them crack. Nausea rose, but he fought that and the wave of dizziness rolling over him as Hanh shoved him backwards again and then spun around and took off, his buddies following him.

Ty stumbled to the porch railing and grasped hold of it to keep himself upright. Well. That had definitely not gone as planned. And now the police were coming. If they arrested him, his parole would be revoked. Likely he should take off too. He took a step away from the porch and stopped as though he'd walked into a wall.

He glanced up at the night sky, only the odd star puncturing the city light pollution and heavy clouds. *Come on. What do you want from me? I dragged myself off the couch to come here, stood still and let the guy beat me up, and now I'm not supposed to leave before the police arrive?*

A strange sensation worked its way through him, like the river flowing gently beneath the bridge. Ty slumped against the railing. *Fine. My way has never taken me anywhere good; maybe it's time to try yours. But stick around, would ya?*

God didn't answer, but the sensation did seem to intensify a little, and, despite the intense throbbing in his ribs, Ty was able to draw in a slow, steadying breath. *Can you do one thing for me? Don't let it be Laken.* He exhaled loudly. There were hundreds of cops in the city, maybe thousands. It was highly unlikely his brother would be the one who happened to answer this call. Blue and red lights reflecting off the buildings around the bar announced the imminent arrival of a cruiser. In seconds, a police car had roared up to the curb in front of The Red Planet and screeched to a stop. Both front doors opened, and a uniformed officer exited the vehicle from each side. As the one who'd been in the passenger seat slammed his door, the glow of the streetlights fell across his face. Ty closed his eyes. *That's just perfect. Thanks for nothing.*

When he opened them, his brother was striding up the walk. His gaze landed on Ty. The look that crossed his face—a mix of pain, frustration, and disappointment—hurt Ty more than any of Hanh's blows.

Laken stopped in front of him. "Seriously?"

"Lake, this isn't what it looks like."

"It looks like you got into a fight in public, someone called it in, and now you're forcing me to arrest you for disturbing the peace or assault or whatever it was you did here and send you back to jail."

Okay, it was what it looked like. Sort of. How could he explain what had happened here to his brother when he didn't fully understand it himself?

Laken studied him. "Have you been drinking or doing drugs?"

"No."

"Are you carrying?"

"No." Although he still had the gun he'd taken to the bridge with him that night stuck in a drawer in his apartment, he wasn't foolish enough to have brought it with him to meet with Hanh.

Laken shot a look at his partner before shifting his gaze to Ty. "I have to check."

"I get it." Ty knew the drill. He turned and gripped the railing with both hands, his feet shoulder width apart.

He winced when his brother patted his throbbing ribs. Laken checked his pockets quickly before stepping back. "Okay, turn around."

When Ty complied, his brother crossed his arms. "First of all, are you okay?"

Ty did a mental check. His face and torso felt as though they were on fire, but he didn't think any of his injuries were serious, other than a cracked rib or two. "I think so."

"Want to tell me what happened?"

"I came here tonight to find a guy I beat up a few years ago."

"Why?"

"To apologize."

Laken cocked his head. Ty met his gaze. Confusion still

played across Laken's face, but something that looked a lot like hope had sparked in his eyes. Ty swallowed, not sure he'd ever loved his brother more. Laken believed him. Or wanted to, at least. Which meant everything to Ty.

"I take it he did not accept your apology?"

Ty managed a wry grin. "No. He did not."

"So, the two of you fought."

"Not exactly. He fought. I didn't."

"You just stood there and let him hit you?"

"Yes."

"Why?"

"Because I deserved it."

Laken blinked, as though trying to comprehend what he was hearing. Ty didn't blame him. Before the last few days, had he ever admitted to his brother—or anyone—that he was in the wrong? That he deserved whatever hardship he was going through in life? Maybe, when he went to prison for shooting that kid. Against his lawyer's advice, Ty had pled guilty, and he'd had no trouble accepting his sentence. He'd spent a lot of his life blaming other people for his troubles though, namely the father who had abandoned them.

Before Laken could speak, his partner came up to stand beside him. "Seems he's telling the truth, Lake."

Laken uncrossed his arms. "Really?"

"Yeah. This guy called it in." His partner nodded toward the porch. Ty glanced over. The man and woman who had come out when the fight was starting and then gone back inside stood at the top of the stairs. A number of other people milled about behind them, including the bartender. Had they all witnessed his humiliating defeat? Ty contemplated that. Somehow that was not what his altercation with Hanh felt like. "They watched from the window and saw everything."

"They confirmed that Tyrone didn't hit the other guy?"

"Yes. Like he said, he appears to have stood there and taken it."

Laken nodded. "You get their contact information?"

"Yep."

"All right then." He lifted a hand in the direction of the couple. "Thanks for your help. We'll contact you if we need to speak with you further."

The man nodded and the two of them wandered down the stairs and along the walkway to the street. Everyone else gradually drifted into the bar, since it appeared the excitement was over.

Laken swung his attention back to Ty. "What was the name of the other guy?"

Ty didn't answer. He'd tell his brother almost anything he wanted to know, but he couldn't rat out Hanh. Like he'd told Laken, he'd deserved the beating he'd gotten.

Laken's partner stepped closer. "Bartender said it was Hanh lo Kongh."

"Ah. Our old buddy Hanh. Can you call that in, Brad? Make sure it gets back to Hanh that it was an unnamed witness who gave us his name."

Ty's eyes met his brother's, and he offered Laken a grateful smile.

"Got it." Brad pulled a cell phone from the inside pocket of his jacket. "And our shift's almost over. Why don't you take off? I'll file the report on this."

"You sure?"

"Absolutely. Take care of your brother. I'll see you tomorrow." His partner inclined his head before walking a few steps away and pressing the phone to his ear.

Laken slapped Ty on the back. "I guess you're off the hook. This time." His grin tempered the words. Ty worked to hide a grimace as white-hot stabs of pain shot across his side.

His brother's grin faded. "All right, that's it. Give me your keys. I'm taking you to the hospital."

"I don't need to go to the hospital."

"Want me to slap you on the back again?"

Ty hesitated before digging into his jacket pocket for his keys and holding them out to his brother.

Laken took them. "Good call." He turned and started along the walkway.

Ty fell into step next to him. So, Hanh had landed *him* in the hospital now. That felt about right. "We have to stop by your place on the way, though. I show up at the hospital with you in a uniform, and my street cred will be completely destroyed."

His brother sent him a heated look and Ty laughed, pressing a hand to his ribs as he did. "Just kidding. About the street cred. Not about you changing into civilian clothes."

"Fine. But you have to do something for me."

"What's that?"

"Before this night is over, I want you to tell me everything that's going on with you. Something's different, and I am very interested to hear what it is."

CHAPTER SEVEN

The X-rays showed three cracked ribs and a number of contusions but no internal injuries. Ty would have to take it easy for a bit, but they didn't need to keep him in the hospital. Not that he would have agreed to that anyway. After the night he'd had, all he wanted was his own place, his own bed.

What he really would have liked was that pizza, his couch, and maybe a little TLC from Gabriella. As much as he knew that, for her sake, he should be trying to put her out of his mind, his mind had other ideas.

"What's that about?"

Ty shifted on the passenger seat of his car, blinking as Laken's voice called him back from the very pleasant place his thoughts had gone. "What's what about?"

"The goofy smile on your face. Did they give you painkillers?"

Oh. They had, but that wasn't what the smile was about. "Yeah, that must be it."

Laken's eyes narrowed. "You met someone, didn't you?"

Ty sighed. He never had been able to keep anything from his brother, something that had gotten him in a lot of trouble over the years. "All right, yes. But it's really new. Nothing much to report at this point."

"Part of what's caused this big transformation in you?"

He mulled that over. "A small part of it, yeah."

"Here." Laken wheeled into the parking lot of a fast-food joint and entered the drive-through lane. "I'm guessing you haven't eaten in a while."

Ty glanced at his watch. Almost three in the morning. Now that his brother mentioned it, he was ravenous. The small car filled with the aroma of hot grease as the teenager at the window handed Laken a paper bag. He passed it over to Ty, nodded at the kid, and pulled away. There was a picnic table near the parking lot exit, and Laken turned into a spot in front of it. "Let's sit for a few minutes."

Ty gingerly settled on the table next to his brother, his feet on the bench. He set the bag between them and grabbed a cardboard container of fries out of it. The pain meds were starting to help, but he still throbbed in numerous places and was starting to stiffen up.

"So, what's going on?"

Where did he even begin? He popped a few fries into his mouth, chewed, and swallowed. "I hit a low point a few nights ago and was out wandering around when I bumped into this homeless guy. Or he might have been an angel—I'm not sure. He wasn't as old, but he reminded me of that guy Clarence in the Christmas movie Iya makes us watch every year."

"*It's a Wonderful Life.*"

"Yeah, that one. Anyway, he said I looked like I needed to talk and that he was a good listener, so we went to a coffee shop. I bought him a sandwich and we had a really interesting conversation."

"About?"

"My past, the guilt I still wrestle with."

"Ah." Laken unwrapped a burger. "Did he have some advice for you?"

"Actually, he did. He suggested I make amends for the things I did, go back and, as much as it is in my power and safe to do so, try to make them right."

Laken frowned. "Tracking down Hanh Lo Kongh at a sketchy bar, even to apologize, was definitely not safe. You're lucky he didn't pull a knife. Or a gun."

"I know. It was a calculated risk."

"That landed you in the hospital."

"Only briefly, and like I said—"

"You deserved it."

"That's right." Ty grabbed more fries out of the container.

"Is this really about making amends then or about punishing yourself for your past?"

Ouch. Ty dropped the fries into the box without eating any. The pointed question competed with the stabbing in his side for the wound causing him the most pain. Ty hadn't thought about this quest as a way to punish himself—could that be what it was, at the heart of it? The number of times he'd told someone recently that he deserved what was happening to him suggested his brother might not be far off. "I don't know. Maybe. Would it be wrong if it was? I do deserve to be punished for all the things I did, the people I hurt."

"And you have been. You've gone to juvenile detention and did six years in prison. At some point, you have to let go of the need to punish yourself, accept that your debt to society has been paid, and that God is ready and willing to forgive that and every other thing you have done wrong. All you need to do is ask. And then accept that forgiveness so you can move on with your life."

Ty's throat tightened. Maybe he was starting to see that God hadn't abandoned him like Ty had long believed he had, but the fact that God was hanging around was one thing. The idea that he might be willing to offer Ty complete forgiveness for all the terrible things he'd done was something else entirely. "I killed a guy."

"I know that. But so did Moses. And David. And a lot of other people God still forgave. Still loved. Still called his children."

Ty propped his elbows on his knees and lowered his forehead to his palms. It was too much for him to wrap his mind around. It wasn't possible. What he'd done was too big. Even God wasn't powerful enough…

He raised his head. The fog from the pain and the meds cleared suddenly. Even he knew that the thought forming in his head was a lie straight from hell. How long had he allowed himself to believe the blatant falsehood that his past transgressions were too much for God to handle? And how had he ever thought that, if God couldn't deal with them, he would have to do it himself with his fumbling attempts to make amends?

Laken rested a hand on Ty's back, warm between his shoulder blades. "There's nothing wrong with trying to make amends."

Ty glanced at his brother. How and when had he become so easy to read? "No?"

"Of course not. Taking responsibility for what we've done and asking others for forgiveness isn't worthless; it's being a decent, honorable person."

"So, growing up."

Laken chuckled. "Exactly. It's just that, ultimately, that's not enough on its own. Apologizing for what we've done, even being genuinely remorseful, can't save us. We need God."

Actually, now that Ty thought about it, Con had basically said the same thing. Ty had latched so eagerly onto the amends idea—something he could do himself without having to ask God for anything—that, in his arrogance, he'd failed to hear the rest of it. Well, he was hearing it now, loud and clear. And he couldn't deny any longer the truth of Laken's words. Ty definitely needed God.

He lowered his forehead to his palms again. *Can you do it? Can you ever forgive me? Not only for everything I've done to hurt you and other people, but for thinking I could make up for all of those things on my own, without you?* The small flicker of warmth that had ignited inside him the night he met Con spread across his chest. What was that, anyway? Whatever it was, Ty knew now, without a doubt, that it came from God.

Which answered the questions he'd just asked.

Tears threatened, and he lowered his palms to cover his eyes, giving in to the warmth that rolled over him like waves scrolling onto soft sand. He lost all track of time as he sat there, his brother's hand solid and steady against his back, the warmth slowly spreading all through his body. Finally, he lifted his head and swiped at a drop of moisture beneath his eye.

Laken was watching him intently. "You okay?"

Ty did a quick assessment, like he had when his brother had asked him that in front of the bar. "Yeah. I'm good. Really good."

His brother smiled, the lines of worry grooved across his forehead easing. "Good."

"You can let it go, Lake."

"What?"

"The need to take care of me. It's not your responsibility anymore. It never should have been."

Laken pulled his hand from Ty's back. "I'm sorry I didn't do a better job." His voice broke.

Ty whirled on him, wincing at the fire that shot across his ribs at the abrupt movement. "No. Don't you dare say that. You're the best brother in the world. You couldn't have done any more for me than you did. Been there for me any more than you were. Everything that happened in the past was my fault. The results of my poor choices. Nothing you did or didn't do."

Laken's smile was weak. "Thank you for saying that."

"I mean it. And I mean it that you can lay that burden down now too. You don't have to be my dad anymore. You can just be my brother."

Laken grasped Ty's ponytail and tugged on it gently. "All right, kid. I hear you. Thanks."

Kid. Laken hadn't called him that in years. That one small word conjured up endless memories of the two of them and everything they'd done together growing up. They'd been so close, virtually inseparable, until Ty had turned his back on everything he'd been raised to believe, everything he'd always known, deep down, was true. Even then, even after Ty had tried to push his family away, after he'd committed unspeakable crimes, Laken hadn't abandoned him. He'd always been there, trying to help, reaching out for his little brother.

How could Ty have doubted that God would do the same?

Laken clambered to the ground and held out a hand. Ty grasped it and his brother hauled him to his feet. The blessed fog from the pain meds was swirling around him again, and it hurt less to move than Ty had expected. Laken slid an arm around his brother's shoulders as they walked toward Ty's car. "Tell me about this woman."

He shook his head. "I don't think so. Too early."

"Fine. Then I'm telling Iya you have a girlfriend. She'll whoop the details out of you."

Ty snorted. "It wouldn't be the first time. It might be the first time you've been the tattletale in the family, though."

"Hey, you're the one who told me I could just be your

brother. I think I'd like to milk that for a little while, make up for lost time."

It hurt to laugh, but the joy of everything that had happened that evening was so profound, Ty couldn't help himself. And maybe none of it would have transpired if God had answered Ty's prayer and Laken hadn't been the one to answer the call about the fight. A good reminder that God's ways were not his ways.

Laken nudged him in the arm. "Can I still take care of you sometimes?"

"Only if you let me take care of you sometimes too."

A thoughtful look crossed his brother's face, as though the idea of someone else taking care of him on occasion had never occurred to him. "I think I could handle that."

"Good. Because it's happening." They were both chuckling when they reached the car and slid onto the front seats.

Ty glanced out his window. One star hung low in the sky, twinkling brighter than the rest—a reminder that Christmas was coming.

For the first time in years, Ty couldn't wait to celebrate the season like he had when he was a child—the Christmas Eve service in a few days and then pancakes on Christmas morning while Iya read from her worn Bible, the ancient story that had taken on a whole new meaning for Ty tonight.

CHAPTER EIGHT

Ty lay on the couch, one arm bent and resting over his eyes, trying not to think about the drugs that would help ease the pain that wracked his body after a long day on his feet at work. He wasn't an addict. Although he'd used drugs whenever he was facing another test while trying to get into the gang, he'd rarely done them any other time and didn't feel a strong urge to. Still, he'd seen the effects of them too often to want to even go close to the edge of that deadly swamp. He could tough this out. Dragging himself off the couch and making himself something to eat was more than he could manage at the moment, though, as much as his growling stomach was demanding that he do so.

A light knock sounded on the door, and he lifted his arm. Who was that?

Maybe if he ignored it, whoever it was would go away. Although … it might be Laken or his mother. He could use their company tonight to take his mind off the ache not only in his ribs but in his chest. He missed Gabriella. After what had happened at the restaurant, he'd realized how unfair it would be to take their relationship any further. Still, it was requiring every bit of strength he had not to grab the phone and call her, just to hear her voice. He couldn't be that selfish. Not anymore.

Ty swung his legs over the side of the couch and sat up slowly. When he made his way across the apartment and pulled open the door, his breath caught in his throat. Gabriella stood in the hallway, holding a square white box with the logo from his favorite pizza place splashed across the top.

His delight at the sight was vastly eclipsed by the sheer joy of seeing her, which told him a lot.

Relief flickered across her face. "Oh good. This is the fourth door I knocked on. I had to wrestle the box away from two other guys."

Ty started to laugh but stopped when pain knifed across his side. "I'm glad you managed to hold on to it."

"I have three older brothers so … years of practice." Her smile looked a little uncertain.

Ty stepped back. "Come in."

She walked into his apartment, and he closed the door behind her. She stopped and faced him. "I'm sorry to drop by without calling."

"No. I'm really glad you did. And not only because you come bearing pizza."

Gabriella laughed, but the sound was more restrained than usual. "It's just, when you didn't call for three days, I thought I'd take a chance and come over, find out what was going on." She set the box on the coffee table and crossed her arms over her chest.

Ty exhaled and ran a hand over his head. "I'm sorry about that. I didn't mean to ghost you. But the other night, when I got you banned from a restaurant for being with me, it struck me that it was too much to ask you to get involved with someone with such a messed-up past."

"Shouldn't I have some say about who I do or do not get involved with?"

"Yes, of course. But you don't have any idea what I've done."

"I never will, you know, if you don't tell me."

She had a point. "I guess that's true."

The aromas of melted cheese and pepperoni wafted from the pizza box. Gabriella picked it up. "Kitchen?"

"That way." Ty waved a hand toward the hallway.

Gabriella headed in the direction he'd indicated. Ty followed her. As apprehensive as he was about everything he needed to tell her, he loved the fact that she was here and that it felt so right, so comfortable to have her in his place. She crossed the kitchen to the table, set the box on it, and pulled off her coat. In a worn pair of jeans and yellow blouse, she looked as lovely as she had in her blue dress the other night. And much more comfortable. She hung her coat on a chair and turned to him. "I'll grab some plates and ..." Her eyes narrowed. "Wait. What happened to you?" She closed the space between them and touched the tips of her fingers to the bruised and slightly swollen spot on his jaw that the softer lighting in the living room had hidden.

Ty swallowed and attempted a grin, trying to ease the concern in her beautiful dark eyes. Not that he didn't appreciate it. "The last guy I tried to make amends with was even less understanding about it than that woman in the restaurant."

"Oh no. I'm sorry." She reached for his hand and led him to the table. "Here. Sit."

Her fingers were warm and soft and fit so perfectly in his that Ty almost couldn't bring himself to let go when she pulled out a chair with her other hand and held it for him.

He tried to hide the wince when he sat, but he obviously didn't do a great job of it because she tilted her head, her long, dark hair cascading over one shoulder. "Did he hurt your ribs?"

"I'm okay, honest."

She didn't answer, only kept looking at him until Ty sighed. "I had X-rays done at the hospital. A couple of cracked ribs and some bruising, nothing major."

"That's major enough." She moved forward, stopping in front of his knees. She was probably five-six or five-seven, but Ty was over six feet. She wasn't that much taller than he was when he was sitting down. He tipped his head back so he could watch her as she brushed her fingers over every bruise on his face. A soft, floral scent drifted from her, and Ty stopped worrying about the pain in his side and drew in a long, slow draught of it.

She trailed her thumb over his jaw. "I wish you'd called me."

He blinked a little at that. "I wanted to. Seeing you was all I could think about, actually. But, like I said, I was hesitant to involve you in any more fallout from my train-wreck of a past. And even if you were okay with that, I assumed it was too soon to make you my emergency contact."

A small smile crossed her lips, although it didn't erase the worry splashed across her face. "It was."

Ty nodded.

"But I would have come anyway."

Her words touched something deep inside him. Gabriella felt it too then, this thing between them. He'd never felt like this around a woman, even one he'd dated for more than a month or two, which hadn't happened often. Whatever it was, he knew inherently that it was special. That it wasn't something that could be rushed. It was too precious, too full of possibilities. And he still had so much to work through in himself.

In spite of the self-admonishment, he couldn't keep from

resting his fingers lightly on her hips. She didn't seem to mind, only leaned in and pressed a soft kiss to the bruise on his cheek. A different kind of warmth coursed through him. It wasn't going to be easy, taking things slowly with her. He almost laughed. Who was he kidding? He knew exactly how difficult it was going to be. But he wasn't afraid of hard things anymore. He'd come to see that it was the hard things that carried the greatest reward. And some things—some people—were worth waiting for.

Although everything in him longed to pull her closer, Ty eased her back a little before taking her hands in his and pulling them to his chest. "Look, Gabriella. Before this goes any further, I want to be completely honest with you."

"Good. I want that too."

"All right then. The truth is, I've been with a lot of women. And I haven't always treated them with the respect they deserved. But I don't want to be that guy anymore. With you, I want to be a better man. Because I think we could have something really special, something worth fighting for. But if you don't, after what I just told you, I completely understand."

In the jury's-out moment of silent deliberation that followed, Ty worked to keep drawing in breaths. Already he knew that, if Gabriella walked out of here tonight, he would have lost something of infinite value. And he would have only himself to blame.

After a few seconds, she exhaled a quivering breath. Her dark eyes locked on his. "Something has changed with you, hasn't it?"

"Yes. Everything has changed."

She nodded. "I can see it in your eyes. The sadness, the desperation I saw in them the day we met, is gone." She tightened her hold on his fingers. "I want to hear all about that. What is happening between us feels very special to me too, like nothing I have ever experienced before."

171

"Me neither."

She contemplated him a moment. "There's something I need to ask you first, though."

Ty braced himself. "Okay."

"When you came into my store that day, you mentioned you were praying that making amends with the people you had hurt would help."

"Yes."

"Does that mean you are a church boy, Tyrone Jones?"

He grinned. "I was, growing up. Then I wasn't for a long time. But yes, now I am most definitely a church boy again." He lifted her hands to his mouth and kissed them. "Are you a church girl, Gabriella Ortiz?"

"Yes, I am most definitely a church girl." Her voice held laughter, like it had that day in the store. "Are you going to a Christmas Eve service?"

"I'm planning to. I told my mother and my brother I would go with them to our Nigerian church."

"That sounds lovely. You should be with your family on Christmas Eve."

The wistfulness in her voice tugged at his chest. "Isn't your family around?"

"No. My mother and father are both gone. I have three brothers and two sisters, but they are all still in Argentina. I am the baby, so by the time my parents moved to Canada when I was ten, they were old enough to stay on their own, and none of them came with us."

Argentina. That must be the flag hanging in the store. "Do you ever think about moving back?" The thought sent a pang through his chest that rivaled the fiery darts that had shot across his ribs the last couple of days.

She shook her head. "No. Canada is my home now. And I grew up working in that store with my dad. I don't know if I will ever be able to give it up."

Relief flooded through him. "Do you want to come to dinner at my mother's and then the service with us?"

She bit her lip. "I don't want to impose."

He squeezed her fingers. "I promise you wouldn't. My mother will be thrilled, and Laken already told me he wants to meet you."

Her eyes widened. "You told your brother about me?"

"No. He guessed. He's the one who took me to the hospital a couple of nights ago, and when we were driving home, I was thinking about you. Apparently, I had a goofy smile on my face, and he put two and two together pretty quickly."

She laughed lightly. "Smart guy."

"He is. And the greatest guy I know. He's also a cop."

"Ah. That must have made for some interesting dinner conversations over the years."

Ty snorted softly. "You could say that. I'm sure I wouldn't be alive, though, without him. Our dad left when I was two, and he really filled that void for me."

"Then I'd like to meet him as well. And your mother. So yes, I'll come with you on Christmas Eve, if you're sure it's all right."

"It's more than all right." Suddenly there was nothing Ty wanted more. Except maybe pizza. He inclined his head toward the box. "Should we ...?"

Gabriella let go of his hands. "We should. It'll be getting cold."

They settled on the couch and ate pizza and talked, like Ty had imagined them doing the night Hanh had beaten him up. He shared with her everything that had happened the last week, even the part about going up on that bridge with a loaded gun. And he told her everything he had done, including the crime that had landed him in prison. He wouldn't hold anything back. Although she hadn't run when he told her about his history with women, she hadn't known about everything else then. It wasn't too late for her to change her mind. If she heard it all, heard the worst, and still wanted to stick around, he'd know for sure what he already strongly suspected—that Gabriella Ortiz was the woman he hadn't even realized he'd been waiting for all his life.

She didn't leave, only listened carefully and asked thoughtful questions, never once making him feel as though she judged him. When he'd finished telling her everything, she set her empty plate on the coffee table. "Did you say you have sketchbooks with your artwork in them?"

"I don't know if I'd call it artwork, but yeah, a bunch of them. Drawing helped pass the time in prison."

"Could I see them?"

Ty hesitated. Was he ready for her to see his work? He'd been excited at the thought of letting the reverend go through his sketchbooks, but that was only because she was offering him work; it wasn't personal. Showing Gabriella that part of himself that he had never shown anyone was deeply, deeply personal. He didn't want to keep anything from her, though. "Sure. I'll get them."

He retrieved the books from the small table next to his bed and carried them to the living room. "Here you go."

She took them from him, handling them reverently, as though they already meant as much to her as they did to him. Another part of Ty's heart slipped from his grasp. Gabriella took her time going through them, turning the pages slowly and commenting on each piece, asking questions that drew from him what he had been thinking when he sketched it, what he'd been feeling. It was the most intimate experience Ty had ever gone through, and by the time she closed the cover on the last book, he was in deep, deep trouble. Those walls Con had mentioned, the ones Ty had erected around himself to block others from hurting him the way his father had done, had crumbled to dust at his feet. Gabriella set the books in her lap and rested her fingers on them protectively, as though they were priceless treasures.

"There is a lot more to you than meets the eye, isn't there, Tyrone Jones?"

The light teasing in her voice eased the intense feelings coursing through him, and he smiled. "I don't know about that."

"I do." She lifted the pile of books and set them on the table. The worn black notebook he'd been using to document his amends journey sat next to the pile, and she picked it up. "Is this more pictures?"

"No, actually. That's where I keep my list."

She raised an eyebrow. "Your list?"

"Of the things I've done that I wanted to apologize and make amends for."

"Ah." She lifted it slightly. "May I?"

"Sure."

Gabriella opened the cover. The Polaroid he'd tucked inside dropped onto her lap, and she stuck a finger in the book to hold the page and reached for it. "What's this?"

"It's what I spray painted on the side of the church that night. The pastor liked it for some reason, enough that she took a picture of it that she's kept all these years."

"For some reason?" Her words were hushed as she stared at the picture. "Ty, this is amazing."

He shrugged, no idea what to do with the praise. "Thanks."

Gabby gazed at the picture a while longer before leaning to the side to set it carefully on top of the stack of sketchbooks. When she straightened, she flipped the small notebook open again and scanned the first page where he had documented each item. He'd already crossed out the first four. Only the last item remained. His chest tightened when she ran the tip of her finger over the words. "You're planning to talk to Zach's parents?"

"I'm going to try. I'm sure they won't want to see me, and if they close the door in my face, I won't blame them. But I need to make the attempt."

"When?"

"Tomorrow, I think."

"Do you want me to come with you?"

Everything in him longed to say yes. Her presence would make the visit to Zach's home easier, but something about the idea didn't feel right. He reached for her hand and lifted the back of it to his cheek. "I really do, but I feel as though this is something I need to do alone."

"I get it. I'll be praying."

"I'd appreciate it."

"Will you call me after, let me know how it went?"

"Absolutely."

Gabriella yawned and set the notebook down to press her fingers to her mouth. Ty glanced at his phone. Quarter after two in the morning. No wonder she was tired. He shook her hand lightly. "You should go home and get some sleep. Do you want me to drive you?"

"I'll be okay. It's not that far."

"All right. I'll walk you to your car."

She didn't protest, only pulled her fingers from his with such a reluctant look on her face that he almost pulled her into his arms, abandoning his resolve to move slowly with her. Instead, he rose and followed her out of the building and across the parking lot to her vehicle.

When she hit the remote to unlock the door, he pulled it open and held it for her. She stopped on the other side of it. "Thank you for sharing all that with me, Ty. I want you to know that I heard everything you said. And it wasn't easy, but I truly believe that you aren't that man anymore. Which is why I'm still here."

"I'm glad you are, Gabby." More glad than he'd been about

almost anything in his life. He grinned and ran his knuckles lightly down the side of her face. "Does this mean we're friends now?"

Gabriella smiled, but her eyes were serious. "We are friends. Good friends. And I can see us becoming best friends, which is the strongest foundation for us to build on."

That had never really been his philosophy in the past, but now he couldn't imagine a better way for this relationship to begin. "I agree." Ty leaned over the car door and pressed his lips to her forehead. "*Buenas noches.*"

In the glow of the streetlamps in the parking lot, her eyes lit up. Ty made a mental note to learn more Spanish so he could speak to her in her native language, something that obviously meant a lot to her.

"*Buenas noches.*" With a final smile, she slid behind the wheel, and Ty closed the door.

He watched until her silver Miata had exited the lot and disappeared down the quiet street. Then Ty tipped back his head and gazed at the hazy sky. "I know I don't deserve her—I don't deserve any of this—but thank you."

Until a few days ago, Ty had never been able to grasp the concept of grace, something his Iya had told him once meant *unmerited favor.* But he'd experienced so much of it this week —from God, Laken, Reverend Milson, and now Gabriella— that he was beginning to catch brief glimmers of what it meant, like rays of sun breaking over the horizon to push back the thick morning mist. Even so, he knew he would never fully grasp the vastness of it.

But he could be grateful for it. And, with God's help, he would extend it to others in his life the way that even those he had grievously wronged in the past had extended it to him.

CHAPTER NINE

He couldn't do it. Ty sat behind the wheel of his car, peering through the front windshield at the massive gray stone house in the suburbs and gripping the steering wheel with shaking hands.

He hadn't been sure he could find this place again; he'd only been here once, years ago, when he and a few other members of the gang had crashed a house party that Zach had thrown while his parents were out of town.

That party had sealed Zach's fate. He'd been completely drunk and high on something and had talked way too freely about the fact that he'd been arrested for stealing a car but was about to make a plea deal. He hadn't gone so far as to say that he would be naming names, but Ty's gang leaders had come to their own conclusions and tried, convicted, and sentenced him, appointing Ty to execute Zach as his final test of loyalty.

Ty scanned the extensive, perfectly landscaped property. Whatever Zach's motivation for joining a gang or for stealing, it wasn't that he'd been desperate for funds.

Poverty wasn't fun, as Ty well knew, but likely the old

adage that money didn't buy happiness was true as well. Light poured from every window, and shadows moved behind the glass. Someone was home. Ty's grip on the wheel tightened. Did Zach's family even live here anymore? If they did, Ty had to be the last person they would expect to show up at their door. The last person they would want to see.

He had never met Zach's parents. Because Ty had pled guilty, there hadn't been a trial, and Zach's family had waived their right to make a victim impact statement. Ty had avoided reading the paper or watching the news, as he'd had no desire to see himself in handcuffs or hear anything about the case when all he wanted was to forget the heinous thing he had done.

It hadn't helped.

He closed his eyes. *Fight the darkness. Focus on the light.*

Like it had when he'd been going through his initiation, this house represented his final test. He felt every bit as terrified now, facing the specter of meeting Zach's parents and somehow trying to express his deep remorse over taking their son's life, as he had felt that night in the car, the handle of the gun cold and hard in his trembling fingers. How could any light possibly come out of this encounter?

It only takes a single spark. Con's voice carried on the wind that rocked the car, sending icy bits of snow skittering across the hood.

Ty ducked his head to peer up at the sky through the front window. *Come with me, please. I can't do this alone.* He unclenched his fingers one at a time from the wheel and shoved open the door before he could change his mind and head back into the city.

His legs were weak, but he managed to stumble between the stone pillars at the end of the driveway and make his way along the walkway and up the three stairs to the front door. Someone passed by the large bay window fronting the porch.

Ty pursed his lips. Might not be a bad idea to see if he could catch a glimpse of whoever was inside, figure out how many people he might be dealing with here. Maybe how big they were.

He grimaced and sidled along the stone wall between the door and the window until he could peer cautiously around the frame. Through sheer curtains, he glimpsed a woman carrying a tray with a teapot, plate of cookies, and two mugs. A man stood with his back to the window, his elbow on the mantel and his foot propped on the stone ledge in front of a massive fireplace, the flickering flames casting a soft glow over the room.

The scene was warm and cozy, and the people appeared to be doing perfectly fine. Ty knocking on their front door would certainly shatter that aura of peace. What right did he have—

The woman set the tray on a coffee table and walked over to the man, who lowered his foot to the ground and turned toward her, a smile on his face.

No. Ty stumbled back a couple of steps, his foot catching a small table and sending a large Poinsettia plant in a ceramic pot crashing onto the porch.

Without checking to see if the people inside had heard anything, Ty spun around, bounded down the stairs, and sprinted for his car.

The front door opened behind him, but he didn't look back, only rounded the hood of his vehicle and jumped behind the wheel. His fingers shook so badly he could barely jam the key into the ignition, but finally he managed it. The man who'd been standing at the fireplace reached the end of the driveway, his footsteps pounding on concrete as he passed the stone columns.

Ty slammed the transmission into drive and pressed down on the gas, hard enough to squeal the tires as he peeled away from the curb. When he reached the end of the street, he glanced in the rear-view mirror. The man still stood on the sidewalk, his hands clasped behind his head, watching him go.

Ty tore his gaze from the mirror, tromped on the accelerator, and tore around the corner, desperate to erase the man's face from his view.

Although it would take far longer to erase it from his mind.

Without consciously planning it, Ty drove to the bridge where he'd met Con that night. Before driving out to Zach's place earlier, he had transferred the pistol from his apartment to the car and stuck it in his glove compartment. Whether or not his last amends went well, he would be finished. He'd have done everything he had set out to do. His conversation with Laken had helped him to see that he didn't have to do any of this to win back favor with God. Still, as his brother had pointed out, it was an honorable thing to do, facing the people he had hurt and expressing his genuine remorse to them, even if they couldn't forgive him.

When he finished this last stop along his journey, Ty had planned to return to the bridge and toss the gun into the river, a symbolic declaration of victory at the end of his amends journey.

Only now he didn't feel victorious. He felt completely and utterly defeated. So maybe he wouldn't be too quick to toss the gun away.

His heart pounded against his still aching ribs as he parked the car on the side of the road at the entrance to the bridge, leaned over and opened the glove compartment, and grabbed the weapon. He stuck it into the pocket of his jacket before clambering out of the vehicle and striding along the cement wall until he reached the midpoint of the structure spanning the snaking water below.

For a long moment he stood staring down at the river, narrower than it had been two weeks earlier now that ice was creeping in from both sides. So cold and dark. A shudder moved through him, and Ty turned and slid his back down the wall until he was sitting on the frigid, snow-covered sidewalk. He bent his knees and dug his elbows into his thighs, lowering his forehead to his palms. Everything in him wanted to cry out to God, but he had no idea what to ask for, what to say.

Be still and know that I am God.

The words hanging on the wall in Gabriella's store echoed through his mind. Maybe it was okay not to know what to ask for. *Be still.* Ty drew in one slow breath after another in an attempt to ease the painful pounding of his heart. *Know.* Warmth flickered in his chest. *I am God.* The warmth spread.

What else did he need to know?

A car door slammed. Ty didn't move as footsteps approached, as someone crossed the bridge toward him. He didn't raise his head and look over until whoever it was had reached him and lowered himself onto the sidewalk next to him.

For a few seconds, Ty gazed at Con without speaking. Then he lifted a hand. "Why didn't you tell me?"

"I figured you'd take off if you realized you were talking to Zach's father."

"I absolutely would have."

"Then nothing that happened the last two weeks would have happened."

"How do you know what happened?"

Con rested his arms on his bent knees and clasped his

hands together. "You wouldn't have shown up at my door unless you'd gone through everything on your list before that, made all the amends you could. And I know from first-hand experience how incredibly powerful and healing that would have been."

"They didn't all go well."

Con grimaced. "I could have told you that from first-hand experience too. But God can also use those moments—to teach us, humble us, remind us that it doesn't matter what others think of us, only what he thinks."

Ty rested his head against the cold cement wall behind him. "You must hate me."

"I did, yes. For a long time." Con drove his fingers through his hair. "But I also hated myself. And I blamed myself for Zach's death as much as I blamed you. More, maybe." He closed his eyes for a moment before opening them and blowing out a breath. "I was a terrible father. All I cared about when Zach was growing up was making money. I was never home. I justified it by telling myself that I was giving my wife and son a good life, everything they could possibly want. When Zach died, my life changed in an instant. I suddenly saw clearly what I had refused to see for years—that the life, the career, I had sacrificed everything for was meaningless. I started drinking, lost my job, nearly lost my wife and home. I fell into a deep black hole. Thankfully, God was there. It was only through his love and grace that I was able to climb out of that pit and begin a whole new life."

"Even so, you weren't the one who pulled the trigger."

"I might as well have been."

Ty turned his head, still pressed to the cold stone, to meet Con's gaze. The man's eyes were haunted, filled with sorrow. Very, very human. "Why do you say that?"

"The last time I spoke to Zach, we had a big fight. He'd been arrested for stealing a car, as you know, and I confronted him, demanded to know why he was stealing when I gave him everything he could possibly want or need." Con scrubbed his face with both hands before meeting Ty's gaze again. If anything, the sorrow had deepened. "He just looked at me and said, in this eerily calm voice, 'Do you?' Then he walked out of the house. I never saw him again."

Ty closed his eyes, unable to bear the grief and guilt in the eyes of the father of the kid he had killed. Or that billowed through him at the realization that he and Zach had been desperately seeking the same thing—a father's presence and love. If Ty had known, if he'd bothered to find out anything about the guy before he'd made the decision to take his life, he'd have understood that. The two of them might have bonded, become friends. The horror and loss of what could have been if not for him twisted his insides into agonizing knots.

When Con spoke again, the words were quiet, threaded through with a sadness that reflected Ty's. "From that night on, I focused all my anger and hatred on you. It took me a couple of years to figure out that I was equally to blame. If I had been a better father to Zach, if I had shown him how much I loved him by being there for him, actually being there, he never would have felt the need to try and get my attention in increasingly extreme and destructive ways. All the signs were there; I simply chose to ignore them until it was too late. Even then, it took another year or two of God working in my heart before I could begin to forgive myself. I'm not sure I fully have yet."

Ty sighed. He knew exactly what that struggle was like. "Did you know who I was when you first saw me up here?"

"Yes. They told us you were getting out of prison, so I was parked outside the day you walked through the gate. I tailed you to your mother's place and then drove by there occasionally to see what you were up to. And I followed you here that night."

Ty rubbed the side of his hand hard across his forehead. "Were you hoping for a chance to get revenge?" That, he would understand.

"I would have been, a few years ago. The irony of me stopping you from shooting yourself the last time we were on this bridge is that for a long time I wanted to do that myself. I pictured it in my head a thousand times—buying a gun, tracking you down, pressing the barrel to your head, seeing the terror in your eyes, and then pulling the trigger."

Ty fumbled in his pocket for the gun, yanked it free, and held it out to Con, handle first. "Do it now. I won't try to stop you."

Con took the pistol from him and held it in both hands, not moving, only staring at it. Ty held his breath. Would Zach's father shoot him? On a human level, there would be poetic justice in that. But neither of them was dealing solely on a human level, not anymore. Still, the darkness was strong, as Ty well knew.

Con took a deep breath. "I can't. It's gone."

"What's gone?"

"The hatred." He shifted to face Ty, keeping the gun pointed at the ground. "I don't hate you anymore, Ty. Once I gave my life to God, I started praying for you. I prayed every time God brought you into my mind, which was often. I admit that, at first, the theme of those prayers ran more along the lines of asking God to strike you down or make you otherwise pay for what you did to my son." He offered Ty a wry grin.

Ty managed a weak grin in return. "Totally fair."

Con nodded. "Gradually, my prayers shifted. I almost didn't see it happening until one day I realized I'd just asked God to protect you and to help you see that you weren't alone

185

in prison, your own black pit. That he was there with you and that he loved you."

Ty's throat tightened. God *had* protected him in prison. And, looking back, Ty could pinpoint many moments where he had felt as though he wasn't alone. It was that feeling, the one that had lingered with him throughout his time behind bars and the months following his release, that had given him the strength to resist being drawn back into his old life. And that sense of someone watching over him had made the events of the past couple of weeks so much easier for him to accept. God had been working in his heart, even in one of the darkest places on earth, just like Con had prayed for. "I think he heard those prayers."

"I know he did. And they didn't affect only you, they affected me. They changed my heart toward you, to the point where I began to care very much about what was happening to you. How you were. That's why I was following you. Not to get revenge, but to make sure you were okay."

Ty's throat tightened until all he could do was nod. Somehow, he cared about this man he had only recently met too. How was that possible?

Con let go of the weapon with one hand and grasped Ty's knee. "I know I'm not your dad, but I kind of feel like I could be that for you. If you'll let me, I want to be there for you. Not because I'm trying to make up for not being there for Zach, but because I have a love for you that could only have come from God himself."

"I'd like that." The words sounded hoarse, and Ty cleared his throat. His dad's abandonment had left a gaping hole in his life that he'd tried to fill by making one bad choice after another. Laken's steady presence in his life had helped, but, like Ty had told him, his brother needed to be free to be exactly that—his brother. Con's nearly incomprehensible desire to step in and do his best to fill the father void inside Ty felt like another precious gift. *More grace.*

"Good." Con squeezed his knee before letting him go. "If we're going to be that close, maybe you should tell me your real name."

"Oh. Right. Sorry about that. I didn't exactly lie to you. Most people do call me Con, a throwback to my college baseball days. But my birth certificate says Brent McConnell."

"Good to know." A gust of wind swept across the bridge, and Ty zipped his jacket up higher. "If it's all right, I think I'll stick with Con, though." A little closer to *Clarence.*

"Yeah. I like that." Con lifted the pistol. "Why did you bring this here with you tonight?"

"I was planning to throw it into the water."

A smile creased Con's features. "Let's do it together."

Ty nodded again and pushed to his feet. He and Con stood at the wall, gazing out over the water below, a brown ribbon threading between fields of white.

"This is our hate, Ty." Con held up the gun. "It's the darkness."

"Our old lives. Our old selves."

"Yes." He shifted the weapon closer to Ty. "Ready to let it all go?"

Ty had never been more ready for anything in his life. "Absolutely." He covered Con's fingers with his, keeping them there as Con drew back his arm a little. The two of them flung the weapon out into the dark night. Neither of them spoke, only listened until a faint splash told them it was over.

Ty lifted his gaze to the horizon, where one star twinkled brighter than the rest. Con draped an arm around Ty's shoulders, his hand clamping onto his shoulder. The two of them stood there for a long time, staring up at the night sky as the flowing water closed over their pasts and carried them far away.

CHAPTER TEN

Ty shook hands with the minister on the way out of the Christmas Eve service, and then he and Laken followed their mother and Gabriella down the steps. Ty couldn't take his eyes from the two of them. They'd just met at dinner a few hours ago, but they already seemed like close friends—or maybe mother and daughter—their heads close as they reached the sidewalk and strolled toward the parking lot, deep in conversation punctuated by bouts of laughter.

Laken rested a hand on Ty's back. "Gabriella's really something."

Ty stopped and faced his brother. "Yes. She is. I mean, it's new, obviously. But it already feels completely different than anything I've ever known."

"I'm happy for you, little brother."

Although Laken had been in a serious relationship himself that had ended not that long ago, his words and the look in his eyes were completely sincere. Which was the amazing thing about Laken. Although he was the one who'd stayed, who'd faithfully been there for their mother, who'd endured tremendous hurt and worry because of Ty, he never played the older brother to Ty's prodigal. He truly wanted the best for him. Ty's throat tightened. How could he ever make up for ...

He stopped himself. As Laken had pointed out, nothing Ty said or did would ever truly make up for the past. All he could do was accept the forgiveness and grace offered him and move on. He shot another look at the retreating backs of his mother and the woman who had recently come into his life. And, with God's help, he would strive to be a better man, a man who didn't hurt his family or the people he loved.

A man who didn't leave.

Ty punched his brother lightly on the upper arm. "Thank you."

"Hey, did you ever see your angel again?"

"Clarence?" Ty grinned. "Yes, I did. I spoke to him last night. Believe it or not, he's actually Brent McConnell."

Laken's dark eyes widened. "Zach McConnell's father?"

"Yeah. I didn't recognize him, but he knew who I was the night we met because he'd kind of been watching out for me since I was released."

Ty could practically see his brother's cop radar going up over that. "Why?"

"He said that for years he hated me, and his own life was spiraling out of control, but then he found God and actually started to pray for me. By the time I got out, he'd started to genuinely care about what happened to me. He ..." Ty scuffed the toe of his brown dress shoe through the inch or two of soft, fluffy snow lining the sidewalk. "He says he wants to be there for me like he never was for Zach. Kind of like a dad."

"And you believe him."

Ty met his brother's gaze. "I do. I know it's almost impossible to believe that he could want that, after what I did ..."

Laken rested a hand on Ty's shoulder. "Did I ever tell you how I met Mr. Yun?"

"The guy you get together with on Sundays?"

"Yeah. He and his wife owned a convenience store in my precinct when I first joined the force. My partner and I went there a lot late at night because Mrs. Yun made these amazing cinnamon buns that they sold in the store. I got to know them, and they became like another mother and father to me. Brad and I were in the store one night when a guy came in, jumped behind the counter, and held a gun to Mrs. Yun's head. I had a chance to take him out, but I hesitated, afraid I would miss and hit her. That hesitation cost Mrs. Yun her life because Mr. Yun lunged at them, and the guy shot her.

"For a long time after that, I was a complete mess. Then I went to see Mr. Yun to tell him how sorry I was. Turned out he had never blamed me for his wife's death; he told me she would have wanted us both to forgive ourselves and move on. We've gotten together pretty much every week since. He fills a huge void in my life as well. And it's every bit as unbelievable to me that he would want to do that, after what I did, as it is to you that Mr. McConnell would want to be part of your life. Only God can do something like that."

Ty nodded. "That's true." He clasped his brother's forearm. "I'm glad you have someone, Lake."

"I'm glad you do too."

They followed the women to Laken's car. His mother let go of the wide-brimmed red hat she'd been holding on her head and gave Gabby a hug. After she let go, Ty walked his mother to the front passenger seat and pulled open the door for her. She stopped and cupped his cheek with one hand. When she spoke, she'd lowered her voice, the words for him alone. "Laken told me what you've gone through the last couple of weeks, what you've been doing. I want you to know that I'm proud of you, son."

A lump rose in Ty's throat. When was the last time his mother had said those words to him? When he was a kid, maybe, and he'd brought a decent report card home or cleaned his room. And she'd said it after he played the wise man in that Christmas pageant when he was eight or nine. But she hadn't offered those words of praise in years. How could she have?

"Thank you, Iya." Ty wrapped his arms around her and held her close for a moment. When he let her go, she squeezed his arms. "See you in the morning?"

Ty grinned. "I'll be there. You know I wouldn't miss Christmas morning pancakes." He helped her into the car and closed the door before joining Laken and Gabriella at the back of the vehicle.

Laken gestured to the car. "Can we give you two a ride home?"

For the first time in days, a cold north wind wasn't buffeting the city. The sky was clear and filled with shining stars, and the temperature had risen from frigid to tolerable. Ty glanced at the woman standing next to him, her dark hair pinned into some kind of up-do tonight, and his chest squeezed. "Do you want to walk?"

She smiled, which weakened his knees a little. "I'd love to."

"All right, then." Laken pulled his brother into a hug. "Merry Christmas, kid."

Ty clapped him on the back a couple of times before stepping back. "Merry Christmas, Lake."

"Merry Christmas to you as well, Gabriella." Laken smiled at her.

"You too. And it's Gabby."

Meaning she and Laken were now friends, which meant a lot to Ty.

"Gabby. Hope to see you again soon."

"I'd like that."

Laken nodded before opening his car door and lowering himself to the driver's seat. Ty closed the door after him, and he and Gabby watched as Laken and their mother backed out of the spot and drove across the parking lot. Then Ty reached for her hand. "Shall we?"

"Yes, let's."

Her eyes glistened in the moonlight, and Ty stilled. "Are you okay?"

"Your mother hugged me."

He laughed. "Yes, she'll do that. You might want to get used to it."

"I think I could." When she smiled at him again, Ty tightened his grip on her fingers.

They wandered the downtown streets, as quiet on this night before Christmas as they ever got. The twinkling lights decorating the lamp stands, shop windows, and every other available surface didn't depress Ty like they had before. Tonight, they filled him with a quiet joy.

Well, the lights and the woman walking at his side. He was so distracted by her presence that they had nearly passed the church with the manger scene on the front lawn before he noticed it. "Hey." Ty tugged on Gabby's hand to stop her. "I walked by this church a couple of weeks ago and saw the manger scene. Kind of reminded me of a Christmas play I was in as a kid."

Her brown eyes were as warm as the twinkling lights around them. "What part did you play?"

"A wise man."

Her smile deepened. "I can see it." She let go of his hand and turned toward the scene, as though she could tell it was meaningful to him and she wanted to give it her full attention.

Ty wrapped his arms around her and, when she leaned back against him, rested his chin on her soft hair, breathing in the light floral scent. He read the words on the wooden sign again. *Peace on Earth.* They struck him completely differently this time than they had the first time he'd seen them. Maybe there was no peace on earth. Wars and discord raged, as they always had. But Ty realized suddenly that the absence of conflict wasn't what the peace on that sign referred to. It meant peace with God.

Warmth spread through his chest, as it had so often the last few days, and his head jerked slightly. That's what it was, this sensation inside him. Peace. Not only because his inner turmoil had calmed, but because, that night on the picnic table with Lake, he'd experienced genuine peace with God for the first time since he was a kid. Maybe ever.

Gabriella turned in his arms. A tear had started down his cheek, and she wiped it off gently with her thumb. "You're crying."

Ty shook his head. "I haven't cried in years. Now it doesn't seem to take a lot to get me going." Although, his dawning understanding that he was now, finally, at peace with the God who had created him, who loved him and had always been with him, was a lot.

She ran her fingers over his cheek again. "You've had to be hard for so long, Ty. Now you're getting all soft." Grinning, she rested her hand on his chest, against the warmth that had flickered to life there over the past few days.

Ty caught the fingers of her other hand in his. "Any chance we could keep that between us?"

Gabriella laughed. "It will be our secret, I promise. Although, it is a good thing, you know."

"I know. And another good thing has happened to me lately too."

"What's that?"

"You."

Her gaze riveted on his. Slowly, Ty bent his head, but stopped a few inches from her. "Too soon?"

"Yes." Her dark eyes gleamed as she slid a hand behind his head and pulled him down until her soft lips touched his. For a moment, she was all that existed for him. Everything he had been through in his life, everything he had done, faded into the background.

When the kiss ended, she rested her head on his chest, and Ty wrapped his arms around her again. They stood like that for a long time, snowflakes drifting around them like a scene from some schmaltzy Hallmark movie. Which felt perfect for this moment. He closed his eyes briefly. He really was getting soft. Although Gabby was right; suddenly that felt like a really good thing.

When he opened his eyes, his gaze fell on the manger, on the baby Jesus lying there. Ty studied it a moment before drawing in a quick breath.

It's you. You are the single spark of light that overcomes the darkness. I've been looking for it everywhere, went on this long journey seeking it, and you were here the whole time, waiting for me to find you.

The warmth spread through him until he felt as though his body might not be able to contain it. It was true that no power on earth could bring back extinguished light or shattered peace. But a power greater than any on earth, a power that, for three decades two thousand years ago, had dwelled here in a human body, walked among them, could do it.

Had done it, for him.

Another tear slid down Ty's cheek, but he didn't move to wipe it away. Although he'd loved Christmas as a kid, this year would be different. This year he had so much to celebrate, so much to be thankful for.

Whatever waited for him and Laken under the tree tomorrow morning would be great, but it would pale in comparison to the gifts God had given him. He had Gabriella, and Con, and the family he belonged to. But even if they were all taken away from him, even if, like his father, they all chose to abandon him, Ty wouldn't lose the warmth that filled him now. Like Con—and Reverend Milson and Laken and his mother—had prayed that he would come to see, Ty had never been alone.

And whatever happened in the future, nothing could ever take that peace from him.

A NOTE FROM THE AUTHOR

Dear Reader,

As it did with Ty, guilt and shame can keep us imprisoned behind bars as strong and unyielding as any jail built by human hands. But Jesus took on human form and came to earth to dwell among us two thousand years ago to set us free from everything that holds us captive. With our finite, human idea of justice, we struggle to comprehend the infinitely vast concepts of forgiveness, grace, and mercy.

And yet they are ours for the asking, for the accepting.

Jesus desires that we live, not in bondage, but in glorious freedom. As he himself said in Luke 4:18, "… He has sent me to proclaim freedom for the prisoners and recovery of sight for the blind, to set the oppressed free."

God does not want us to live lives that are burdened down by our past sins, guilt, and trauma. He longs for us to be free and waits to take those burdens from us the moment we turn to him and ask. The moment we let go.

My hope and prayer for each of you is that you will be able to lay the burdens of whatever you might have done—and everything that might have been done to you—at the foot of the cross, accept the grace and mercy Jesus died to attain for you, and believe that our great God is powerful enough to forgive you, to enable you to forgive others, and to set you free.

In the words of Paul the apostle in 2 Thessalonians 3:16, "… may the Lord of peace himself give you peace at all times and in every way. The Lord be with all of you."

Sara

ACKNOWLEDGMENTS

Deepest thanks always to my family for your love and support.

To the members of my writer's groups who are a constant source of encouragement and advice. Thank you for listening to rough drafts and believing (and helping me to believe) that there might be something there worth sharing with the world.

To my dear friend and brilliant writer and editor, Deb Elkink, who so generously shares her time, expertise, and insights on my work. You make my stories better every time.

To my Mosaic Collection sisters—I love doing this writing journey with you!!

And always and above all, to the One who pours out grace upon us all and longs for us to live in the freedom only He can provide. It is all from you and for you.

ABOUT SARA DAVISON

SARA DAVISON is the author of four romantic suspense series—The Seven Trilogy, The Night Guardians, The Rose Tattoo Trilogy, and Two Sparrows for a Penny, as well as the standalone, *The Watcher*. A finalist for more than a dozen national writing awards, she is a Word, Cascade, and Carol Award winner. She currently resides in Ontario with her husband Michael and their three mostly grown kids. Like every good Canadian, she loves coffee, hockey, poutine, and apologizing for no particular reason.

Get to know Sara better at www.saradavison.org and @sarajdavison, or find her on Amazon, BookBub, Goodreads, and Facebook.

TITLES BY SARA DAVISON

THE MOSAIC COLLECTION: NOVELS
Rose Tattoo Trilogy
Lost Down Deep
Written in Ink

two sparrows for a penny series
Every Star in the Sky

THE MOSAIC COLLECTION: ANTHOLOGY STORIES
"Taste of Heaven"
(*Hope is Born: A Mosaic Christmas Anthology*)
"Ten Bottles of Sand"
(*Before Summer's End: Stories to Touch the Soul*)
"Sixty Feet to Home"
(*A Star Will Rise: A Mosaic Christmas Anthology II*)
"I'd Like to Thank the Academy"
(*Song of Grace: Stories to Amaze the Soul*)
"Scarlet"
(*All Things New: Stories to Refresh the Soul*)
"A Single Spark of Light"
(*A Whisper of Peace: A Mosaic Christmas Anthology IV*)

THE NIGHT GUARDIANS SERIES
Vigilant
Guarded

Driven
Forged

THE SEVEN TRILOGY
The End Begins
The Darkness Deepens
The Morning Star Rises

UPCOMING
Every Flower of the Field
Sharp Like Glass

RECLAIMING TOMORROW

Angela D. Meyer

* * *

An old threat resurfaces, forcing Josie to face her greatest fear.

Josie Ferris is making strides to build a new life when an old threat resurfaces. Will Josie trust her new friend Daniel enough to let him teach her how to defend herself so that she can stand up to the man determined to destroy her future?

To all the women facing their fears and rebuilding their lives.

CHAPTER ONE

Susan and I clamber into the front seat of my car and buckle up. I twist in my seat to check that I don't back up over someone. A shadow moves to my left. A tallish, broad-shouldered man slips down the trail between the buildings of the complex. He's favoring his right leg. His hoody covers his face. The logo on his back sends a shiver up my spine. Where have I seen that before?

"Did you see that guy?" I point out the window.

"What guy?" She peers behind her, then squints at me. "What's wrong?"

"It's probably my overactive imagination." Then why the fear? I shake off the memories of my past and pull into traffic. I am much too suspicious.

Susan, my best—and only—friend from Tulsa, Oklahoma, where I lived for the worst years of my life, has been here for two days now. Our reunion is long overdue. An apartment search is much better with a friend along. I sigh. The prices on the apartment brochure where we last stopped tell me I can't afford to live here. The magic genie syndrome I seem to live by some days is the only reason I stopped by the most prestigious complex in Christmas. I'm grateful that my nine-year-old and I live with my parents. But though we have the run of the house, it's not ours. It's time we have our own place. But it won't be this spot.

Fifteen minutes later, we're at a table inside my favorite pizza joint. The waitress sets our hot chocolate in front of us and takes our order for a medium veggie pie before she retreats to the kitchen. I warm my hands around my mug. I should have worn gloves today.

"Spill it. Start with Daniel." Susan twirls her long blond braid between her fingers.

And so, the interrogation starts. I shake my head. I might as well get this part over with. "He's a friend."

"A *good* friend from what you say."

"Yes."

"With the possibility of more?" She sips her cocoa.

"Maybe, but trust doesn't come easy. My counselor is helping, but it requires that I relearn a lot." I crinkle up the wrapper from my straw.

She places her hand over mine. "Give it time. Tell me about Jason."

Grateful she doesn't push it about Daniel, I launch into Jason stories. I tell Susan about his science project last year in school and the little girl who was assigned as his partner and then he ended up with a crush on her. We giggle like schoolgirls with stars in our eyes over the football hunk we wish would ask us out.

"Did Jason ever get a dog? He was always good with ours."

"Not yet. That's all he asked for this year, but I don't know if I can swing it."

Someone waved in our direction from the door.

My heart does a summersault when I see Daniel. Why, oh why, does my body betray me like this at the mere sight of the man? My brother, Steven, comes inside the restaurant and the two men shake hands, then walk in our direction.

I take a shaky breath. "Don't. Say. Anything."

"Wouldn't dare." She laughs at my consternation.

The guys stop next to our table, and I introduce them to Susan. They start to head off, then Daniel makes a U-turn.

"If Jason comes by the dojang early on Friday before testing, I'll review his forms with him. Might even have a few extra boards I can let him practice breaking."

"He'll like that. Thanks. His goal is to earn his brown belt this time."

"I'll be ready for him." He joins my brother across the room.

The waitress places our food between us, then ensures we're set before she takes the order at the next table.

"Brown belt?"

"Daniel teaches taekwondo." I put two slices on my plate.

"Maybe you should take lessons from him." Susan wiggles her eyebrows as she dishes up her food.

"Stop it." Not that I haven't thought about it. But I will never tell. I dig into my lunch and ignore Susan's attempts to tease me. I won't admit it to anyone yet, but it does kind of, sort of thrill me to my toes to consider the possibilities with Daniel. But could someone like him really be happy with someone like me?

CHAPTER TWO

At the end of my shift at Coffee Joe's, I grab my coat and scarf. The plan is to meet up with Susan and Charice for lunch, but since I have about half an hour to get to the restaurant only a few blocks away, I decide to walk. I'll come back later and get my car. Charice has been such a dear friend since I came back to Christmas, and I'm confident that she and Susan will hit it off.

As I walk, I daydream about how I'll fix up our new apartment. Yesterday, Susan and I toured several apartment complexes in and around Christmas until I finally landed on a two-bedroom within my budget. Money would be tight, and Christmas may be meager this year, but I could do it. Later today, Jason and I will stop by to see it.

Lost in my head, I don't notice Daniel until I'm almost right in front of him. I would have passed him if he hadn't said my name. I still haven't gotten used to his more frequent presence now that he lives in Christmas.

I laugh at myself and glance at the building behind him. "I didn't expect to see you today. Did you find a new group to volunteer for?" I've always appreciated Daniel's willingness to help others.

"Just a meeting." Someone waves at Daniel and he waves their direction as they step inside. "Can I tell you about it later? I need to get inside."

"Sure." There's still a lot I don't know about him. But my brother trusts him, and that's enough for me to count him as a friend. I hum a tune I heard recently on the radio as I finish my trek to meet my friends. They are already at a table and chatting like they've been acquainted for years. It does my soul good to see.

I scoot into the booth next to Susan. "Am I interrupting?"

The two bust out laughing, but quiet down when a few other patrons look our way.

This will be good. "Do tell."

Charice embarks on a story about them at the mall this morning and how a misunderstanding almost got them in trouble with the mall security. Susan inserts several explanations that I'm sure Charice hoped to avoid telling. Our conversation lulls while the waitress takes our order, then picks back up where the mall security cameras proved their innocence.

"Basically, an uneventful morning?"

Charice and Susan roll their eyes in unison.

"I'm glad you two get along. One of these days, I'll plan a time that Tiffany can join in on the fun."

"I would love to finally meet her." Susan takes a drink of water.

"That would be great. Maybe a girls' vacation." Charice digs in her purse for something then gives up and sets it aside.

"That's a great idea." I lead the debate about where we would go until the waitress arrives with our food.

Charice passes the basket of bread around. "Susan says you found a nice apartment."

"Finally. I'm excited to decorate it." I take another bite of my chicken.

Susan clears her throat. "We're getting a new apartment, too, since we've about outgrown our little studio."

I pick up my water glass. "I can't believe you stayed there for as long as you did. I could never live in a—wait." I set my glass down. "You said ... are you—"

"Pregnant? Yes!"

I let out a small whoop. "Congratulations! When are you due?"

"End of May. Can you come for a visit?"

I stare at her like a deer in the headlights. Images of my past in Tulsa fill my head. It's hard to breathe. My landlord threatened me shortly before I left Tulsa, and I wouldn't put it past him to follow through if he ever figured out where I was. He is a vindictive man and because of my husband, he lost a lot on unpaid rent. Besides the fact that he's a pervert. I take a few deep breaths and alternately tap my knees until my body calms down. "I'm sorry, Susan. What if the landlord saw me? I can't."

Susan pulls me close. "I'm sorry, Josie. I wasn't thinking. Of course, I wouldn't ask you to come back. That jerk will never find you."

Charice furrows her forehead. She's never heard this part of my story.

"Before I left Tulsa, our landlord, a total jerk and pervert, warned me he would get the rent my husband owed him by reaching an ... understanding ... between the two of us."

"Oh, no." Charice squeezes my hand. "Anything you need. Anything. I'm here for you."

"What would I do without you guys?" I sit back against the booth. "Enough of this. I plan to enjoy today." It takes a beat, but within a few minutes, we've left all talk about my landlord behind, although I can't get him out of my mind.

CHAPTER THREE

"What's new, Josie?" My counselor sits poised with a pen and notepad, ready to record anything pertinent I might say.

"Susan came for a visit this week. She left this morning."

"That's wonderful. Did you have a good time?"

"She helped me find an apartment."

"Good for you. When do you move in?"

"In two weeks. Saturday after Thanksgiving."

"This is great, but I doubt that's why you came in to talk. You sounded a bit frantic on the phone."

I swallow hard. Not talking about it won't make it go away, but these healthier approaches don't seem to get the job done either. It's like fear is on a stakeout in my head, waiting for the first opportunity to pounce. I'd much rather knock it on the ground and kick it to bits than ruminate over the issue.

"Josie? What's going through your head?"

"I saw someone who reminded me of my landlord from Tulsa." My muscles tighten and heaviness lands on my chest.

"Reminded you or do you think it's him?"

I open my mouth, then press my lips together. If I say the words, it will feel more real. I avert my gaze. I don't want to go back to the place in my mind where I lived for eight years. "It's not fair."

My counselor remains silent, waiting me out. She's done it plenty over the past six months and she won't give in. I might as well get this over with.

"I'm afraid." All the thoughts I've bottled up the last couple days pour out, and by the time my session is almost up, I've concluded that what really has me unnerved is the possibility that I would ever be put into a situation again where I was overpowered. Whether by my landlord or someone else.

My counselor closes her notebook. "Between now and our next session, what is one thing you can do to make yourself less vulnerable?"

Charice's suggestion to take taekwondo reverberates in my head. Maybe she was onto something. "I will check into a self-defense class." It's time to fight for my future.

After counseling, I hustle over to the dojang for Jason's testing. I'm ready for a less hectic schedule. Between my job at Coffee Joe's, my VA work for Charice, my last college classes, and Jason's activities, I'm exhausted. Fortunately, my family has helped me pick up the slack here and there and in two weeks I'll be done with school. If I were a cheerleader, I'd yell at the top of my lungs right now.

I pull into a parking space with a few minutes to spare before testing begins. There won't be any chairs left if I don't get inside, but I need a minute to catch my breath. I usually plan for a bit of decompression after counseling, but today, joy of all joys, I get to jump right back into life. I tell myself that it's for Jason, then take a few deep breaths. Heaven knows, my old habit of compartmentalizing still comes in handy at times. I blow out a last breath and shake my hands to release some tension before I climb out of the car and join the other parents eager to see their children test for their next belt.

I find a spot toward the side to stand and make eye contact with Daniel. He nods, then focuses on his students. His words rise above the din, as he tells the kids they'll be great. He speaks to Jason, then my son waves at me. Daniel must have told him I was here and I'm grateful. I wave back, then Jason faces the front when the lead instructor calls out. All the kids stand at attention.

Testing starts with the lower belts, then advances in difficulty. Each child works through their forms, then in the higher ranks, sparring and breaking boards are included in the skills required for advancement. The self-control is impressive. These kids have really worked. Jason steps in position and I focus on his every move. His forms are perfect as far as I can see, and he wins his sparring match. Now board breaking. He's the first one to break boards tonight. I hold my breath.

The first time Jason tested for his brown belt, he couldn't break the board and was ready to give up. But Daniel challenged him to keep after it and worked with him overtime to help him prepare, both in mind as well as skill. The room is silent as Jason gathers his concentration. The board holders signal they're ready and Jason runs toward them. At precisely the right moment, he jumps and kicks. The boards fly to the side and the room cheers. Jason stands tall and bows to the board holders. His chest puffs out a bit as he takes a seat. I'm proud of him.

The rest of the evening passes in a blur. I clap at the right time, but otherwise lose my thoughts to my future. I'm eager to have our new place, be done with college, and move forward. I'm done with the past.

After the new belts are awarded, the crowd begins to disperse. I spot Daniel tying Jason's new belt. If only Jason had experienced that kind of encouragement in his early years. I shake off the melancholy and walk over to join them.

Jason wraps his arms around my waist. "I did it, Mom!"

"You sure did. And I'm proud of you."

"Can I go talk with my friends?"

"Sure."

He runs off, as Daniel joins me.

"Thanks for all your work with him."

"You're welcome. He's a good kid. Lucky to have a mom like you."

I shrug. How could I possibly qualify as a good mother when I stayed with an abusive man as long as I did? I'm trying do better now, but those early years hold a ton of regret.

Daniel places his hands on my shoulders. "You are a great mother. You did the best you could in the position you were in. Don't listen to those voices inside your head."

"It's hard not to."

"I understand. I'll repeat myself until you get it." His smile assures me he wants the best for me. "Even though Jason has things he has to work through, he wouldn't be where he is now if you weren't his mother." Daniel drops his hands and stuffs them in his pockets. "Can I take you guys for ice cream? To celebrate Jason's new belt?"

I miss the warmth of his hands. "Yeah, that would be nice." Spending more time with him sounds comforting. I'm not ready to go back to my parents' house tonight. *My parents.* I forgot they would be here. I spot them on the other side of the dojang talking with Jason. I excuse myself and hurry over. I'm sure they have plans to celebrate with Jason, too. By the time I reach them, they've already promised Jason to take him to his favorite spot to eat on Saturday as a reward. Relieved, I visit a few minutes, then Jason and I find Daniel, who's already changed out of his uniform. As soon as Jason hears there's ice cream in his near future, he runs into the locker room to change.

While we wait, I help Daniel stack chairs "Do you guys offer self-defense classes?"

"We've talked about it. Are you interested?"

"It's time."

He tilts his head. "Something happen?"

I pull my bottom lip between my teeth. "Sort of."

"Mom. Daniel. I'm ready." Jason jumps and lands in front of us.

Daniel tussles his hair. I'm amazed that he gets away with it. But then again, Jason thinks the world of Daniel.

"Ready." I stack the last chair.

"Yes." Jason throws a fist pump in the air.

I pull on my coat and pause to check notifications on my phone. Susan texted that she arrived safely back in Tulsa. I shoot off a quick reply then walk back to Jason and Daniel, who are in quiet conversation. As I approach, they start in on a loud senseless conversation about video games.

"What's up with you two boys?"

"What?" Jason and Daniel look at each other.

I cross my arms. "Like that isn't fishy."

"I plead the Fifth." Daniel winks at Jason.

"Fine. Leave me out in the cold." It is the time of year for Santa secrets.

After double dips of peppermint for Daniel and me and a triple scoop cone with chocolate, peppermint, and vanilla for Jason, we load up in Daniel's truck and drive to my parents' house. Jason is nodding off in the back seat. He'll sleep well tonight. As soon as we pull in the drive, though, he wakes up, jumps out of the truck, and dashes into the house.

Inside, Jason gushes about how good his ice cream was, followed by a lot of laughter. I plop my purse on the entry table and walk toward the living room with Daniel at my heels. My parents mention puppies and Jason lets out a squeal. I enter the room and my parents look up sheepishly. I doubt I'll be happy about what they have in mind. I ignore the natural path of the conversation for the moment and tell Jason it's time to get ready for bed and since Daniel will be taking me to pick up my car, he can read until I get back.

He gives me a hug, then runs down the stairs, his voice trailing back to me. "I can't wait to get my puppy."

"What's this?" I tilt my head in question.

"We want to get him a puppy for Christmas."

"Why didn't you ask me first? What if I had planned to do that?"

"Were you?"

Really? "That's beside the point. I'm his mother. Besides, this isn't the best time for a new dog. And my rent will go up if I have a dog in our apartment."

"We can help with that." Mom reaches for Dad's hand.

"No."

"Why not?" Dad sat forward on the edge of the couch.

I'm about to explode, but I keep my voice low. "I need to do some things on my own."

"Does it need to be this?" Mom's posture slumps.

My whole body feels tight. Like it's all my fault and I'm supposed to let everyone else do what they deem best regardless of what I need. I clench my fists at my side, fighting

216

the urge to say all the things bursting to come out from inside me. But I know that once they're said, they can't be taken back. Daniel places his hand on my back and my emotions begin to settle. I hold up my hands and sidestep a bit closer to Daniel. "I need to take a breather and think about this. Daniel, I'm ready to go."

I march out of the room, tuck my purse under my arm, and then pull on my gloves as we leave the house. Daniel closes the door behind us, and we walk in silence to the car. The ride is tense, but he waits me out. He's better than my counselor at this. He stops at the town square, gets out, and tilts his head toward the swing in invitation. I join him and he places his arm along the back. After a few minutes, the turbulent undertow subsides.

"Why can't they check with me first? They mean well, but I'm a grown woman." I stare out across the lawn.

"You are."

"Jason would like a dog, but there are a crazy bunch of changes right now."

"True."

"And then there's the cost." I chance a peek at Daniel.

"There's that to consider."

"But they did say they would help with the cost."

"They really are thoughtful." He gazes at the sky.

"And I'm not getting him a dog this year."

"Hmm."

"Jason will be disappointed if he doesn't get a puppy."

"That he would." Daniel nods.

"I suppose it would be okay if they helped."

"How would you feel if they did?"

I let out a sigh. "Really grateful. Christmas will be simple this year."

"Sounds like you've made a decision."

"I guess so. Thanks for listening."

"Anytime." He rests his elbows on his knees. "So why take self-defense?"

"Remember my old landlord I told you about?"

"The one who demanded the past rent due even if it meant … never mind. Yeah, I remember." His expression hardens.

"I thought I saw him the other day, which doesn't make a lick of sense. I'm sure it's fear talking." I take a shaky breath. "Regardless, it's time I learn how to defend myself because I won't be a victim again. Whether to my landlord or anyone else."

"I can teach you how."

Tension drains from my body. "I'd like that."

"We can start tomorrow. The dojang is always empty on Saturday afternoon."

"Thank you." I place my hand on top of his. "This means a lot."

He stands and allows my hand to slip away. "Go for a walk?"

"That would be nice."

We circle the square in the quiet of the evening, the sound broken by the occasional car passing. Next week, the square will dance with Christmas lights. "Hard to believe it's been almost two years since I came back."

"And almost two years since we met."

"I gave you quite the brush off."

He chuckles. "With good reason. A stranger on a road trip asking you out?"

"Sounds humorous on this side of things. Especially if you consider that the next time I saw you was here in Christmas handling camels for the nativity program."

"Would you consider it now?"

"What's that?"

"A date."

"Oh." I stop walking.

He pauses and takes both my hands in his. He seems sad. And a bit apprehensive. "There are some things about my past that I don't tell everyone. But you need to know before you answer. Can I take you to lunch tomorrow and fill you in?"

I pull my hands from his and back up a step. A part of me screams to escape. But another part of me longs to rush into his embrace and never leave. Despite his past, he's the same man I've learned to trust the last six months. The same man who treats my son the way a son should be treated by a father. The same man who is always there for me. The same man whom I trust to teach me self-defense. The same man I am with alone on a walk in the darkness of evening.

"If you're not ready, that's okay."

"Can I tell you in the morning?"

"Absolutely."

"Thank you. Can you take me to my car, now? I need to check in on Jason."

CHAPTER FOUR

On my shift this morning at Coffee Joe's, I decide to listen to Daniel's story. As I slide into my car to go meet him for lunch, my gaze wanders across the park and settles on a man leaving a park bench. Panic seizes me. I dig my fingernails into the palms of my hand. *It isn't my landlord. There is nothing to be afraid of. I'm overreacting.* My heartrate slows and I take another look at the man who triggered my panic. His height and build are similar to my old landlord, but he doesn't favor his right leg. There's no familiar image on his clothing.

I put the car in gear and start to back out, then it strikes me. The logo of a hammer on top of a white and blue square was for a handyman company that frequently worked at the apartment building. It was a locally owned business in Tulsa. Someone who is connected to my former city of residence *is* in Christmas. I put the car in park and call Susan. I fill her in, and she promises to nose around and make sure that the jerk of a landlord hasn't left Tulsa. Until there's something definitive, I'll stay alert, but try to assume the best.

A few minutes later, I pull up to the restaurant where I'm

meeting Daniel. Bundled against the cold, he waits for me in front. I take a few minutes to gather my things so that I can switch gears in my head. Daniel isn't someone I need to be afraid of, even if I'm terrified at the thought of a relationship with him. I climb out of the car and join him at the same moment the hostess calls out his name.

After we place our order and the waitress is out of earshot, I make eye contact with Daniel. "What's up?"

"Do you want to eat first?"

I lift my right shoulder a bit. "No need to waste time."

"I'll give you the quick version, then I'll answer any questions you have." He steeples his fingers underneath his chin. "When you ran into me the other day and asked what I was up to?"

"Yeah?"

"AA. I'm fifteen years sober."

A shiver of apprehension runs up my back as I remember what drinking can do to a man. "And you waited till now to tell me?"

"I'm sorry about that. There aren't many people I trust with that information. And fewer that I believe would trust me if they knew. Or give me a chance to earn that trust." He grunts and shakes his head. "I'm working to be more open about it, but I've had bad experiences sharing outside of AA. Yet ever since you chose to let me be your friend, I've debated about when to tell you. Your brother suggested I allow you a chance to get to know me first."

My brother accurately assessed that I probably wouldn't have given Daniel a chance even as a friend if he had told me at the beginning. I unroll my silverware and put my napkin in my lap. "There's more to your story, I take it?"

"I started drinking in high school. In college, that was part of the culture with more liquor more easily accessible. My dependance on alcohol worsened and my relationship with my parents grew strained. That's when I walked away from God."

I blink. Who was I to judge, really? His story echoed my own to some degree. "Go on."

"After graduation, I moved in with my girlfriend. That worked—more or less—for about two years. She couldn't handle my drunken mood swings or always being short on money. When she left, I hit bottom." He pinches the bridge of his nose. "I tried to take my own life. My parents paid for me to go to rehab and after a month sober, I decided to give AA a shot." Daniel runs a hand through his hair. "I met your brother at a church I visited, and he took me under his wing. I got right with God and eventually, I reconnected with my parents and moved back to Nebraska. That's the nutshell version. Any questions?"

"Not right now. Thanks for sharing." I reach across the table and cover his hand with my own. "I'm sure that was hard. You are still my friend, but I need to process this before I can give you an answer about our relationship."

"I get it." He covers my hand with his other. "Thank you."

I pull my hand out from under his and awkwardness stretches across the table as we attempt to find our way back to some sort of normalcy while we wait on our meal. After chatting with a passing friend for a couple minutes, we meander our way around to talking about Jason and his most recent adventures at school. Bit by bit we find our way to more comfortable chatter.

When the waitress finally approaches, I lean out of the way so that she can place our food on the table.

I would be a fool to not give this relationship with Daniel a chance. But almost more than I'm afraid he'll hurt me, I'm afraid I'll hurt him with all the baggage I would bring to the relationship. He's had fifteen years to heal, while I'm at the start of my journey. But who better to understand?

I check the clock, anxious for my last shift this week at Coffee Joe's to be over with. I've had finals all week, and my brain is ready for a break. I am beyond grateful that my boss always closes shop over Thanksgiving weekend. Daniel waits at the corner table for me to get off work. I meet his gaze and my heart begins its slow melt that it does when he is around, despite what he told me about his past. I break eye contact. We're talking after work today.

The door chimes when a small group enters the shop, and we're busy for an additional half hour.

My boss locks the door behind them when they leave. "Hey, Josie. Go ahead and clock out. I'll finish up here."

"But I'm supposed to …"

"Take the offer, Josie. You have better things to do." He tilts his head toward Daniel's table.

"That I do. Thank you." I toss my apron into the hamper. "Happy Thanksgiving. I'll see you Monday." I pull on my jacket, then Daniel and I head out into the chill of the evening. My breath floats away like a small cloud. Christmas lights are hung up and down the block, in shop windows and on the light poles that line the streets. I haven't felt this alive in a long time.

"You're happy."

"I am." I clasp my hands behind my back.

"Intriguing."

"I've made a decision." I lead the way across the grass toward the swing.

"And?"

"Yes. I'll go out on a date with you."

"Only one?"

"Hopefully a lot more than one." I smile.

"You're sure?"

"I couldn't be surer." I step closer to him. "But … I can't promise you a smooth ride. I'm bound to be triggered. I still need to heal."

"It will take work on both our parts, but I won't run out on you."

Daniel touches my cheek with his right hand and a shiver runs up my spine. The things this man does to my insides. A part of me hopes he'll kiss me, but another part of me realizes it would be wise to take it slow. We haven't even gone on a date yet. The longing in me for connection wars against the desire to flee.

He takes my hand in his. "Would you like to sit a while?"

"Can we walk?"

"As long as I can hold your hand."

"I wouldn't have it any other way."

We continue to the other side of the town square, then down another street and check out Christmas decorations in the store windows. I tuck my hand in the nook of his elbow. "I wish we were going to be together tomorrow for Thanksgiving."

"Me too. Is it okay if I tell my family we're dating?"

"I guess. I need to inform my family, too. But we need to tell Jason first."

"Think he'll mind?"

"Ha. He'll be excited. We'll have a hard time getting time to ourselves if we're not careful."

"You've done a great job with him."

"Thanks."

We arrive back at Daniel's truck, and he unlocks the door. "There's no time like the present. Shall we head over to your parents' house now? I couldn't keep the secret tomorrow if I tried. My family has a way to crack the code when it comes to each other's personal life."

CHAPTER FIVE

The day after Thanksgiving, I finish packing. A crew of family and friends will be here at seven a.m. tomorrow to help us move into the apartment. Last summer, I cruised the garage sales and with my measly budget found the basics I need to set up my own home, so there's more to pack than I realized.

"Knock, knock." Mom picks up an empty box. "What needs to go in here?"

"If you could load up the books left on the shelf, that would be great."

"I'll miss you guys. I like our spontaneous moments."

"Me, too. But consider the bright side. You and Dad can go crazy any time without worry over the noise." I hope Mom doesn't go emotional on me. I'll miss being here, too, but not for the same reason. Their home is my safety net and a part of me is scared to leave, but it's time I take ownership of my future.

Mom pulls books off the shelf. "You and Daniel. That's some news."

"You must have seen it coming."

"I did, but I didn't think it would be this soon. Are you sure you're ready for a relationship?"

"Honestly, no, but Daniel is a good man. Steven approves, and as protective as he is, that means a lot. I like him, Mom. Jason does, too. Most importantly, I trust him. I didn't know if I would ever trust a man again."

Mom wraps me in a hug. "I'll be praying for you guys. And if you ever need us, we're here for you."

"Where should we put the white dresser?" Daniel's brother hollers up the stairs.

"My bedroom, next to the door." I scoot out of the way while he and Daniel maneuver the dresser through the door and across the living room. Most of the boxes are in and we only have a few pieces of furniture left to unload.

"Hey, Sis, what about this shelf?"

"Jason's room. Next to his bed." I direct traffic in between helping my mom and Charice unpack my dishes and making sure Jason doesn't get into trouble. He's with a neighbor kid, so I check out the window to make sure they haven't wandered off. I gasp. Jason is talking to a man that I haven't met yet. Heaviness descends on my chest and it's hard to breath.

"Josie?" Daniel rubs my back. "What's wrong?"

I point outside and in a flash he's out the door. His action spurs me on and I catch up as the man walks off and Jason gives Daniel a high five before he runs back to the apartment. I didn't see the man's face, but this close encounter sends dread coursing through my body.

"He's safe, Josie."

"For now. When will I be able to live without this ... dread?"

"You'll get there. You're a strong woman and you've already come a long way." He draws me into his arms.

"I feel like I'm constantly back tracking."

"Healing is not a linear process. Be patient with yourself."

"I'll try." I rest my head against his chest and allow myself to relax.

"Hey, you two. Is this your plan? Letting us do all the hard work?" Steven laughs.

"Ha ha." I pull away from Daniel. It's going to take a quick minute to get used to being part of a couple.

"Who wants pizza and ice cream?"

"Me!" Jason takes the ice cream from Daniel and pushes it into the freezer, then skids along the kitchen floor in his sock feet to the table where our supper invites us to indulge.

We each slide a couple pieces onto our plates and silence reigns while we take the edge off our hunger. By the time boxes were unpacked and everything had a place, it was late afternoon. Other than a sandwich around lunch, we hadn't eaten much today, and Daniel's suggestion was perfect.

Jason fairly inhales his serving, takes a gulp of his soda, then burps.

"Jason." I fight against a chuckle.

He scrunches his shoulders and takes another drink, longer then the first, and lets out a second burp. Longer and louder than the first.

I roll my eyes. Boys will be boys. "Tell us about your new friend."

"Mikey has the coolest bedroom and lots of Legos. And he has comic books and action figures."

My mind freezes as he carries on about all the toys and gadgets his new friend owns and how his room is all decked out as a jungle. How can I possibly compete if Jason asks for all the things, too? Christmas will be here before we know it and I still have no idea what I can afford that he'll enjoy. Maybe Mom was right, and I shouldn't have rented an apartment.

Daniel seems to sense my tension and takes my hand in his as he addresses Jason. "Has he ever ridden a camel?"

Jason's eyes light up. "Oh. I bet he hasn't done that."

"Maybe we could take him sometime."

"Can we?"

"Absolutely." Daniel rubs his hands together like a little kid excited about an adventure.

"But for now, let Daniel and me finish our dinner. You can pick out the movie?"

Jason tosses his plate into the trash then takes up a position in front of the television to scroll through the options.

Daniel scoops up more pizza. "What's on your mind?"

"Christmas." I pull the cheese off the top of my piece and pop it into my mouth.

"Ahh. You said a lot with one word." He pours another glass of soda for himself.

"How can I make this year special? I scrape by to pay the bills and put food on the table. Maybe I should have waited till after Christmas to move. Or until my VA business really takes off." I get up from the table and throw away my plate, then gather the leftovers and put them in the fridge for another meal.

Daniel follows me to the counter. "You've got a lot of people behind you more than willing to help if you need."

"If I ask for help, it'll be like I've thrown in the towel."

"Hardly that." He pulls me close. "I understand that you need to be independent, but all of us need help from time to time."

I relax against him. How can I explain the turmoil inside me? "I feel disqualified."

Daniel lifts my chin with his finger. "What your ex drilled into you are all lies. You can do this. Look at how much you've accomplished. You're a manager at the coffee shop and you're starting your own business. You have what it takes, Josie."

"I can't see it sometimes."

"I'll keep reminding you."

"Thanks." I pull away. "But that still leaves Christmas. I don't even have a tree or decorations and my parents are getting Jason a puppy for Christmas. Anything I do for him will pale in comparison."

"I doubt your parents see it that way."

Tears pool in my eyes.

"You don't need to prove anything. Jason already thinks you hung the moon."

"My ex always gave Jason lavish gifts and was very clear they were from him. I was left to squeeze a bit out of the grocery budget in order to put a little something under the tree from me."

"Which gift did he still play with six months later?"

"Mine." It's like a lightbulb turns on in my head. Maybe I am overreacting.

"I'm sure you'll figure out the perfect gift for Jason. But in the meantime, how about tomorrow after church we go pick out a tree for the apartment?"

"I don't have the money to—"

Daniel puts a finger on my lips to quiet my objections. "Can I do this one thing for you? Can I buy you a tree?"

I fill my cart with another box of ornaments, grateful that this thrift store has a rather large collection of Christmas decorations. Jason is exuberant about all the baubles he finds for our tree. Without the high price tags of a retail store, I let him choose what he likes. I almost squeal when I find a wreath that will blend perfectly with the other items we've chosen.

I agreed to let Daniel buy the tree if we tried a thrift store first. He protested, so I promised that if we didn't find a tree at the first stop, he could take me to the tree farm and buy us a live tree. Now, I can't help but be excited that they have no trees, and we'll get a live one this year. I add a box of tangled lights to the cart and lead our little parade to the line at check out, as we enjoy the carols playing in the store. I smile as the Christmas spirit lifts me out of the doldrums. This will be a great Christmas.

Half an hour later, we head out the door and walk a couple blocks to the car. Along the way, Daniel stops to visit with a man and his family huddled next to a building. He holds a sign asking for money. I'm embarrassed at the way I complained about not having enough for a nice Christmas when there are people who have much less than I do. Their coats aren't even sufficient for the weather.

Jason tugs on my coat sleeve. "Can I give them some money?"

I swallow the lump in my throat. "That would be good." I fish out my baggie of change swimming at the bottom of my purse. Our Christmas money, as I'd dubbed it.

"Can I give them all of it?"

Hope shines on my son's face. Would I have enough

money for his gift without it?

Daniel leans close. "Letting him give is a present to him that you can't replicate with any physical item."

The man makes a lot of sense. Not that I'm comfortable with it. I hand the bag to Jason.

"Thanks, Mom."

He runs over to the family and gives the money to them. The man gives Jason a hug. The woman mouths "thank you" to me. The joy I experience far outweighs any concern over my own lack that I had a few minutes ago.

Jason pulls his bouncy ball out of his pocket and hands it to the kids before skipping back to me. "I have lots of toys at home." He grabs my hand and skips alongside me all the way back to the car.

Later that evening, the is tree set up with strings of lights covering its branches. I tuck Jason into bed, then pull out a couple of bowls for ice cream. The day happened differently than I'd expected, but I wouldn't change a thing. My phone rings as I head to the living room to join Daniel for a Christmas movie. I stop and check the notifications. Susan. Chill bumps run up my arm. Not now. I won't let news about the landlord ruin the day. I'll call her later.

I hand Daniel a bowl and sit next to him with my legs tucked to the side. "Thank you for today. You're great with Jason. And thanks for the tree."

"I enjoyed it. Got to be around my favorite girl."

"I like the sound of that."

I snuggle closer to him. This must be a bit like heaven. Next to him, I feel safe.

My phone rings again. Probably Susan. A niggling urge to run for the hills steals my moment of peace. I might as well get this over with. I excuse myself and pick up my phone. I swipe to answer.

"What's up?"

CHAPTER SIX

I almost didn't come to the shelter after the news from Susan, but I hashed it out with Daniel and decided I wouldn't cower. I fill another plate and hand it to the woman in front of me. I ache for the residents here, but I'm in awe of their strength and determination to leave abusive situations. When I found out about this place last summer, I decided to be a part of the serve team. With the shelter located in Omaha and my schedule busy, I'm only able to come once a month. Charice and I usually come at the same time, but our schedules didn't match up this month. Now that I'm done with school, I plan to be more involved in the new year. I wish Christmas had a place like this.

"Ma'am?"

I focus on the next woman in line. Each hand hangs on to a child. A baby rests secure against her in a snuggly. My breath hitches at the sight of a bruise on her cheek. The anxiousness in her voice reminds me of a place I have visited too often in my mind. "My name's Josie. What do you need?"

"Can you help me get food? My boys won't let go of me."

"Absolutely." I wave over another volunteer to take my place and step out of line. "What's your name?"

"Isabella."

"Well, Isabella, let's get your family some food."

Daniel is outside, watching out for me, just as he promised. I'm grateful that I have someone to protect me, and I pray all these women find that, too, someday.

I break Daniel's hold around my neck and flip him over my back. He lands with a thud, and I cringe.

"Did I hurt you?"

It's Sunday afternoon, so Daniel and I have the dojang to ourselves while he teaches me more self-defense moves.

He laughs. "I hope you don't apologize if you throw some jerk to the ground."

"I doubt I'll have any problems leaving that creep in the dust and making my escape." There's a part of me that kind of, sort of hopes that I do get to show my stalker that I'm not easy prey. Susan's news chilled both Daniel and me to the bone. The landlord was indeed in town. Evidently, he shadowed Susan for some time and made several brags at his local bar that he would get himself a prime chunk of meat by Christmas. Me being the meat, from what Susan was able to ascertain. While she and her husband weren't rich, they did have contacts. One of her husband's best friends was a private investigator. He got the landlord to talk while he was drunk and found out what he planned. I am forever thankful. The police were alerted, but by the time they were involved, the landlord had already left Tulsa.

After I had got off the phone with Susan, I'd started

shaking, curled into a ball, and rocked. Daniel gathered me onto his lap and held me like a small child until I calmed down enough to fill him in. He stayed late. I was too scared to be alone and clung to the only comfort I wanted. This man who saw past all my gunk and chose to be here and protect me and Jason. Somewhere after midnight, a righteous anger took over. I was determined not to let this dangerous man win. Daniel and I laid out a plan. Follow up with the police, increase my self-defense lessons, and get some mace. Jason is jealous that I'm at the dojang more than he is.

"Josie?" Daniel walks over and stands in front of me. "You lost in all the what ifs?"

"Some. But mostly, thinking about how thankful I am that you're a part of my life."

"Same." He lets out a sigh and steps back. "Ready for the next move?"

"Bring it on."

"Congratulations, Josie." My boss delivers coffees all around to me, my friends, and family who are enjoying an after-graduation ceremony celebration. "I'm not losing you yet, am I?"

"Nope. I need to build up my VA business before I can hand in my resignation. You have to put up with me for a while yet." I'm blessed with a boss who cheers me on my journey. He's like a protective father, too. God has put all sorts of guardians around me. I don't understand how He could love me.

"That I will do happily. In the meantime, I posted next week's schedule." He heads back behind the counter.

I appreciate each person here and the courage they give me to move beyond my past. My gaze passes around our tables. Since the call from Susan, I've been in a state of tension while I studied for finals and practiced self-defense. My mind is tired and I'm very thankful to be done with school. If the police can arrest my former landlord, I might be able to enjoy Christmas.

"Mom?"

I startle and look at Jason standing next to me. I didn't even notice when he came over from two tables down. Daniel's words echo in my head to not get lost in my thoughts and stay aware of my surroundings. I look around at the other customers in the shop then give my attention to Jason. "What's up?"

"Can I go outside and play?"

A few weeks ago, maybe, but now there's too much at risk, especially with the light waning. "Not tonight."

"Mom." Jason is not one to whine, so his tone catches me off guard.

He's probably as antsy as I am but doesn't have any explanation. I asked Daniel's opinion about telling Jason there was potential danger for us and we both decided it would be best not to yet, although I did tell my parents, since he spends a lot of time with them. I catch Daniel's eye. He points at himself, then outside.

Relieved, I whisper to Jason. "Daniel has something in mind. You can go with him."

Jason meets Daniel at the door, and they head outside.

An hour later, I meet them on the sidewalk outside the coffee shop. Someone hollers at Daniel from across the street and he jogs over to say hi before we head back to my apartment. Jason skips back and forth on the sidewalk between Coffee Joe's and where Daniel's truck is parked. I'm in the middle and each time he passes me, he gives me a high five. I glance across the street where Daniel chats with his friend. We may be here a while.

"Mom."

The fear in his voice signals danger. I spin around. The landlord stands next to Jason, gripping his shoulder. "Sorry to interrupt your little celebration."

The sound of his voice sends chills through my body. We're out of the line of sight of anyone inside the coffee shop. I glance across the street. Daniel's view is blocked by the truck.

"Don't even think about calling your friend over."

"You okay, Jason?" *Stay calm. Daniel, look over here.* I will him to sense the danger.

Jason nods.

The landlord squeezes Jason's shoulder and he winces. "I'm the one you need to be concerned about."

I swallow hard. "What do you want?"

"To collect what you owe me."

"My husband's name was on the lease. He's the one who shortchanged you. There's no way you can legally collect from me."

"Who said anything about legal? Between the two of you, I have enough to repay your debt."

Chills run up my back. What is he talking about? I need to get Jason away from him. I take a step in their direction. *God, help.*

"If you know what's good for your son, don't come any closer. Unless of course you *want* to come along for the fun." The landlord leers at me, lust written on his face. Then he backs up, taking Jason with him.

"Mom?"

Jason's expression calls out the fighter in me. I take a step to follow, then a hand stops me.

"Get away from the boy." Daniel's voice beside me brings me strength.

"You get away." The man points his finger at Daniel.

"Jason. Remember Tuesday?" Daniel drops his hand from my arm.

The landlord snorts. "What is this? Code?" He shifts his position to stand behind Jason, his arm snug against the front of Jason's neck.

Daniel nods and the next few seconds are a blur and now Jason is tucked behind me. Daniel takes a step toward the landlord.

"Go ahead, attack me." The man glares at Daniel." I'll press charges, and then where would your little tramp be?"

I grab Daniel's arm. "It's not worth it."

The landlord sneers at us and backs away. "I'll see you again soon, Josie." He spits on the ground then blends into the shadows.

Daniel puts a call in to the police, then pulls us both into the circle of his arms. I begin to shake. How are we ever to get through this? On my own, maybe I could defend myself. Maybe. But with Jason in the mix?

Daniel whispers reassurances in my ear. "Until that man is behind bars, if I can't be at your and Jason's side, I'll make sure someone is."

CHAPTER SEVEN

Daniel has kept his word. Someone is always nearby watching for any sign of danger. Along with a couple good friends of his and my brother, the police are involved in our protection as well. Once Jason is out of school for the holidays, it will be much easier. For now, there are undercover police stationed inside the school. In truth, it's for more than Jason's sake. Evidently, there is a warrant out for the man's arrest for some sort of involvement in human trafficking. The thought of it sends chills up my spine. If put in a dangerous situation again, I hope I do as well as Jason did with what Daniel has taught me about self-defense.

I thought Jason would be freaked out over the altercation last week, but he came out of it standing a bit taller. Able to do his part to keep us safe gave him a new confidence. Evidently, in addition to taekwondo classes, Daniel taught him a few tricks to protect himself. My counselor warned me that Jason needs to deal with the trauma, and I've set up an appointment for him, but so far, he hasn't missed a beat.

With only two weeks till Christmas, I try to get my mind off current events by going full holiday mode. Our apartment is fully decked out with our thrift store finds and our fresh-cut tree. The wall of lights we bought is my favorite accent and gives a soft glow in the evening. Last weekend we baked cookies for some elderly neighbors, and Jason wrapped some of the treasure he's collected over the years to give to the kids who live a couple doors down when we discovered they don't have much money for gifts this year. We also took a few outerwear items to the local homeless shelter. We tried to locate the family we saw on the streets, but they must have found a place to shelter in the cold.

A snowball hits me in the arm and pulls me out of my thoughts. Snow has finally visited us for the season, dropping almost two feet, and Daniel's family invited Jason and me to come spend the weekend at their place in the country, about forty-five minutes outside of Christmas. His family knows how to play. Laughing, I pull behind the wall of snow that Daniel and I have piled in front of us. "Your mom has good aim."

"And she doesn't go easy on anyone. With a house of testosterone, she couldn't afford to." He lobs another ball over the wall toward his parents.

"Come on, Daniel. You can do better than that." His dad's voice carries on the still wintery air.

"Wimpy, if you ask me." His mother snickers and tosses another snowball our way.

It hits the shed behind us and sprays all over us. His parents have taken up the most secure spot in the battle— behind a snow packed yard swing.

"Yeah, Daniel." Jason giggles. His taunt comes from behind the third point in the triangle of our battle where he aids Daniel's two brothers.

"Can you distract them?" Daniel eyeballs the pile of ammunition between us.

I flex my muscles. "You can count on me. What are you up to?"

"I've learned a few tricks over the years, but I'm usually on my own. This should be fun. Keep those balls flying and if you run out, distract them with your charms. I need about five minutes."

"You got it." He sneaks around the shed behind us, while I engage in the battle in front of us. "Is that all you have?" I peek out from behind my hill of snow.

"Incoming." Daniel's younger brother stands up and pulls back his arm like a pitcher.

I duck and shield my head as more balls break apart on the ground around me. I throw a fist pump in the air that Jason would be proud of. They're doing half my job for me by using up more of their ammunition. I toss out a couple of balls from my side of the hill, then crawl over to Daniel's side and throw a few more. The exchange continues for a few more minutes, then a lull. They must be making more balls. I scoop up some snow and form another half dozen. From my position in the fort, I spy Daniel high up in the evergreen tree directly behind our opponents. Not sure what he's up to, but I better distract his family. I pull the bottom edge of my coat out and pile it with snowballs, then dash out and throw them with a more direct aim than before. One pops his dad in the head. I zigzag out of his range as he throws one my way. I toss another one at his older brother, then Jason. He picks up several and chases me. I run back toward my hiding place. Daniel's family cheers for my son.

The otherwise quiet of the afternoon is suddenly broken by a swooshing sound. His family looks up in time to see snow falling from a branch that Daniel has bent to release its white burden. They try to get out of the way and trip over each other. Within seconds they're covered in white. Another swoosh and more snow lands on top of the first layer.

Daniel's cheer of victory has everyone in stitches and he and I are declared the official winners.

"Who's ready for some hot chocolate?" His mother leads the way back to the patio where a hot cocoa buffet is set up, so we won't traipse back into the house with snow clinging to our boots.

Daniel's mom loops her arm through mine. "I thoroughly approve."

"What?"

"I've never seen him this happy."

I kick at the snow. This is new territory for me.

"We didn't ask you here to decide if we approve of you or not. We asked you here because we wanted to meet the girl that is making him happy. Don't ever doubt that you're welcome in this family." She pulls me into a hug.

The welcome touches me somewhere deep inside that I didn't realize needed to be loved. In my peripheral vision, I notice Daniel watching us. I don't understand why God saw fit to surround me with people who care for me. But I'm glad He did.

Jason runs over to me. "Mom. Daniel said we can go on a real sleigh ride. Can you believe it?"

Daniel comes up behind Jason. "If that's okay with you?"

"I would never live it down if I told Jason no to a sleigh ride."

"This is the best day ever." Jason jumps off the patio and creates a snow angel.

"We'll get this cleaned up and supper on the table while you guys enjoy the ride." Daniel's mom leads her husband to the patio door and calls back to her other sons. "You boys take care of the mess out here, then I could use a hand inside."

The sound of the horses' hoofs hitting the ground breaks the quiet. Even Jason is awed into stillness by our surroundings. At one point on the trail, we come to the top of a hill, where we can see the countryside dotted with the lights. We stop and silence descends on us with only the occasional creak of a limb bowing under the weight of the snow.

The moon overhead casts a soft shadow around us. I take a deep breath and enjoy the view. It's like peace has taken on a form I can see, hear, and touch. In this moment, it's easy to believe that even though the threat of danger waits for us as soon as we leave this sanctuary, everything will be okay. A branch cracks and snow swooshes to the ground.

Daniel squeezes my hand. "Ready to head back?"

"Not really."

"I'm hungry." Jason pipes up, making our decision for us.

As Daniel urges the horses homeward, I look behind us at the receding scene. The last two days have been a retreat from the darkness that shadows us. I wish I could take a dose of this peace with me.

CHAPTER EIGHT

Since the town square Christmas village is open, Daniel does his part to help to create the Christmas spirit by taking Jason with him on the weekends to help with the nativity camels. The bond between the two of them is something I never dreamed possible. But tonight, the camels can wait. It's my turn to explore the Christmas village with my son. Two of Daniel's friends trail not too far behind us. A couple who could easily be someone else on a Christmas outing, they are both black belts at the dojang where Daniel teaches. With him busy, the pair volunteered to keep Jason and me company. I'm beyond ready for this protection detail to be over and done with.

Jason bumps up against me. "Mom. Can we do the gingerbread house decorating contest?"

"Sure, kiddo." He pulls me toward the prefab building housing the contest. Inside, we choose our supplies and hunt for a table.

"Josie."

Charice's voice is music to my ears. My local bestie wraps me in a hug. "You guys just get here?"

"Yep. Let's share a table."

Charice attempts to corral her youngest, who is following her older brother and Jason on what appears to be a parade around the tables.

She finally gives up. "Why fight it?"

I chuckle at her kids' antics. "They'll probably get ideas for their own houses."

"True that."

Charice and I lay claim to a recently vacated table, then wave down the boys, who run a crazy path in our direction. Once our supplies are set up, the boys clamor to decorate a house with no help from adults. Happy to acquiesce, Charice and I work on our own.

Charice spreads icing on the roof of our creation. "Have they caught that guy who's intimidating you?"

"Not yet." I open a bag of chocolate candies and pour them on the table.

"You okay?"

"Between our bodyguards and the self-defense classes, we'll be fine."

There's a commotion at the door. I glance up before placing candy canes along the side of our little gingerbread cottage. Something niggles in my mind and a shiver runs up my back. I had assumed Daniel's friends had stayed outside, but what if we got separated? I brush away the thought and sprinkle coconut flakes around the house.

Before another half hour is gone, we finish our entries, label them, and place them with the others for judging. Charice's husband is waiting for her when we step outside. She gives me a hug and her little family aims for Santa Claus. A must-have for her boys.

I lead Jason out of the flow of traffic and look around for Daniel's friends. When I don't see them, I pull out my phone to call Daniel. No service. *Drats.* They instructed me that if we got separated, I should meet them under the canopy in the middle of the park.

I try to stay calm and reach for Jason's hand. "Let's go see Daniel."

"Can we walk through the tunnel of lights?"

"We'll do that later." We thread our way through the crowds, stopping under every other lamppost to try my phone. This town needs a cell tower of its own. There are too many dead spots in Christmas. Up ahead, in the shadows, I think I spot Daniel's friends. But even if it is them, we're heading further away from the center of activity. Not good. We head back in the direction we came from, and I pick up the pace. "Jason?"

"Yeah, Mom?"

"Don't be afraid, but something isn't right. We need to stay alert."

"I wish Daniel was here."

"You and me both. That's where we're going now. But, if anything happens, run as fast as you can to Daniel. He'll come." And Jason will be out of harm's way.

His grip tightens. "But I could help you."

"Getting to Daniel is the best way you can do that." I take a deep breath. "Remember everything Daniel's taught you. Okay?"

He stands a bit taller. "You can count on me."

I hate that he's experiencing this. That he has to be a part of making sure we're okay. But right now, right here, all we have is each other. There are a few stragglers ahead and we'll catch up with them quickly. I'll feel a lot better then. Footsteps come up behind us. I tense, ready to run, when a man with a diaper bag hurries past. The image would be humorous if not for our situation.

"Jason, let's double time it and catch up with that couple ahead of us." We start out at a jog.

A man steps out of the shadows, bringing us to a halt. I suck in my breath at the sight of my old landlord.

I look down at Jason and see bravery reflected in his eyes. "Run."

Jason sprints across the lawn, taking a direct route toward Daniel. And safety.

"I don't need him anyway. I'll get what I need from you." The landlord steps toward me. "And we'll be gone before he can fetch help." He grabs my left bicep.

I bring my left forearm up on the inside of his arm and twist back to the left, knocking his hand to the side, then step off the sidewalk to my right, in the direction of the people I was trying to catch up to.

His eyes light up with surprise. "Okay, then. I like a bit of a challenge. This will be fun." He looks past me and shakes his head. "I got this."

I chance a peek behind me. A man several inches taller than me and with arms as big around as my legs stands in my path to freedom. I turn back to the landlord. *Run Jason.*

The landlord spits on the ground. "And, in case you wonder, that couple guarding you? They won't be any help either."

This man makes me mad. I back up a few steps closer to the hub of activity in the park. *My whistle.* Daniel got it for me after the encounter outside of the coffee shop, but I forgot about it. I reach into my jacket pocket. The can of mace is there, too. Not enough to win, but enough to give me an edge till help arrives. I pull out my whistle and blow as hard as I can. Quick short blasts.

The landlord snares the cord dangling from the whistle and yanks it away from me. I take a few steps back and glance behind me. Muscle man glares at me. *God help me.* I attempt to stay in the light of park lamps and Christmas lights as I zigzag across the grass, a few more feet at a time away from the landlord. Muscle man maneuvers around me and blocks my path again.

"Hey, you! Leave her alone." A stranger runs toward us, phone in hand. "My girlfriend is calling the police."

The landlord, attention locked on me, motions his goon toward the interruption. The larger man stomps toward the stranger, now filming the conflict. The landlord rushes me and starts to drag me away. I scratch at his hand gripped around my wrist. To my side, I see two men tussle with the landlord's muscle. I can't be taken away from here. I wrap my free hand around the can of mace in my pocket. I dig in my heels and bring our progress to a halt.

The landlord sticks his nose in my face. "Move. Or you'll be sorry."

I pull out the mace and spray it in his eyes. When his grip loosens, I knee him in the groin. As he grunts and bends forward, I push his head down at the same time I raise my knee, nailing him in the nose.

He stumbles backward and I kick him. Momentum takes him to the ground. He gapes at me in disbelief as he wipes blood off his face. "You good for nothing little—"

Before he can rise to his feet, two police officers run past me, flip him on his stomach, and cuff him. *Thank you, God.* My body starts to shake. I did it. I protected myself. I drop to the ground and wrap my arms around myself, rocking. A crowd is gathered nearby—phones out—filming, I suppose. The two men who fought with the landlord's goon now have him on the ground. A police officer puts cuffs on him. My heart rate begins to slow. A police officer drapes a blanket around me and makes sure I'm okay, then tells me she'll be right back. I'm not up to going anywhere, anyway. The crowd dissipates as they're directed away from the scene.

"Mom. Mom." Jason throws himself at me. "I ran as fast as I could."

"You did good. Thank you." I hold him close, relieved this nightmare is close to an end.

"You did good, too, Josie girl." Daniel kneels in front of me and touches my cheek.

"I got separated from your friends. Did he hurt them?"

Daniel shakes his head and sits next to me. "They texted me about the same time Jason reached me. They'll have headaches and wounded egos, otherwise, they're fine."

I let out a pent-up breath as my phone notifications start going off. Susan texts and asks if I'm okay. Next, my brother Stephen asks if they got the guy. Then Charice promises to be right over as they are still at the park.

Daniel glances at my phone. "What's all that about?"

I read the next text. "According to my dad, someone posted a video of the incident to social media."

"Can I see? I bet you were great." Jason reaches for the phone.

"Why not? But hold it where we all can see it."

"Okay. Wow, Mom. Wait till I show my friends."

Daniel chuckles. "That's my girl." He pulls me into a hug.

Someone nearby clears their throat. "Excuse me. I need to get a statement. If I could."

I pull away from Daniel and join the officer. I'm ready to tell my side of the story so that I can go home.

Two hours later, I pull into my parking spot at the apartment and Daniel slides into a space next to mine. He insisted on making sure we got home okay. Even though my old landlord is in jail, I'm grateful for Daniel's presence.

The police had taken a short statement at the park, then

after what felt like the tenth time of Jason interrupting me to ask when we could go home, the officer took mercy on him and instructed us to come by the station tomorrow for a fuller account.

Climbing out of the car, I look in the back seat where Jason has fallen asleep. I hate to wake him.

Daniel places a hand on my back. "Let him sleep. I'll get him inside for you." Daniel opens the back door and scoops Jason into his arms.

"You're handy to have around." I speak in a low tone to avoid waking Jason.

"My plan worked."

I chuckle nervously as I lead the way upstairs and let us inside. Daniel heads to Jason's room and by the time I catch up, he's already removing Jason's shoes and pulling the covers over him.

I wait for him to finish. Jason moves restlessly in his bed. His eyelids flash open and he scoots over in the bed away from what must be our shadows towering over him and cries out. I kneel next to the bed to comfort him.

Daniel rubs Jason's back. "Shh. It's okay. Your mom is right here with us. Go back to sleep." He rubs Jason's back and my son stills under his touch. I drop to my knees next to his bed and lay my hand on Jason's chest. "I'm right here."

Like he used to as a much younger, scared child, Jason touches my cheek as though to confirm it's me, then drops his hand and rolls over.

I look up at Daniel. He's a good man and I'm thankful for the tenderness he has for my son. Daniel tilts his head to the door and takes hold of my hand. I leave Jason's door cracked and follow Daniel to the living room. "Finally. I've got you to myself." He pulls me into a hug.

I relax in the comfort of his arms and cry.

"What's wrong, Josie girl?" He caresses my cheek.

"Relief, I guess. I don't know what I'd do without you."

"That's a two-way street."

I hug him tight and hope he's telling the truth. He releases a deep sigh as I rest my cheek against his chest. His heartbeat soothes my thoughts. I could stay here forever, I think, but all too soon, Daniel needs to leave. I watch out the front window as he walks to his truck. A part of me is afraid that this won't last and that I'll be lost again, but for tonight, I'll hold on to the possibilities. After pulling the curtain closed, I head to bed.

CHAPTER NINE

"Pass the bread."

The basket makes its way down the table to me, passing from one person to the next. The table is filled with family, and I'm thankful for each one. I wouldn't have made it through the last couple of years without them. I only wish Daniel could have joined us for Christmas Eve dinner, but he's with his family. I'm content that he'll be with Jason and me on Christmas Day.

My brother pushes away from the table and claims to be stuffed. Wait till dessert is brought out. He'll change his tune. The others scoot back from the table as well, but I want more bread. I slather butter on my slice and the aroma delights my senses. Mom always sets the Christmas table with sourdough. I really need to learn how to make it myself.

The last few days were a flurry of final gift buying, last-minute tradition making, and surprise planning. With the matter of my landlord fully behind me, I'm able to enjoy my favorite time of year.

"Who's ready for presents?" Dad stands at the head of the table.

"Me!" Jason jumps up and runs for the living room and we all join him around the Christmas tree.

"Who wants to play Santa this year?" My dad looks over at Jason.

"I will." My son, ever the eager one when Santa is involved, volunteers for the job that is invariably his, ever since we came home to Christmas.

He crawls under the tree and, one by one, pulls out packages and passes them around. Now that we're all grown, except for Jason, the gifts are far fewer, but typically much more meaningful, and within half an hour, most of the gifts have been opened.

Jason crawls under the tree one more time and comes out disappointed when he can't find a gift for himself.

"Oh my. We must have forgotten to put your gift under the tree." Dad winks at Jason.

Jason's smile grows.

"I wonder where it could be." Mom joins the game.

Jason runs around the house, hunting in all the rooms, then finally stops in front of his grandparents. "Where is it?"

Dad looks at Mom. "Do you remember where you put it?"

"Dad." Stephen interrupts. "Enough already. Can't you see how miserable Jason is?"

Jason jumps up and down. "Please, tell me."

"Should we?" Mom wiggles her eyebrows.

"Mom." Stephen and I speak in unison.

"Now I remember where it is." Dad slaps his knees. "Wait here. I'll go get it." A few minutes later, the door to the garage opens and closes, and then a ball of fur bolts into the living room.

Jason's eyes widen. "A puppy?"

"Yep." I finally agreed to let Mom and Dad get Jason a dog as long as it was apartment size, and they landed on a standard schnauzer. Smart, the perfect size for an apartment, and a plus, protective. They promised to get all the startup supplies necessary and if the occasion arose that I needed help with the extra rent or dog food, they would chip in. Daniel was right. There was no reason I should deny them the pleasure of giving their grandson a dog. They had missed enough of his life already. And Jason's joy is the last evidence I need to convince me that it was the right choice.

"Yay!" Jason dances around the room, then drops to the floor. He pats his lap to get the dog to come to him, but the puppy makes its rounds and sniffs everyone's shoes before it finally stops in front of Jason and licks his face. Jason giggles and pulls it onto his lap. "What's his name?"

"That's for you to decide." Mom scratches the puppy's head. "But it's a girl."

Jason spends the rest of the afternoon with his new friend while the grownups play table games and dig into the pies Mom made for dessert.

By five o'clock, I'm beat. Dad loads up all the puppy supplies into my car and secures the carrier on the seat next to Jason. I'm not ready to allow the puppy full roaming privileges in the car while I drive. No matter how much Jason pleads.

While I prepare breakfast, Jason stands sentinel at the window waiting for Daniel. "Mom! He's here. I'm going to help him bring in stuff from his truck."

"Make sure your dog's shut up in your room. Don't want her to escape."

"Done." The front door opens, then slams shut.

Jason still hasn't settled on a name for his new companion.

I chuckle. Jason—the one who never wants to get out of bed—woke me up early today to help him take his puppy out for a walk. We bundled up over our pajamas and shivered our way into the darkness of morning. I had every intention of snuggling back into the comfort of my bed but was wide awake after tromping through new fallen snow for fifteen minutes while we waited for his puppy to do her business.

I hear Jason and Daniel at the door, stomping off snow from their shoes. I hurry to set the pitcher of orange juice on the table. I'm as excited as Jason is for Daniel to be with us for the day. I was surprised that Jason agreed to wait for Daniel before we opened gifts. My stomach growls. He'll have to wait till after breakfast, too.

The door opens and I peek around the corner. "Merry Christmas!"

Hands behind their backs, Daniel and Jason cast not-so-innocent looks at me like I've caught them doing something they're not supposed to.

"You're not allowed in here yet, right, Daniel?"

"Absolutely."

I tap my foot. "This is all very suspicious." The timer on the stove dings and I let out an exaggerated sigh. "I better get the cinnamon rolls, so they don't burn, but I'll figure this out later." I give them my best mom look before I retreat to the kitchen. There's a bunch of whispering, then rustling noises around the Christmas tree before Jason lets his dog out of his room. Daniel wanders into the kitchen and offers to help while Jason takes his four-legged friend on a walk.

Jason is back in record time and kerplunks himself at the table. "Is it time to eat yet?"

"What's got you in a hurry?" Daniel takes the platter of bacon to the table with Jason's puppy dancing around his feet.

"Daniel." Jason draws out his name like a slinky strung across a room. "It's Christmas."

I set the pan of cinnamon rolls on the table and my stomach growls loud enough to draw an eye roll from my son.

An hour later, the leftovers are put away and dishes sit in the sink to be washed later. We're gathered around the tree, admiring the packages underneath.

"Mom, can I give you my gift first?"

"Sure. I'm not used to being first to get a present."

Jason hops up and grabs a large, flat package wrapped with a huge bow, leaning against the wall behind the tree. I hadn't even noticed it. That must be what he and Daniel were being sneaky about.

I take it out of Jason's hand and place it on my lap. I untie the bow and pull off the paper. I gasp when I see the picture.

"Do you like it, Mom? Daniel helped me pick it out and get it framed."

The picture of Jason and me is from Daniel's house at Thanksgiving. We're tossing snow over each other, a snowman in the background. Pure joy radiates from us.

I dab at my eyes. "I love it. Thank you."

Jason kisses me on the cheek. "You're the best mom in the world." He looks at Daniel. "I told you she would cry."

"She's allowed."

I wipe the tears off my cheek. "Who's next?"

"Me, me!" Jason hops up from the floor. "Can I pick out my own?"

"Go for it." Daniel points out the one from him.

Jason dashes for the gifts and pulls out the rectangular box wrapped in white paper with camels in front of tiny Christmas trees. He guffaws as he rips off the paper, then does a happy dance when he sees one of the Lego sets that he asked for. I breathe a sigh of relief that Daniel and I hadn't doubled up.

A few minutes later, Jason offers an enthusiastic thank you to my choice of Lego sets for his gift. He crumples the gift paper and tosses it across the room. His dog chases it, then shakes it to death. Jason pulls the tape off the first box of Legos and pulls out the tiny packages with various colored pieces inside.

"Jason. Give Daniel his gifts from us."

Jason's gift is a new winter hat and Daniel immediately puts it on. Then he gets to my package, and I hold my breath. I had followed his mom's suggestion and I hope I got it right. He lets out a whoop and holds up the two tickets to an upcoming concert with his favorite band and kisses them. An overgrown kid freaking out over VIP tickets.

"Thank you, Josie girl. This is perfect. Now it's your turn." He pulls a gift bag from the side of the couch and holds it out to me.

I accept it from him and pull out the red and green tissue paper. In the bottom of the bag is a rectangular jewelry box. Daniel watches me closely as I pull it out. Blushing, I open it to reveal a folded-up piece of paper. "What are you up to?" I drop the box and unfold the paper. My mouth drops open at the amount of the gift certificate.

Daniel chuckles. "I thought you might like to get another tattoo."

I press my hand against my chest. I've been wanting to get another tat. "This is perfect. Thank you." I squeeze his hand.

"Cool." Jason scoots next to me. "What kind of tattoo will it be?"

"I'll let you know once I decide." I tap the end of his nose, then push up off the floor.

"Plenty of leftovers from breakfast if anyone is hungry. The roast won't be ready till midafternoon."

Later that night, after we tuck Jason into bed, Daniel and I settle on the couch for a movie. Daniel angles his body toward me. "This has been one of my best Christmases ever. But I'm missing one thing." He cups my cheek in his hand, and I lift my face. His first kiss is gentle, almost tentative, and then he pulls away. He caresses my cheek, then kisses me one more time before taking my hand in his. I wonder what life would have been like if I had met Daniel before my ex. At that point in our lives, we probably would have hurt each other. I'm thankful God brought us together now.

We watch *Miracle on 34th Street*, but before we get to the most satisfying part of the movie, I begin to doze off. At some point, I quit fighting it and enjoy resting against Daniel.

"Josie? I should probably head home." His voice sounds far off.

I want him to stay longer, so I allow myself to drift back toward sleep. I'm vaguely aware of Daniel's warmth moving away from me as he guides my head to lie against the pillow. He covers me with a blanket, and I nestle into the comfort, too tired to go to bed. I start to reach out from under the blanket to hold on to him when his voice stops me.

"I hope you realize I plan to marry you someday, Josie Ferris." He kisses me on the forehead.

I pretend I'm still asleep while Daniel makes his exit. But I'm wide awake now. *Oh, what I have gotten myself into?* Daniel's intentions unnerve me, but I have to admit that the idea of someday being his wife thrills me to no end.

A NOTE FROM THE AUTHOR

I'm always awed by God's ability to redeem and restore no matter what the brokenness is in our life. He is never short on grace and mercy, always patient in our attempts to connect with him.

Having been the recipient of this grace in the midst of my own encounter with brokenness in my marriage, I hope that through this story you find encouragement to bring your hurt, your fears, your pain to God. Your pain may not be anything like Josie's, but the same grace which helps her is available to all who call on Jesus.

He is trustworthy, even when someone close to us may not be. He is faithful even when a loved one fails us. He is kind when we are offered anything but kindness by those around us.

Hang in there my friend. Turn to God. Let Him bring you the comfort and healing you so desperately need.

"The LORD is close to the brokenhearted
and saves those who are crushed in spirit."

Psalm 34:18 NIV

ACKNOWLEDGMENTS

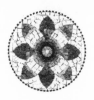

I want to thank my Mosaic sisters who are wonderful journey mates on this publishing adventure!

ABOUT ANGELA D. MEYER

ANGELA D. MEYER writes fiction that showcases God's ability to redeem and restore the brokenness in our lives. Now that her two children are grown, she spends her time writing instead of homeschooling, stays active at church, and she is plotting how to reclaim her tomorrows during the next season of life. She enjoys sunrises and sunsets, hanging out with friends, a good laugh, and reading. Someday, she would love to vacation by the ocean.

Learn more about Angela's books on her website, www. angeladmeyer.com. Sign up for her newsletter to be among the first to hear about her new book releases.

TITLES BY ANGELA D. MEYER

THE MOSAIC COLLECTION: NOVELS
This Side of Yesterday

Applewood Hill series
Where Hope Starts
Where Healing Starts

THE MOSAIC COLLECTION: ANTHOLOGY STORIES
"The Jukebox Café"
(*Hope is Born: A Mosaic Christmas Anthology*)
"Returning to Christmas"
(*A Star Will Rise: A Mosaic Christmas Anthology II*)
"Jillian's Refuge"
(*Song of Grace: Stories to Amaze the Soul*)
"Reinventing Josie"
(*All Things New: Stories to Refresh the Soul*)
"Reclaiming Tomorrow"
(*A Whisper of Peace: A Mosaic Christmas Anthology IV*)

UPCOMING
Applewood Hill series
Where Joy Starts

WHISPERED MIRACLE

Stacy Monson

* * *

Casey Younghans has bounced around foster care most of her life. About to age out and unprepared to be on her own, she faces an uncertain future alone. Being sent to Outlook Adventure Camp for Christmas is just one more place she won't be welcome. Then she meets Lula, the tiny dog with understanding eyes, and the camp staff who seem to accept her, attitude and all. Could she actually find a way to fit into the world just the way she is? It would be a miracle.

To all who have traveled a lonely path in life: Scripture promises that God is with you, that Jesus understands what you are going through, and that all who believe are welcome and invited to approach God's throne for help.

For we do not have a high priest who is unable to empathize with our weaknesses, but we have one who has been tempted in every way, just as we are—yet he did not sin. Let us then approach God's throne of grace with confidence, so that we may receive mercy and find grace to help us in our time of need.

Hebrews 4:15-16

CHAPTER ONE

Spend Christmas with strangers? Wasn't it bad enough that this was her first Christmas without Gigi? Casey Younghans reread the text from her older brother. Now he expected her to go to some camp he'd gone to years ago and hang out with people she didn't know?

Her typed response was simply, "No."

Somewhere across the world, Jeff was no doubt frowning at his laptop, muttering about how stubborn she was. Probably throwing in some cuss words he'd acquired from his years in the Marines. The flicker of satisfaction evaporated when his answer appeared.

"All set up. Expecting you Thurs 1200 hours at Denver airport. Details in email. Out 4 now. –J"

She opened her mouth to scream in frustration but could only manage a sound like a strangled cat, another lasting reminder of the accident. Who made him boss of her life? Just because she wasn't quite 18 and he was 20-whatever didn't mean he got to make decisions for her. He was traveling the world in the military while she sat alone in the empty apartment trying to figure out how to go forward. *Why* go forward. Nobody but Gigi, her final foster mom, had ever cared about her; a bunch of mountain people sure wouldn't. And obviously her own brother didn't.

Tears welling, she threw her phone at the bed and watched it bounce off and land on the carpet. Her shoulders drooped. What did it matter where she spent Christmas? She didn't have anything to celebrate anyway, especially without Gigi.

She flopped onto her back and stared at the ceiling. She could be alone here or alone on a mountain somewhere. Alone was alone. Maybe she could go to the camp and then find some place to live up there by herself. Where Jeff couldn't find her, not that he'd look. Tears slid down her temples. He wouldn't even know she was gone for months. No one would. Gigi had been the only one who cared, and she was gone.

"All because of me." Her raspy whisper floated aimlessly around the tiny, empty apartment, like she'd been doing since the accident. She rolled over and buried her face in her arms. She'd go to the mountains but not because he ordered her to. Because it's what Gigi would expect.

Entry #240 – 49 days to freedom

On the plane to some camp up on some mountain. Jeff's probably celebrating Xmas with a buncha friends somewhere in Paris or London. How come he's got a great life and I have no life, but then he can still send me wherever just becuz?! I'm SO done with him. He doesn't care about me. Only Gigi did, but maybe that's becuz she got paid to. Duzn't matter. At least I had someone to talk to, who listened. Now I can't make enough noise to be heard even if I had something to say. Had another dream about the accident last night. It all seemed so real, like it just happened. Will I ever get a full night's sleep? I'm T.I.R.E.D. OK, plane's landing. Wish me luck. I hope it's not some weirdo camp. Scary thought.

Approaching the end of the jetway, Casey's heart ramped

up. There was still time to change her ticket and go home. Home to the silent apartment with reminders of Gigi. She straightened her backpack and tightened her grip on the rolling carry-on. Turning up the volume on her earbuds, she followed the crowd into the Denver terminal.

This couldn't be worse than the loneliness and grief she'd been stuck in these past months. Or the foster homes that had barely acknowledged her existence. Right? In the baggage claim area, she kept her head down as she waited for her suitcases, earbuds firmly in place. The longer she went without making eye contact with anyone, the longer she could pretend she was a famous chef hiding from the paparazzi, on a dream vacation with a handsome—

"Casey?"

She looked up at the female voice, encountering smiling blue eyes over a sign that read "Casey Younghans!" She nodded at the young woman.

"You look just like the photo your brother sent. I'm Mikayla, part of the Outlook staff. I'm glad you're here to spend the holiday with us."

Casey turned back to the baggage carousel. This girl was pretty and not that old, and short and blonde like her. Not too scary. She turned the volume down but left her earbuds in place.

Once the overloaded suitcases appeared, they headed out of the terminal. The other girl didn't make conversation, just smiled reassuringly as she directed Casey through the parking ramp. Stopping behind an old brown jeep, she hoisted Casey's heavy suitcases into the back like they were pillows.

Denver was a mass of traffic, Christmas lights, and people. Casey stared out the window to avoid conversation.

"Are you a coffee drinker?"

Startled, Casey looked at Mikayla and shook her head, nose wrinkled. "Cocoa," she rasped.

Mikayla's face brightened. "Me too! Well, I do like coffee but I looove cocoa. Let's get some before we head up to camp. There's a super cute coffee shop just over here I always stop by when I come into the city. It's the first place I visited when I got to Denver last summer."

She wasn't from here? The jeep zipped into a parking lot and slid into the only open spot, right by the back door.

Inside, Casey drew a deep breath, tugging out the earbuds. She might not like the taste of coffee but there was something warm and inviting about coffee shops. She'd usually done her homework after school at the shop near the apartment she shared with Gigi. When she was going to school. Now she did it all online. When she had the energy.

There was a boisterous welcome from the baristas as she followed Mikayla toward the counter. "MinnieSOHtah Mikayla!" Laughter, hugs, excited chatter.

Casey watched from the side. What would it be like to have friends like that? To have people who were happy to see her? To be recognized and welcomed?

"And this is my new friend, Casey." Mikayla gestured her closer. "She'll be spending Christmas at Outlook while her brother is away in the military."

The women greeted her with hugs, introducing themselves and thanking her for her brother's service. Resisting the urge to stuff her earbuds back in, she smiled awkwardly and nodded. Jeff, the hero, the wonder military man. She looked away and rolled her eyes. Jeff, the rotten brother.

"Okay, we'd better order and get going," Mikayla said. "I want to be up at camp before dark so Casey can get settled."

Ten minutes later they were on their way. Casey savored the flavorful cocoa and ate every crumb of the chocolate chip muffin. Mikayla pointed out areas of interest as they wound up the mountain toward Winter Park. They paused at the

Continental Divide so she could take Casey's picture by the sign "to send to her friends." That would be nice, if she had any. Eight foster homes in the last nine years had kept that from happening. Maybe if she'd had more than a year with Gigi, things would've been different.

As they passed a ski resort, Mikayla asked if she skied. She shook her head. Not a lot of mountains in Iowa. She didn't have money for it anyway.

"Me either. I'm afraid of heights."

"But you live in the mountains," she managed to say loud enough to be heard.

"With my feet planted firmly on the ground," came the cheerful response. "Not interested in flying down a steep hill on little wooden sticks. Do you snowshoe?"

Another no.

"Now *that* is fun. And not scary. We can give it a try if you'd like. It's not hard to do. There's something magical about walking through the woods in the quiet of winter." She smiled to herself. "Peaceful and far from the crowds. Not," she added, glancing at Casey, "that there are crowds at camp right now."

Casey shrugged. Too bad. She was good at getting lost in crowds. The more people, the less attention focused on her.

Finally, the jeep rattled down a long driveway and under a sign that read Outlook Adventure Camp then stopped beside a lodge. In the center of the circle drive stood a tall carved statue of a smiling man pointing upwards. Casey climbed out of the jeep and moved around the car toward the figure, studying the amazing detail carved into the wood. A hatchet, a stringer of fish, sunglasses propped on a head of curls.

Mikayla stood next to her, squinting up at the guy with an odd frown. "This is Walter Smith, the founder of the camp. I never met him, but I hear he was quite the character. A professional skier before he started the camp." She turned toward Casey and motioned with her head. "Let's get you settled. I'll give you a tour of the camp later."

Casey pulled one of the suitcases and the carry-on behind Mikayla who carried the other suitcase. Instead of going into the single-story log lodge, they headed to a nearby two-story building.

"The Bunkhouse," Mikayla explained, "is housing for staff only. They come from all around the country for the whole summer, and sometimes the whole year, so this is their home away from home. During the summer, campers stay in tents onsite or up on the mountain. During the winter, we just offer day camps."

There were two levels of bedrooms, along with a laundry, kitchen, and main living space. Casey was surprised to find she had her own room, next to Mikayla's on the upper level. Small and clean—a single bed, a closet, a dresser and desk, and a sink in the corner. Bathrooms with showers were communal, girls' on this level and boys' on the lower level.

With the luggage deposited in Casey's room, Mikayla paused in the doorway. "I'm glad you're here, Casey. I know we're strangers to you, but I hope you'll soon feel part of the family. There are no campers these next couple of weeks, so feel free to explore, ask questions, sleep, eat. Whatever you feel like. And since there's just a handful of staff onsite right now, we eat meals here in the bunkhouse kitchen. A little homier. I hope you'll join us.

"Now, you get unpacked and take a snooze. I'll be over in the lodge. My phone number is on that paper on the desk. Holler if you need anything. Welcome to Outlook!"

Earbuds back in, Casey took her time unpacking, pausing often to look out at the towering pine trees and snow-covered grounds. There was a strange peacefulness here, a quiet that whispered to her, inviting her to release the breath she didn't know she'd been holding.

Climbing under a down comforter, she pulled her beloved, battered notebook and ever-present sketch pad from her backpack. She'd journal first, and then, if she could stay awake, there were images she wanted to sketch before she forgot.

Entry #241 – Still 49 days to freedom

Day 1 of Mountain Captivity

So far this place doesn't look like a commune. Not that I know what that looks like. LOL The 1 person I've met seems normal. We had AMAZING cocoa in Denver. I've said it a bazillion times but someday I wanna run a coffee shop. Or maybe just serve cocoa. Is there such a thing? Maybe a cocoa beverage bus! It's pretty cool out my window. Wish we had mountains in Iowa. Gotta take lots of pics. Man, I need Zzzzs. Gonna take a nap. Will sketch later. If you don't hear from me by tomorrow, this place IS a commune and they locked me up somewhere. Come find me! LOL. And then blame Jeff.
:(

CHAPTER TWO

For her first full day of "mountain captivity," Casey explored the quiet bunkhouse, earbuds in place. Even when she didn't have music playing, it kept her from having to talk to anyone. She felt exposed without them.

The kitchen was super well-stocked. Gigi could never have afforded this much food. A note invited her to eat whatever she wanted. Definitely would, since it was probably all she'd have to do for two weeks.

"More food in the lodge," the note concluded in what had to be Mikayla's handwriting. The heart was a giveaway. She fixed herself several small meals through the day and ate them in her room where she journaled and doodled in the notebook, combining words and drawings of this first day. And although she'd kept to herself, the loneliness that had silenced her life since Gigi's funeral was a little less suffocating.

Entry #242 – STILL 49 days to freedom
End of Day 1 of Mountain Captivity
Made it thru the first day alive. I like having my own room, but

it'd be way creepy if Mikayla's wasn't next to mine. Brenda's is at the end of the hall. Not thinkin I could live in this little room 4ever but 2 weeks is ok.

Didn't feel like eating with everyone tonight. Maybe tomorrow. Or not. At least there aren't any rules that I know of. But plenty of food!! I could get used to that! LOL Jeff hasn't called to check up on me. Like usual. Just assumes I followed his orders. Which I did becuz I'm a loser with no life. Getting closer to freedom is sorta freaking me out. I don't wanna be homeless. Maybe I should join the army just to bug Jeff. HA! But at least I'd have a place to sleep and food every day. I could open my coffee shop when I get out.

Girl, what are you even saying?? You are NOT going military. No way could u shoot someone. I wonder if Jeff has. Ewww. That'd be awful.

Anyway, goin to bed. I might do some exploring outside tomorrow. Or just stay in my room, eat all day and get fat. LOLOL

Day Two of Mountain Captivity, she pulled on boots and her jacket to explore the grounds. For some weird reason she was drawn to the statue. Standing beside it, she studied the details. The joy on the man's face pinged her aching heart. Almost childlike in his delight, she could hear his laughter. She folded her arms against the ache that grew. Could she ever be happy like that? Did she even know how?

"Amazingly real, don't you think?"

She started at the man's voice and turned, tugging her earbuds out. He was looking up at the statue, hands on his hips, dark curls showing under his knit cap.

"Sometimes I come out here to talk to him," he added, then smiled at her. "Sorry I missed you yesterday. I'm Dawson. The camp director. Walt here was my boss. And my best friend."

"He died?" Casey rasped.

He looked back at the statue, smile gone. "Ten months ago.

Feels like yesterday. And then it feels like ten years. Grief is a strange, unpredictable thing."

She wasn't crazy for feeling that way? One minute she missed Gigi so much she was sure her heart was literally breaking, then ten minutes later she'd start humming a song.

"I wasn't sure I'd ever feel normal again," he said. "What I've learned is that we all grieve in different ways, and we need to take as long as necessary to get back on our feet. There's no right or wrong way. It just is what it is."

She turned those simple words over in her mind. *It just is what it is.*

"So." The muffled clap of his gloved hands pulled her attention back. "I'm heading into the lodge to find Mikayla. Want to join me? I'm hoping she's whipping up some of her world-famous hot chocolate."

Casey turned a doubtful lift of her brow to him, and he laughed.

"Okay, maybe just camp-famous." They started toward the wide lodge steps. "I was strictly a coffee guy until she made me try it. Now I'm sold. *After* I have coffee, of course." He pulled the door open, then followed her in. "Yup, I can smell it already. Let's go check the kitchen. It's through the swinging doors over there."

The heavenly aroma of chocolate drew them around long tables, where campers probably ate, and through the doors.

Mikayla looked up from where she stood at the large stainless island, pouring steaming chocolate into mugs. Her bright smile warmed Casey's heart. "Good morning, you two lovely people. You're just in time for cocoa and cookies."

Something Gigi had done on occasion.

Dawson kissed Mikayla's cheek then put the mugs on a nearby platter. "The perfect mid-morning treat."

Casey blinked. Did he kiss all his staff? Kinda gross to think your boss would kiss you every day.

"Nice fire you've got going out there, by the way," he told Mikayla.

"Thanks. The forecast says snow later today so I thought it would be good to get the fire going early. Casey, will you please grab the bowl of whipped cream from the fridge behind you? Oh, and three spoons from that middle drawer over there? Thanks, hon."

In the main room, Mikayla and Dawson settled next to each other on one of the worn leather couches, Casey on the adjacent one. Warmed by the fire, they munched sugar cookies and sipped cocoa smothered with amazingly fresh whipped cream and chocolate sprinkles. Dawson was right; this cocoa was easily as good as the coffee shop's in Denver.

Casey looked around the spacious room. Worn wood plank floors. Real log walls. The stone fireplace rose to the rafters, a huge wood mantel stretching across it. Like they chopped down a tree and stuck half of it there. Sorta cool. More couches and chairs filled the room in groupings that invited hanging out.

Mikayla encouraged Dawson to share the story behind Outlook which he seemed happy to do. He talked about how the statue guy, Walt, had come to Winter Park after a series of bad decisions that included jail time. He'd needed a place to work on some major character flaws. Creating the camp had been the start of his relationship with Jesus, which changed everything—for him, and for the thousands of kids that would eventually visit. Especially for Dawson.

"And me," Mikayla added, sharing a smiling glance with him.

"God is good," he answered, then got to his feet. "And on that note, I have an online meeting in ten minutes, so I'd better get ready. Leave the dishes and I'll clean up later," he told Mikayla. "Thanks for the treat, sweetheart."

Casey nodded to herself. Definitely something more than a boss/employee thing.

Mikayla waved him off and turned her attention to Casey. "I love hearing him tell the Outlook story. Especially about how coming here changed *him*, inside and out. We'll have to get him to share his own story later."

Casey nodded. She'd been disappointed when he stopped. This place stood on a lot of pain, sweat and tears. Could she build something out of her own bad decisions and character flaws? Nothing this amazing, of course. But maybe a decent life.

"Outlook changed me and my life as well," Mikayla mused. "I came here angry at God and my family and the world in general. But this place has a way of welcoming you in, accepting you, and breaking down the walls that have kept you locked in your own private jail. All without you knowing it's happening."

Casey turned her gaze to the fire. There was no key for her private jail. No door even. And this pretty girl with what appeared to be a cute boyfriend, living in this amazing place, couldn't have a story that came close to hers. God had been nowhere in her life as she bounced around in foster care year after year. She'd finally gotten comfortable at Gigi's and then He'd—

The front door opened, and Mikayla straightened. "They're back! I've been dying for you to meet Lula."

A black and white blur raced toward them and launched from several feet away, landing on Mikayla and licking her face as its feathery tail wagged furiously. A young woman with dark braids hanging over her shoulders plopped down on Casey's couch. "You must be Casey. I'm Brenda, part of the staff here. Glad you're joining us for Christmas. The more the merrier."

She nodded. They sure acted happy to have her there. So had all those foster parents.

"And this little creature is Lula," Mikayla said. "Lu, go over and welcome our guest, please." As the dog leaped from Mikayla's lap onto Casey's, she added, "She and Brenda were in Denver visiting a couple of rehab centers."

"And she was the star of the show, as usual," Brenda said. "Well, I've got work to catch up on so it's into the office for me. Good to meet you, Casey. Hopefully we can chat over lunch today."

Casey ran her hand over Lula's silky coat, marveling at the tiny black nose and eyes framed by large, feathery ears. Cutest. Thing. Ever. Gigi's big black labs had been her only friends, but after Gigi died, they'd been given to neighbors. Something else ripped from her life after not being asked what *she* wanted.

Snuggling Lula close, she released a long breath. Good thing she wouldn't be here long enough to get attached to this adorable little thing. That would be super easy to do.

"Lula brought me so much comfort last summer when I was at my lowest," Mikayla said. "My life had pretty much imploded, and I wasn't sure what to do or where to go. Lula became my unexpected travel buddy, the one being I could talk to honestly without worrying about being judged."

She smiled affectionately at the dog. "God used her to bring me back to life, to a place where I could start to heal and move forward. And that was when I wanted nothing to do with God. I blamed Him for everything that had happened." Looking around the room, she shook her head. "This place does something to people."

"Kayla?" Dawson's voice came from behind them. "Can you get on this call with me? I need your opinion."

"Sure." She grinned at Casey. "Always happy to share my opinion. There's more cocoa on the stove in the kitchen. And there are some great books over there on the bookshelf. Make yourself at home, hon."

As Mikayla disappeared into the corner office, Casey relaxed against the couch, still cradling Lula. These people were awfully chatty, but at least they were pleasant. Like Gigi. Good thing they didn't seem to care if she talked. She could barely make enough sound to be heard most of the time. The doctor had said maybe her bruised voice box would heal. Or maybe not. Not talking was just easier.

Lula looked up and licked her chin. Casey smiled, sticking her earbuds back in. But maybe she could practice by talking to this little friend.

At the end of a busy day of exploring, having dinner with the staff, and taking a moonlit walk with Brenda, Casey snuggled into bed and pulled her notebook close.

Entry #243 – 48 days to freedom

Day 2 of Mountain Captivity

Had another dream about Gigi and the accident last night. My sheets were all tangled when I woke up. Took a looong time to go back to sleep. HATE those dreams.

In happy news—I'm in love! With LULA!! Cutest thing ever. Mikayla let her hang with me most of the day. She's so easy to cuddle. Can't get enough. I told her a little about Gigi. She's a good listener. And she agreed with me that Jeff is a rotten brother. It was worth coming here just for her. Wish I could take her home with me. But since I don't know where I'll live or if I'll have enough $$ for food, how could I take care of her? No way. She's so sweet. She deserves better than me. This is a good place for her. But how can I say goodbye to her? Makes me cry just thinking about it. ☹ I gotta spend as much time with her as I can and take a bunch of pics to remember her by. I wonder how fast she'll forget me. Now I'm really crying. This stinks.

CHAPTER THREE

Over the following days of mountain captivity, Casey relaxed into a habit of sketching in the morning and then mid-morning cocoa with Dawson, Mikayla, Lula, and Brenda in the lodge. Afternoons she explored the camp and surrounding trails, and then dinner in the Bunkhouse with whoever was around. Evenings were spent in her room journaling and listening to music. And talking to Lula. By the end of the week, she could actually make decent noise as she shared thoughts, fears, and feelings with her sweet companion.

A main topic of conversation with Lula was that ignoring Jeff's texts was both satisfying and guilt-inducing. Maybe this wasn't the worst place she could be, but he'd never even asked what she thought. She wasn't a baby, but he treated her like one. That original text still made her stomping mad. If he'd asked, she might even have said okay.

Christmas was next week, and she'd be alone. Well, with the camp people but no family. Since Jeff couldn't treat her like a grown-up, she basically had no family. There sure wouldn't be any celebrating. Her life was stupid.

Sitting on the front steps of the lodge after lunch, she

scribbled furiously in the notebook. Even poked a hole in the thick paper when she crossed out Jeff's name.

Entry #251 – 46 days to Freedom
Day 5 of Mountain Captivity
Freedom is coming. Inch by inch. Then what? I have no money, no place to live. Aging out is good. And not. What am I supposed to do? It's not like anyone has helped me get ready. Well, Gigi was starting to, but now... I'm scared. I wanna be free but I don't know what to do. I don't even know how to get a job. Loser. No wonder I don't have friends. Maybe these guys can help me get a job at that coffee shop in Denver. Right. With all my experience.

She stopped writing to wipe impatiently at her eyes. Like crying would help. If she acted like a baby, that's how everyone would treat her. She pulled in a sharp breath and sat up straight. When the lodge door opened behind her, she slapped the notebook closed.

"Hey, Casey." Mikayla settled next to her. "I'm walking to Vi's bakery in town. Whenever I'm sad, Vi is my go-to person." She laughed. "Actually, I think she's everyone's go-to person. Care to join me?"

Casey glanced sideways at her. What did she have to be sad about? Stuffing her earbuds in her jacket pocket and the notebook in her backpack, she shrugged. "Okay."

They headed toward town in a comfortable silence, snow crunching under their steps. Lula pranced ahead of them, her tiny feet making no sound and barely an imprint. Mikayla lifted her face to the sun and sighed. "I'm from Minnesota so I'm used to winter, but I've decided I like it a lot more out here in the mountains. Tons more snow but the temps aren't as extreme."

"Why are you sad?" Casey blurted.

Mikayla stopped abruptly, eyes wide, and Casey kicked herself. What a loser.

"Casey! Your voice!"

Casey blinked, a smile tugging at her mouth. "It's getting better," she acknowledged. "I'm practicing with Lula."

Mikayla gave her a quick hug, Lula dancing around them, front paws waving in the air. "That's wonderful!"

Casey swept her tiny friend into her arms and buried her nose in the silky fur. "I'm trying. With Lula's help."

"You sure are. I'm so excited for you." Mikayla reached over and ran her hand over Lula's head. "And you, sweet girl, are a great helper."

As they continued toward town, now just a few blocks ahead, Mikayla sighed. "Back to your question. I'm sad because this will be my first Christmas away from my family. Sounds silly at my age, but I've never been away from home during the holiday. My twin sister got married in September and will be with her hubby's family in North Carolina. Our older sister has to work; she's a pediatric surgeon in Boston. And my parents decided to go on a second honeymoon."

Two sisters sounded great, and a twin even more amazing. So much better than one brother who didn't care.

"Selfishly," Mikayla continued, "I was glad to hear you were coming. I was hoping you'd be fun, and it would be like having another sister. And that's just what happened. But I'm sad you aren't with your own family for Christmas."

Casey set the wiggling Lula down and shrugged. "Just the one brother and he's away."

"Do you live with anyone?"

Pain shot through her heart. She used to. "No."

Mikayla hooked her arm through Casey's and hugged gently. "Then I'm extra glad you're here with us. And speaking of here, this is the Wildflower Bakery and Café. Come on. I can't wait for you to experience Vi."

Experience was the right word for the bakery owner and her shop. Casey was sure she'd stepped into an alternate universe once they passed through the doorway. Amazing, mouth-watering smells, bright colors, walls filled with photographs and knick-knacks, and a larger-than-life woman who enveloped Casey in a hug she never wanted to leave.

"Well, now I have an Iowa darlin'," Vi said, hands on her broad hips, "*and* a Minnesota darlin'. You two sit right here at the counter and I'll get you some treats."

Mikayla leaned toward Casey as they settled onto the stools and whispered, "Prepare to be amazed. She's known all over Colorado for her treats."

Through the wide glass window behind the counter, Casey watched Vi bustle about the kitchen, sliding trays into a large oven and pulling others out, setting timers. Moments later she came through the swinging doors, a tray of assorted bars and cookies in hand.

"Here we go. A little of this and some of that," she said, setting the tray on the counter. "What would you like to drink?"

Glancing at the chalkboard menu pricing, Casey requested water. She would owe Mikayla for her share of the treats since she hadn't brought money. No need to add more cost.

"I've found a kindred cocoa lover," Mikayla said, "so could we please have two with extra whipped cream?"

Casey opened her mouth to decline, but Vi patted her hand and smiled. "Two cocoas for my Midwest girls comin' right up."

"Thanks, Vi." Mikayla turned toward Casey, blue eyes sparkling. "I love these sampler platters. So where should we start? Ooo, those brownies look fabulous. Looks like they have mint in them."

"Yum. And these Christmas cookies are darling." Casey

pointed to six decorated sugar cookies. "Makes me think of Gigi."

As they split each delicious treat, Mikayla asked about Gigi and then Jeff. Casey focused on making her answers loud enough to be heard in the crowded café. Gigi, in her late 60's, had taken Casey in just over a year ago. After so many foster homes, it was finally the right fit.

She licked minty chocolate from her fingers. There was so much more to say about Gigi but that would mean she had to explain how Gigi died. Couldn't do that yet.

"Jeff has been in the marines for…a lot of years. Maybe 10? Right after he aged out of foster care. Haven't seen him since before last Christmas." The mint flavor soured in her mouth. How could you both hate and miss someone? "He sent me here."

Mikayla bumped her shoulder against Casey's. "And I, for one, am glad he did. We're not all that bad, are we?"

Casey couldn't stop the smile that wavered when Mikayla blinked her blue eyes innocently. "Not *all* bad," she admitted.

"Yes! Okay, you pick the next treat."

Vi finished ringing up a customer and joined them. "So what's the verdict, girls?"

Casey gave a thumbs up, her mouth full and her throat tired from straining to be heard. Mikayla added two thumbs up and Vi smiled.

"That's what we want to hear. Or see." She leaned dimpled elbows on the counter. "Maybe I should hire the two of you to be the Wildflower's official taste testers."

Casey nodded quickly. "Yes, please," she rasped. It would be amazing to be part of this. Vi reminded her of Gigi. Sorta. Not as old but fun and accepting. Or maybe it was just how she acted with everyone.

"I sure could use an assistant," Vi said. "Business has been almost too good. I'm wearin' out with all the serving and baking and decorating."

"I want to have a coffee shop one day," Casey said.

"Nothing better," Vi said. "Hard work but worth it. If you're staying around a while, I'll hire you on the spot."

What? Casey's eyes burned as she blinked at the large woman. A real job?

"That will be something to talk to Jeff about," Mikayla said.

The joyful throbbing in her heart waned. Jeff. He'd say no just because he could. She straightened on the stool. But only for another month. Then she was free. Of him and the system and everything but the guilt she would always carry over Gigi. "I turn 18 soon. Then I won't have to ask him," she forced out loudly, then glanced around. Maybe too loudly.

"Darlin', you get things worked out and then come back here when you can." Vi's smile was warm. Genuine. "I'll hold a spot for you."

Biting her lip to keep the tears back, Casey nodded. If only that would be true.

CHAPTER FOUR

Entry #269 – 43 days to Freedom
Day Whatever of Mountain Life
I love it here. Can't believe I'm saying that. Don't tell Jeff. LOL.
People see me. Like really SEE me! They remember stuff I say, and
they ask questions and listen. It's. So. Weird. Feels like I've always
been here, and Mikayla has always been my sister and Dawson is
my REAL brother. And of course I have Lula. Well, not like I get to
keep her or anything, but she's my absolute BESTIE. And Vi is like
what a real mom is like. I've gotten to clean in the café and try some
new treats she was creating. And I even cleaned the bathroom.
Gross. But not too bad. Christmas is coming and Vi is decorating
cookies like crazy. I stink at that (she let me try!) but I luv watching,
and I keep the icing bags full. Gonna have a bonfire outside tonight.
Cool!

As her first week at Outlook drew to a close, Casey continued
journaling and sketching, even hung new drawings of Lula
and the lodge and the mountains on the walls of her room.
Only one more week here. She stuffed the thought and the

tape dispenser into the desk drawer and surveyed her room. It was starting to feel like home.

A knock at the door sent Lula flying off the bed, barking. Casey laughed. Like that teeny creature could actually save her from danger. "Come on in."

Brenda popped her head around the door. "Ready to get supper started?"

"Yup." Her second cooking lesson from Brenda. The first, spaghetti, had been sort of a disaster but no noodles tonight so it should go better.

Working side-by-side in the Bunkhouse kitchen, Brenda shared stories of camp life, raising dogs when she was growing up, and learning to downhill ski. Casey plopped her meatloaf into the loaf pan and grimaced at the meaty slime on her hands. "Yuck."

"Cooking can be pretty messy," Brenda agreed, "but the outcome is worth it." Their gazes met and they burst into laughter. "Okay, maybe not spaghetti the first time."

Sitting down an hour later with Brenda, Mikayla and Dawson, Casey enjoyed the triumph swelling in her chest. It looked great, from the crispy brown meatloaf to the biscuits, and the not-too-lumpy gravy over sorta-lumpy mashed potatoes.

Conversation followed its usual course of banter, new camp activity ideas, and this time compliments on Casey's meal. Then Mikayla encouraged Dawson to share the rest of his Outlook story.

Casey was surprised to hear of the difficulties he'd encountered growing up. While he'd grown up with a mom and a grandma, he'd still made one bad decision after another. Given the choice of coming to Outlook or going to jail, he'd finally, though reluctantly, made a wise decision. She realized she'd done the same.

Mikayla added her story onto his, sharing how her journey to find her biological father last summer had intersected with Dawson's decision to return to Outlook as the director after Walt's death. Her anger and hurt had driven her here, but it was Dawson's patience and God's relentless pursuit that finally led her to her forever home here in the mountains.

Casey looked from Dawson to Mikayla. Walt was Mikayla's actual dad? Statue Walt? That was crazy.

Mikayla chuckled. "That was one of my expressions when I first realized it. I didn't get to meet him, but I've learned a lot about him from these guys. There are plenty of stories."

Brenda chimed in with a brief story of having grown up in Winter Park watching Outlook become a place of peace, restoration, and love for both campers and staff. She'd been thrilled to learn they needed an office manager and had jumped in with both feet.

"No big a-ha moment for me," she concluded, "but they'll have to drag me kicking and screaming if they want me out of here."

As their laughter died down, Casey drew a deep breath. Her turn. "So, you all know when I got to Outlook, but there's a little more that came before it."

"We'd love to hear it," Mikayla said with an encouraging lift to her brow. Dawson and Brenda nodded.

"Okay. Well..." Where to start? "So my dad wasn't around after I was born. Not much before either, I guess. Spent most of his time in jail. And my mom... She tried to stay clean but that didn't go so well most of the time. By the time I was eight I was permanently in the system."

"Foster care?" Dawson asked.

"Yup. The system where everybody wants the money but not the kid." Except Gigi. "So in the past nine years, I've been in at least eight different homes."

Mikayla laid a warm hand on her arm. "I'm sorry, hon. That must have been awful."

"Yeah," Casey sighed. "Teaches you how to take care of yourself."

"Must have been pretty lonely," Brenda said, dark eyebrows tented.

Casey shrugged. "Most of the time. I learned to be okay on my own."

Dawson studied her across the table, arms folded. "You've learned lots of lessons you shouldn't have had to," he said. "The adults in your life failed you big time."

His understanding stung her eyes and she looked away. "Yeah. Including Jeff."

"But Gigi was different, right?" Mikayla asked.

The bittersweet ache she'd become accustomed to swept through her. "She was different. She'd had a lot of foster kids, I guess, and had pretty much stopped fostering before I came along. For some reason she decided to take me." A corner of her mouth lifted, then dropped and she closed her eyes. "It didn't turn out very good for her."

After a silence, she looked around at the sympathy and compassion on their faces. They wouldn't push her for more, although they'd shared the details of their difficult journeys. She sat up straight and pulled in a breath. It was time to share the whole story.

"It took a while for me to get comfortable, but she was super patient. We had fun doing stuff and just hanging out at home. She listened to me. Nobody ever did that. When I told her I wanted to own a coffee shop someday, she didn't even laugh. I think she believed I could do it.

"She was teaching me to drive. She was really patient because I wasn't very good at first." She smiled to herself at the memories of mistakes and laughter. "But she wouldn't give up and I finally got better. And then..."

Memories turned dark, those sounds she heard in her dreams as clear now as all those months ago. Heart pounding, she folded her arms across her chest. "It was raining that night. And sorta cold. We were driving home from a movie and she had me drive, although I didn't want to. She said...she said I needed to know how to drive in all kinds of weather."

The wipers were going full speed, tossing water across the windshield, mixing stoplights and brake lights and streetlights. Casey's fingers curled on her lap now as they had around the steering wheel, neck muscles knotted. She'd squinted into the darkness, Gigi's calm guidance barely registering. Water sprayed from the tires of the truck she followed.

Unable to draw a full breath, Casey looked at Mikayla through tears. "I was so scared. And then that truck, it stopped. Just stopped for no reason! But I couldn't because the road was slippery. I think I hit the brakes too hard. I didn't mean to. The car spun around, like slow motion, you know? And then...then we hit the truck. On Gigi's side."

Metal screeching, glass breaking, being tossed around in the car as they hit. The airbags didn't go off, and Casey slammed forward into the steering wheel. Gigi cried out and then was silent.

Hot tears rolled down her face. "I couldn't stop. I tried! It's my fault she's gone."

Mikayla's arms wrapped firmly around her as the initial tears turned into a torrent. She leaned into the embrace and sobbed, clinging to Mikayla to keep from drowning in the sorrow and guilt.

Just as in her nightmares, she saw Gigi's pale, bloodied face, the flashing lights when help arrived. And then the doctor's face as she shared the awful news about Gigi, holding Casey's hand between hers. When she mentioned the injury to

Casey's throat, it seemed fitting then that the last words Casey might ever speak had been calling out for Gigi.

The tears finally slowed, and Casey released her hold on Mikayla, accepting the dish towel Brenda held out. Struggling to catch her breath, she mopped her face and gave a shuddering sigh.

"Casey." Dawson sat beside her. "Would you mind if we prayed for you?"

She shrugged and nodded. It wouldn't change anything. As they gathered closer, she closed her eyes.

"God, we know you are the God of forgiveness and restoration. You've invited us, through your Son Jesus, to bring our pain, our sadness, and our shame right to your throne. So we bring our hurting friend, Casey, to you for healing. You know all that she's been through in her life, and you know the healing she needs now. Most of all, she needs your love and grace and mercy."

He prayed a bit more, followed by Mikayla, then Brenda. With their hands warm on her head, her shoulders, and her hands, Casey relaxed into the words, into the love that seemed to flow from them to her. And the pain in her heart lost its edge.

CHAPTER FIVE

Something had shifted since that dinner and revelation a few nights ago. She'd tried to journal about it but strangely had no words. She tried sketching but struggled to draw feelings she couldn't identify. So she walked the grounds and played with Lula, and took countless photos of everything—the amazing blue sky, snow on pine trees, Dawson standing by Walt's statue. And Vi's bakery, Mikayla and Brenda building snowpeople, and of course sweet Lula.

She'd caught on easily to using snowshoes and made short treks along the marked paths, always with a walkie talkie like the staff used. Thoughts of Gigi didn't bring tears now, only bittersweet sighs. Even her anger at Jeff seemed muted, more like the grief of losing yet another person from her life.

The early morning sun on Christmas Eve splashed across the sketch pad she was bent over. With little money for presents, she'd decided she'd give her camp friends something personal. The drawings for Vi, Brenda, Dawson, and Mikayla were done and wrapped. Now she worked on Jeff's. He wouldn't get it for a few months, but she wanted it done before leaving camp for...wherever she landed. There might not be privacy like this again for quite a while.

She turned up the music on her phone to drown out the questions and fears that hovered at the edge of every day. Where would she end up? How would she find a job? Nope. She'd deal with that on the plane home after New Year's. No way was it going to wreck the time she had left here. She should check the ticket to see exactly how much time she had left.

A rapid knock at the door made her jump and close the sketch pad. "Come in."

Mikayla's ever-present smile appeared as she opened the door. "Come on, slowpoke! We've got to get cooking if we want the feast ready by 6:00."

Casey glanced at the clock as she slid the sketch pad into the desk. Three hours had gone by? "Sorry! Didn't know it was so late. I'll meet you over there in five."

Through the afternoon she worked alongside Brenda, Dawson, and Mikayla in the lodge kitchen as each prepared their chosen, secret dish for the Christmas Eve dinner. Vi had shared her secret recipe for chocolate raspberry cheesecake with Casey after they created one together two days ago. Now she focused carefully on the instructions, praying it wouldn't be a total flop.

Just before six that evening, Casey stood in front of the mirror giving her hair a few last strokes of the brush. The reflection looked surreal, like she'd sketched a self-portrait. But that girl had color in her cheeks, life in her eyes. And she looked almost pretty in the sequined navy dress Gigi had bought her before the accident.

Lowering the hair brush she smiled tentatively at the girl who smiled back. She winked and got one in return. She cleared her throat and said "Hello" in an almost normal voice. The girl sounded even stronger somehow.

She rolled her eyes and tossed the brush on her bed. "You are so weird." Sliding into a red cardigan, she gathered the bags of carefully wrapped sketchings and left the room. Under a black sky glittering with stars, she hurried along the path to the lodge. Stepping into warmth, she stopped abruptly.

The lodge glowed, lights twinkled, Christmas music filled the air along with a mouth-watering aroma. Candles flickered along the mantel and in every window. Wrapped gifts filled the floor around the ten-foot tree. The long dining table had been transformed by greens and candles spread along the center of a red tablecloth, place settings and glassware sparkling in the light.

"Welcome to Christmas at Outlook." Dawson stood in front of her, transformed as well by a navy suit and white shirt. "You look amazing, Casey Younghans. May I escort you into the festivities?" He held out an arm and winked.

A smile filled Casey's heart and tickled her cheeks. Shifting the bags to her left hand, she shyly took his arm and let him lead her toward the people visiting near the fireplace, including several she didn't know.

Mikayla joined them, stunning in an off-white sweater and long black skirt, her blonde hair swept up and back. She reached for the gift bags. "I'll put these by the tree, then let's get you some cider. You look amazing, Casey! I love all the sequins."

Lula danced around their feet, the plaid bow on her collar adding to her adorableness. Casey remained silent even after a warm mug of apple cider was put in her hands. Brenda joined them, her tan and black suit highlighting brown curls Casey had never seen out of braids. She and Mikayla chatted about the evening schedule, what time the church service started, and giggled at Casey's wide-eyed silence.

"I've never seen anyone so quiet on Christmas Eve."

Mikayla waved a hand toward the decorations. "Didn't Brenda do a beautiful job?"

"You did all this?" Casey asked. "It's amazing. I feel like I'm in a whole different place."

"Thanks. It does feel completely different from our everyday lodge," Brenda said, nodding. "I love decorating. Oh, there's the alarm on my phone. Time to start getting the food out."

She headed toward the kitchen, but Casey stopped Mikayla before following. "Who are the extra people here?"

"Oh! I suppose that surprised you. The couple over there," she gestured toward an older couple chatting with Dawson, "are from church. They're usually in Arizona for the winter but Bob is having surgery in a few days, so they stayed home with no family around. And that's Shelly, our church secretary."

She took Casey's arm and started toward the kitchen. "I guess Dawson has always invited anyone who would be alone on Christmas Eve. We were going to visit his mom and grandma but had to put it off because his mom's been sick, so here we all are." She gave Casey a happy squeeze and pushed through the swinging doors. "You're one of us now, hon."

Her words echoed in Casey's heart as she helped set food out on the table. *One of us.* She'd never been part of anything, any group. *You're one of us now.* Leaving in a week was going to hurt a lot more than she'd expected.

Once everyone was settled around the table and introductions were made, Casey asked about the empty place setting to her right.

"We always leave a chair open to welcome unexpected guests," Dawson said. "And to remind us that we always have room for Jesus at our table."

She nodded in response although the part about Jesus was sort of confusing. Then everyone joined hands as Dawson welcomed them to the Outlook Christmas Feast and said a blessing over the meal.

Bowls and platters were passed, exclamations made over delicious smells and unexpected items. Brenda's crescent rolls melted in Casey's mouth. Dawson's roast was better than anything she'd tasted before. Both of Mikayla's salads were amazing. And then there was cranberries, jello, something with green beans and those crumbly onions that Gigi loved, corn, squash, and a fruit platter.

Casey looked at her full plate and then at Mikayla's. "I've never seen so much food in my life. There's no way I can eat all of this."

Mikayla laughed, nodding. "I bet you'll surprise yourself. Doesn't it all look amazing?"

Chatter, laughter, and the clink of silverware filled the room. Casey ate, watched, listened to the varied conversations, and ate more. She needed to soak this moment into her heart, burn it into her memory for comfort in the coming lonely months.

A knock at the door brought conversations to a halt. Dawson exchanged a glance with Mikayla before excusing himself to welcome another guest to their feast. Casey took a second roll as the basket passed and slathered it with Brenda's homemade butter. Lifting it to her mouth, she glanced toward Dawson and his guest and stared.

Her brother approached wearing a Santa hat on his short hair, military duffel bag in one hand and a box filled with gifts under his arm. His cocky, lopsided grin was familiar but the uncertainty in his eyes was new.

Setting the roll back on her plate, Casey stood slowly, legs shaking, heart pounding. He'd said he couldn't come home. He'd said he didn't have any leave. He'd said...

Stopping in front of her, Jeff dropped the duffel at his feet and let Dawson silently take the box of gifts. "Hey, kid."

She put her hands on her hips, the anger that had muted rushing back like a tidal wave. "What are you doing here?"

"Right now, I'm looking at my little sister who isn't so little anymore. You look...great. Grown up."

"Yeah. Surprise."

He nodded. "I didn't want to believe it, so I had to come see for myself." Uncertainty darkened his eyes. "Forgive me?"

"For?"

"Not believing you. Not being with you when Gigi died. And mainly for not letting you know I love you." A corner of his mouth lifted. "Even when you give me attitude."

In the silence, it seemed everyone around the table held their breath.

Forgive him for abandoning her? For ordering her around like she was a mindless child? For lying to her? Gigi would prod her to say yes, but Gigi hadn't spent her childhood alone, forgotten by the only family she had. Countless nights crying herself to sleep, wondering what was wrong with her that no one cared about her.

And now he showed up like some bigshot with presents and a stupid Santa hat, expecting everything to be okay. He had a place to go back to after his short visit. She had nothing.

She bit hard on her lower lip, willing the tears back. She wasn't a kid anymore asking Santa to bring her brother home. She understood how it worked now. He dropped in and out of her life when it suited him, not her. She couldn't do it anymore. *Wouldn't* do it anymore.

"So you finally decide to show up wearing a stupid hat and I'm supposed to feel honored by your presence and say all's forgiven? All these years, and you want me to pretend I didn't mind being ignored? That being alone was no big deal? Forget it. Forget *you*."

She dashed toward the kitchen and pushed through the swinging doors, crossed the room and went out the back door. Moments later she locked her door in the bunkhouse and threw herself across the bed, sobbing into the crook of her arm.

Why did he have to show up now and ruin Christmas? Why show up at all? Like bringing a bunch of presents made everything okay. She wasn't ten and content to get a few toys. But he wouldn't know that because he'd never bothered to spend time with her. He didn't get to make all the rules anymore, deciding when to come home, expecting her to be happy to see him.

When the tears slowed, she rolled to her back and stared up at the ceiling, pressing a hand over the decades-old ache in her heart. No more. She was done letting him hurt her. She'd just figure out life on her own. A light knock at the door, followed by the familiar sound of Lula's scratching, made her wipe her face and climb off the bed.

"It's just me and Lula, hon." Mikayla's voice was muffled.

Casey opened the door without meeting her gaze and went back to sit on the edge of her bed. Lula was on her lap in an instant, ears at high alert, black eyes watching. Casey gave her a gentle hug and then set her aside as Mikayla closed the door and sat in the desk chair.

"I'm sorry if I wrecked the dinner," Casey said finally.

"You didn't. Casey, that was a really brave and honest reaction to what I'm sure was quite a shock."

Casey's head came up. "It was?"

"You didn't know he was coming, and it sounds like you haven't seen him in a while?"

"Since before last Christmas."

"Wow. So to be faced with not only seeing him for the first time in a long time, but then expected to play nice in front of complete strangers, you reacted far better than I would have."

"I'm not even sure what I said," Casey admitted. "I was so shocked. Did you know he was coming?"

"I heard about it last night. And I told Dawson I didn't think it would be a good idea to spring it on you, but...guys." She rolled her eyes. "I guess when Jeff first came to Outlook years ago, it was Dawson's first year on staff, and they hit it off. They've stayed in touch all these years—same sense of humor, same faith, same—"

"Wait. Faith?" No way. "Jeff never talks about God. And he swears sometimes." They rarely talked for more than ten minutes, but he could have at least said something about having faith. Whatever that meant. She massaged her temples. This was so confusing.

"From what Dawson has said, it's been a slow progression but now it sounds like Jeff talks about it when he's deployed, and on base. I guess he's even given a few sermons."

Casey stared at her. "Are we still talking about my brother?"

Mikayla smiled. "Maybe you can ask him about it sometime. This is just my guess, but I don't think Jeff has a clue how to be a big brother. Dawson said he enlisted right out of high school, right? About your age now. He had to do his maturing in the military, which hardly encourages relationship-building. And long-distance relationships take a lot of intentional focus and energy. Especially for guys."

She settled next to Casey on the bed and faced her. "Hon, I honestly don't think he thought through how you'd react to seeing him after so long."

"Well, he got a rude awakening."

"I'm sure he's trying to figure out how to fix this. Maybe starting fresh would be a good idea. Not rushing right into forgiveness but taking time to get to know each other, build a relationship as adults, not kids."

Casey folded her arms, eyes burning. "What if it's too late?"

"It's never too late to start over, Casey, but it will take

work. And you might have to be the one teaching him how to be the big brother. Or at least your equal."

She frowned. Equals. He'd never go for it. But if that were the only option he had in order to have a relationship with her... She nodded slowly. "I'd be willing to try as equals." She was tired of being angry, and pitiful, and lonely.

"Trying is good. God will help you," Mikayla assured her, getting to her feet. "Ask Him for the right words and *lots* of patience. Thank goodness it's an unending supply. I'm going to head back to the lodge. We'll be going to the 11:00 church service tonight. Want to join us?"

"Would it be bad if I said no?"

"Not at all. We'll leave about twenty to 11, so meet us at the lodge before then if you change your mind. Otherwise, we'll see you in the morning to open gifts by the tree?"

"Tomorrow, for sure. Tonight, I just need to think. And pray. And sleep."

"Sounds good." Mikayla scooped Lula from where she'd been snuggled next to Casey, then paused at the door. "I'll pray for a restful sleep for you, and for God to provide whatever you need going forward with Jeff. Good night, hon."

When she left, Casey changed into her sleep shirt and shorts, and climbed under the comforter. There was a lot to think about. Where to even start?

CHAPTER SIX

Climbing the wide porch steps of the lodge, Casey paused to draw a breath of crisp morning air before pulling the door open. While it had taken hours to fall asleep, she'd woken rested and weirdly calm. Maybe that praying thing actually worked.

"There she is!" Brenda crossed the room wearing a wide grin and a sparkly green sweater, and hugged Casey. "Merry Christmas."

"Merry Christmas." She returned the hug, then looked past her. Mikayla, Dawson, and Jeff stood by the table.

"Come on." Brenda kept an arm around her shoulder. "You've gotta try Dawson's bacon and eggs."

Mikayla and Dawson greeted her with cheerful hugs, then stepped aside to let Jeff approach.

"Merry Christmas, Casey." Towering over her, in a regular flannel shirt and jeans, he didn't look like her marine brother. The cocky grin was gone. "I'm sorry for just showing up like that last night. That wasn't fair to you."

She blinked several times. "No, it wasn't."

He folded and unfolded his arms. "So, I was thinking... Maybe we could start over?"

"The visit or our relationship?" She glanced at Mikayla who was setting food on the table with Dawson. She'd talked to him too?

A smile flickered across his face. "Good question. You really have grown up. I'd say both."

Start fresh as adults. Maybe she could try looking at him as just her brother, not a big scary marine who dropped in and out of her life. Maybe live her life without counting on him. Although that still sounded lonely. She was tired of being lonely.

She lifted her shoulders. "We could try."

Jeff held out his arms and she went into his hug, pressing against his solid frame. She hadn't known how much she needed a hug. From him.

When he sniffed, she leaned back, eyebrows lifted. "Wait. Marines cry?"

He laughed, wiping his eyes on his sleeve. "Only over their kid sister. Merry Christmas, Case."

"Merry Christmas, old man."

Once they'd enjoyed the breakfast pastries Vi had sent over, and Dawson's camp-famous bacon and eggs, Mikayla brought out Casey's cheesecake.

"You didn't eat it last night?" It looked good. Like really good.

"Nope," Mikayla said, placing it before her. "This is yours."

The oohs and aahs made her laugh, as did the shock on her brother's face.

"*You* made this?" he asked.

"With no help from anyone," Mikayla replied firmly. "This is just the start of an illustrious career as a coffee shop owner and budding baker."

Mikayla's pronouncement sent Casey's heart singing. Even Jeff's raised eyebrow couldn't squelch it.

He took his first bite and closed his eyes, a smile growing. "Okay. I stand corrected. And I'll be your first investor." He looked at Casey with a proud grin. "This is like store-quality good."

She huffed. "Better than that, I hope."

"Okay, restaurant-quality good. Man, you are full of surprises."

Casey smiled and silently thanked Vi.

Gift opening by the fire was filled with laughter, hugs, and more than a few tears. Casey's drawings were widely praised after stunned silence. Dawson teared up over the sketch of him standing at Walt's statue. Mikayla hugged the likeness of her and Lula. And Brenda was speechless at seeing herself looking at the fire, coffee mug in hand. Casey assured Jeff his gift would be ready in another day or so.

Jeff had brought gifts for everyone. Candles, scarves, intricate figurines. A hand-carved knife for Dawson included a funny story about getting it through airport security. Casey opened gift after gift from Jeff—a new sketch book and pencils, a camera, a cashmere sweater, gorgeous hairclips that sparkled in the firelight. He'd obviously put thought into them. Maybe there was hope for them after all.

Then Mikayla brought out a large, wrapped box, the colorful ribbons on top dancing as she approached. She set it at Casey's feet, excitement sparkling in her eyes. "This is from all of us—me, Dawson, Brenda, and Jeff. And Vi too. We're so glad you decided to come to Outlook."

"Me too. And not just for the gifts," she added with a giggle, ripping off the wrapping paper. Digging into the shredded crinkle paper, she pulled out a Wildflower Café apron and a floppy chef's hat that made her laugh. New earbuds. A pair of bright blue snowshoes. A handmade candle smelling of pine, campfire, and sunshine. At the bottom was an envelope. The Christmas card, made by Brenda, was signed by everyone. Casey unfolded the paper tucked inside and started to read.

"Wait...what?" She looked from Mikayla to Jeff, heart pounding against her ribs. "Is this real?"

"Yup. You're officially out of foster care," he told her with a firm nod. "I have all the paperwork."

Tears burned at the rush of relief. "But..."

"No reason to wait another month," he said. "You're free as a bird. But now you have to adult like the rest of us."

The others laughed. Casey had no words.

"We heard you have to vacate Gigi's apartment," Mikayla said, "so we really want you to stay on here. With us. You can finish your high school work here. Please?"

"Stay here?" This had to be a dream. Mikayla's warm hand squeezing hers made it very real. "Like live here?"

"Yes! You're one of us, hon."

Casey's new favorite phrase. And it would be her mantra going forward.

"But," Dawson added, his dark eyes sparkling above his mock frown, "this isn't a free ride. Everyone here pulls their weight, so you'll need to find a job, at least part-time."

Casey nodded. She could find a job. Right?

"I need an assistant," Brenda said. "Not terribly glamorous work but Outlook keeps expanding, and I'm having a hard time keeping up with phone calls, paperwork, grant applications. You know—office work."

Work with Brenda? Cool! She didn't know anything about office work, but she could learn. Hopefully.

"That would only be part-time," Mikayla clarified, then added, "because the rest of the time you'll be an apprentice at the Wildflower Café. The apron and chef's hat aren't just for fun. It's your new uniform."

What? Casey dropped her face into her hands, unable to control the tears. This couldn't be real. It was everything she'd dreamed of, prayed for through dark, silent nights alone. Freedom. A place to live. A real job. Friends.

"Hey." Jeff's arm came around her. "This is supposed to be good news."

She nodded, face still buried.

He chuckled. "I'll take this as a yes?"

She nodded again and sat up, mopping her face with the tissue Mikayla offered. "I c-can't b-believe it," she hiccupped. "Is t-this real?"

"Oh, it's real," Brenda assured her with a grin and added, "I've got a ton of stuff piling up I need help with. You start in two days."

"I need a homebase when I get leave," Jeff said, "so I told Dawson I'd do whatever heavy lifting he needs when I'm here."

"But you don't come home for leave," Casey reminded him. That truth stung.

He sighed. "I figured it was hard on you when I came and went. It sure was hard on me. So I thought staying away was better. I was wrong," he admitted, "about that and so many other things. Think you can get used to seeing me more often, kid?"

She leaned her head against his shoulder. "Okay, I guess."

"Gee, thanks."

Casey stood and hugged each of them several times, repeatedly asking if it were true, and if Vi was really okay with it. Their laughing assurances overwhelmed her heart that only weeks ago had been empty.

With her mug refilled, she wandered to the fireplace,

studying the wooden manger scene on the mantle. Gigi told her the Baby Jesus had come to set everyone free, but Casey had figured it didn't include her. God had never seemed real or remotely interested in her messy life.

She'd been sure her life would remain dark and lonely, as it had always been. And though she'd whispered prayers for something, anything to change, she'd never truly believed it would happen. Now she knew differently. She heard God's whispered response, His promise that there was indeed a life waiting to be lived. *Her* life.

She'd come to the mountains reluctantly, protesting every step, barely able to speak. She would never have believed this was where her life would truly start. Now she couldn't wait to step into the future and live life out loud. She'd hold this whispered miracle close to her heart forever.

With a gentle finger, she touched the tiny baby figurine. She wasn't a loser, unloved, and abandoned. Jesus had indeed come for her as well.

Entry #352 – Freedom!

Livin' my new Mountain Life

I'm free! F.R.E.E!!!! In so many ways. Free of foster care. Free of beating myself up (well, I'm trying). Free of being mad at Jeff. And I'm learning about freedom with Jesus. That's gonna take forever to understand. LOL! I still can't believe this is my life. MY LIFE! I have 2 jobs! I have friends. Jeff is already planning his leave to come back here in July. I wonder what summer is like in the mountains?? Winter is SO cool! Dawson, Mikayla, Brenda and I did some winter camping. WAY cold but glad I tried it. I've tried so

many new things. Never thought I was brave but look out world!
I'm a warrior! Haha!

So thankful for what God has done in my life. So glad for miracles. So glad for – oops, there's the lunch bell. So glad for lunch! Ha. I wonder what tomorrow will bring. Can't. Wait.

The End

A NOTE FROM THE AUTHOR

Dearest Reader,

Thank you for reading *Whispered Miracle*. I've been away from writing for a few years, as I care for my husband with dementia, so to write Casey's story was very exciting for me. As He did for Casey, God has provided everything I need as we make this dementia journey. He is good, all the time! My prayer now is to write book 2 in the *My Father's House series*, *When Valleys Mourn*, within the year. I know Lindy Gordon Spencer's journey and I'm excited to finally share it with you!

Praying you experience God's love, mercy, and provision every day.

Until we meet again on the page,

Stacy

ACKNOWLEDGMENTS

This simple story wouldn't have happened without the brainstorming, encouragement, and love of my Mosaic sisters-in-Christ: Angela Reed Meyer, Brenda Bryant Anderson, Camry Crist, Candace West Posey, Chautona Havig, Deb Elkink, Eleanor Bertin, Elizabeth Bråten, Johnnie Alexander, Lorna Seilstad, and Sara Davison. All gifted, award-winning writers in their own right, but who are also focused on furthering the Kingdom in countless ways (including pushing/dragging me along!).

I'm also beyond grateful for those who have allowed me space (mentally and physically) to focus on life outside of dementia; who have encouraged me, made me laugh, slapped me upside the head on occasion, and prayed with and for me.

And as always, thank you, Sweet Jesus, for allowing me to serve you and the Kingdom in this way.

ABOUT STACY MONSON

STACY MONSON is the award-winning author of The Chain of Lakes series, including *Shattered Image, Dance of Grace,* and *The Color of Truth,* and also *Open Circle.* Her stories reveal an extraordinary God at work in ordinary life. Residing just outside the Twin Cities, she is the wife of a recently retired physical education teacher, mom to two amazing kids and two wonderful in-law kids, and a very proud grandma of 6 (and counting) grands.

Please visit Stacy's website, www.stacymonson.com, to learn more about her books and to subscribe to her newsletter. Find Stacy on Amazon, BookBub, Goodreads, and Facebook.

TITLES BY STACY MONSON

THE MOSAIC COLLECTION: NOVELS
When Mountains Sing

THE MOSAIC COLLECTION: ANTHOLOGY STORIES
"Mountaintop Christmas"
(*Hope is Born: A Mosaic Christmas Anthology*)
"A Summer of Reckoning"
(*Before Summer's End: Stories to Touch the Soul*)
"The Sweetest Sound"
(*Song of Grace: Stories to Amaze the Soul*)
"Whispered Miracle"
(*A Whisper of Peace: A Mosaic Christmas Anthology IV*)

THE CHAIN OF LAKES SERIES
Shattered Image
Dance of Grace
The Color of Truth

Open Circle

UPCOMING
When Valleys Mourn

THANK YOU FOR READING!

We hope you enjoyed reading *A Whisper of Peace,* Mosaic's 2022 Christmas anthology. If you did, please consider leaving a short review on Amazon, Goodreads, or BookBub. Positive reviews and word-of-mouth recommendations count as they honor an author and help other readers to find quality Christian fiction to read.

Thank you so much!

If you'd like to receive information on new releases and writing news, please subscribe to Mosaic's newsletter, Grace & Glory.

If only owning a bookstore didn't mean dealing with people.

No one was more surprised than Harper Brevig when Great Aunt Lorene (not "Lori," thank-you-very-much) died and left her least favorite niece her bookstore–including a prime piece of real estate in downtown Red Wing, Minnesota.

Making a go of the place shouldn't be too hard. With her library science degree, she should be set. Then again, the website describing library degrees had said it would teach her excellent communication skills. It had not. Could she get a partial refund?

Still, owning the building should mean crazy-low overhead to offset her less than optimal "book-side" manner. Ahem. So when yet another huge bill arrives, and she starts getting twitchy about the low bank balance, Harper does the only thing she can think of.

Enter Milton Coleridge. He'd been excited about the possibilities of the store last year, but Harper had sent him packing before he could talk to her about them. Now he has a chance to make a difference. But she's right. She's bleeding money, and it doesn't make sense!

Milton's job is to figure out what's going on, plug the financial leak, and maybe... do a little matchmaking. That dad with the adorable little boy would be good for her... and she'd be good for him. Probably.

Made in the USA
Middletown, DE
27 October 2022

13627613R00187